Aaron Bagley was the bartender on duty on May 29, 2008, when Kelley Cannon walked into the Hickory Falls Grille & Bar in Smyrna, Tennessee.

"A lady came in and sat at the end of the bar and started to tell me about her and her husband going through a divorce," Bagley testified. "She found out she was being cheated on. She had caught him flying women to come see him in other states. [She said] if he tried to take the babies from her that she would kill him."

To Bagley, Kelley seemed very distraught, very angry and very bitter. Not to mention, really emotional and unstable.

"And did you actually spend a good bit of time interacting with this customer?" prosecutor Sharon Reddick asked.

"Yes, ma'am. Well, I mean, she sat down, and I was a bartender working on tips. And she had a nice wedding ring on her finger, so I kind of spent a little more time with her. She was giving a lot of information out, so you had to listen."

"Now, did she make the statement about killing her husband more than once throughout the course of the time you were listening to her?"

"Yes, ma'am. She said it in a couple of different contexts—that she was so mad that she could kill him. That if he took the babies—tried to take the babies from her—that she would kill him."

Also by Linda Rosencrance

HOUSE
OF LIES

LINDA
ROSENCRANCE

PINNACLE BOOKS
Kensington Publishing Corp.
http://www.kensingtonbooks.com

PINNACLE BOOKS are published by

Kensington Publishing Corp.
119 West 40th Street
New York, NY 10018

All Kensington Titles, Imprints, and Distributed Lines are available at special quantity discounts for bulk purchases for sales promotions, premiums, fund-raising, and educational or institutional use. Special book excerpts or customized printings can also be created to fit specific needs. For details, write or phone the office of the Kensington special sales manager: Kensington Publishing Corp., 119 West 40th Street, New York, NY 10018, attn: Special Sales Department, Phone: 1-800-221-2647.

Pinnacle and the P logo Reg. U.S. Pat. & TM Off.

ISBN-13: 978-0-7860-2794-1
ISBN-10: 0-7860-2794-0

First Printing: January 2013

10 9 8 7 6 5 4 3 2 1

Printed in the United States of America

For Sylvia, Penny, Mario, Mark and Cindy.
And to all the gang at Heidi's Restaurant—you rock!

PROLOGUE

One of the most dangerous species of spiders found in North America belongs to the genus *Latrodectus*. They are known as black widows because of the female's reputation for devouring the male after mating. The female black widow has a shiny black bulbous body, with long, extended legs and a distinctive red hourglass shape on the bottom of her abdomen. Beautiful, but deadly.

The male black widow approaches his mate cautiously, crawling slowly onto the web toward his target. Moving closer, he taps his legs in a courting ritual to entice the female. If she accepts his proposition, she will stay still while he climbs onto her larger body and starts inserting his sperm. When he's finished, part of his body may break off and remain in the female's body.

And then she eats him.

CHAPTER 1

Kelley Cannon wriggled into the low-cut, long-sleeved white dress, with the green and blue circles, then slipped into her white Candie's sandals, with the wedge heels. She put the finishing touches on her makeup, grabbed her white puffy jacket and headed outside to her rented gray Pontiac. At half past nine, she was going to meet Amy Huston for dinner at BrickTop's Restaurant on West End Avenue in Nashville. It was Sunday, June 22, 2008.

Although Kelley hadn't talked to Amy for quite some time, she had called her earlier that evening. Kelley was distraught and depressed and needed a friend. She was at the end of her rope and didn't know what else to do. Already in her pajamas, Amy was in bed reading the newspaper. She was tired from a trip to Atlanta and just wanted to relax before going to the office the next day. But hearing how upset Kelley was, Amy agreed to meet her.

When Kelley arrived at BrickTop's, she parked across the street. She walked inside, where Amy was already waiting. The two women hugged; then they sat down. Kelley ordered macaroni and cheese and a piece of key lime pie. During the evening she ate a bit of the pie, but she asked the server to pack up the macaroni and cheese to go. Amy had already eaten dinner, so she just ordered a glass of wine. She ordered another glass later. Kelley also ordered a glass of wine—the first of three she would have that evening.

As they talked, Amy couldn't help but notice the Band-Aid on one of Kelley's thumbs. Despite the Band-Aid, Amy could still see the cut. It was unusual—sort of a straight-line razor cut down her thumb.

The two discussed the problems Kelley had been having with her husband, Jim, who had asked for a divorce earlier that year. Jim and Kelley, who had married in 1996, had three children—two boys, nine-year-old Tim and seven-year-old Henry, and a girl, eighteen-month-old Sophie. And Kelley wasn't about to lose custody of them.

As Amy listened, Kelley went on and on about her marital problems.

"I just don't know what to do. How dare he? How dare he divorce me? I'm the primary caregiver," Kelley told Amy, sounding more angry than distraught.

After hearing Kelley's tale of woe, Amy suggested she get a job. Amy thought if she had a job, at least she could pay her attorneys' fees. Amy also figured, since Kelley said she was no longer taking the sedatives and painkillers she had been prescribed, she wouldn't have to worry about getting drug tested. As could be expected, Kelley wasn't too thrilled with Amy's suggestion.

Kelley and Amy talked and drank for about an

hour. At about ten-thirty, Kelley's cell phone rang. Amy couldn't see the number that came up on the caller ID; but from Kelley's end of the conversation, she knew it had to be Jim. During their brief conversation they argued about custody of their children, who were living with Jim.

"I don't know what to do. I can't get up in the morning, and, you know, you can't—they're mine," Kelley told her husband.

As Kelley and Jim argued over the custody of the children, Amy realized that Kelley never once asked him how they were. And she thought that was a bit odd. Although Amy didn't have any kids, most of her friends did. And she knew that if they were out for the evening and they called home, they always asked how the kids were doing. And what, specifically, was she saying on the phone call to the person about not being able to see her children or taking her children?

After about five minutes Kelley ended her call. Amy had the distinct impression that Kelley was planning to continue the conversation with Jim later because she didn't want her friend to hear what she was saying.

The friends sat at BrickTop's for another ten or fifteen minutes. They paid the check and walked out of the restaurant together around eleven o'clock. An obviously agitated Kelley crossed the street to her car, and Amy walked to the parking lot behind the restaurant, where she had parked her car.

When she pulled out onto the street, she could see that Kelley was still sitting in her car. Amy thought that Kelley was talking on her cell phone, but it was hard to tell in the dark.

Shortly after Amy drove past, Kelley made the four-minute drive home, changed into black jeans, a light-colored silky top and a dark sweater. Then she got back in her car and drove to the Walgreens located at the intersection of Charlotte Pike and White Bridge Road.

Carrying a light-colored purse, Kelley entered the store and casually walked to the aisle where the latex gloves were displayed. She picked up a box of store-brand latex gloves from the shelf, tucked the box in the crook of her right arm, then walked to the patient-consultation window of the pharmacy to speak with someone. A short time later, Kelley walked toward the front of the store, the box of gloves still tucked in her arm. She passed the checkout counter and left the store, around eleven-thirty, without paying for the gloves.

Kelley then went to Jim's house on Bowling Avenue—the house she once shared with her husband and children. When she arrived, she realized she didn't have a key. She went to the back door and noticed it was slightly ajar. She opened it farther and called out Jim's name. No answer. She went inside. All the lights were on downstairs, and the house was in total disarray. There were beer bottles everywhere. The kitchen was a total mess; there were towels all over the floor. The baby was crying, so Kelley went upstairs to get her. All the while, she was calling out for Jim—still, no answer. The upstairs was dark, except for the light in the bathroom.

From the hallway Kelley could see into the boys'

bedroom, where Jim often slept. His briefcase was on the floor, as were a number of water bottles. The chest of drawers had been knocked over on its side. She was scared to death. Not knowing what was going on, her first instinct was to protect her children. She already had Sophie, so she went to the master bedroom, where the boys were sleeping, and woke up her sons. She gathered as many of their things as she could and put everything in the car. She drove as fast as possible to her apartment. She never thought about calling the police. All she thought of was getting her children to a safe place.

At least . . . that's what she said.

CHAPTER 2

It was around half past eight in the morning on Monday, June 23, 2008, when Jean Armstrong arrived at her housekeeping job on Bowling Avenue. She took out her key as she walked to the front door. As she was about to put the key in the lock, she discovered something odd—the front door was already unlocked. It was closed, but unlocked.

The first thing she noticed when she went inside was that the house was a complete mess. Granted, she hadn't been there for days, but still. And it was quiet, eerily quiet. There didn't seem to be anybody around—not the three young children or their dad, Jim Cannon. They were usually up by the time she got there.

And something else was strange—the door that led to the backyard was opened fully. Jean went to the back door and looked outside. There were two cars in the driveway, and there was a beer can on the lawn. Not sure what to make of the situation, Jean decided she'd just start her chores, like she did every morning. She grabbed some dirty clothes out of the hamper in the laundry room and threw them in the washing machine. Then she went to the kitchen, picked up the trash and did the dishes.

At about nine, Maria Cross, one of the children's nannies, showed up. Now Jean was getting a little concerned. Where was everybody? Certainly the baby, Sophie, should have been up by then. Jean told Maria she was going upstairs to check on her. But when she got to Sophie's room, her crib was empty. She went to the bedroom that the two boys shared, but there was no sign of Tim or Henry. Something else was odd—the chest of drawers in their room had been moved in front of the closet— the drawers facing the door. And everything that had been on top of the chest, a lamp and other items had fallen to the floor.

There was no one in the master bedroom, either. But it, too, was a total mess. Jean walked into the master bathroom. The wastebasket had been tipped over, spilling trash all over the floor. There was a dirty wineglass on the counter. She grabbed the glass and went back into the bedroom. That's when she saw the bloody towel on the floor beside the bed. Shaking her head, Jean picked it up, took it downstairs and threw it in the washer with the rest of the clothes. She put the wineglass in the kitchen sink. Then she told Maria about the total destruction upstairs.

"What the hell is going on here? Where is everybody?" Jean asked Maria. "The two cars are here, but there's no sign of Mr. Cannon or the children. Maybe one of the children got hurt and he had to call an ambulance to take them to the hospital. That would explain the bloody towel and why there's nobody home. Maybe we should try calling Mr. Cannon on his cell phone."

Maria took out her phone and dialed Jim's number—no answer. She left a message.

"Let's go back upstairs and look around," Jean said.

When the two women got to the boys' bedroom, Jean asked Maria to help her move the chest away from the closet because she was afraid she'd break something if she did it herself. Once they had moved it partway, Jean told Maria she could finish the job herself.

When the chest was out of the way, Jean went back to the closet and opened the door. It was dark inside. She squinted a little; then she saw it—the palm of Jim Cannon's hand. It was as black as charcoal. Shocked, Jean slammed the door shut again. Then she turned around and just stared at Maria. Her heart was racing.

"What's wrong?" Maria asked. The horror in Jean's eyes startled her.

"Jim's in the closet," Jean said.

"I'll call 911," Maria said as she bolted out of the room.

All kinds of thoughts went through Jean's mind. What if Jim was passed out? Maybe she should try to wake him? She didn't want him to be embarrassed when the police and paramedics arrived. Jean cautiously opened the closet door again. A strong odor of bleach hit her nose. She leaned down to check on Jim. She moved a pillow out from under the side of his face. It was then she knew he'd never be embarrassed again. Jim Cannon was dead.

* * *

"Nine-one-one. What's the address of the emergency?"

"We need an ambulance immediately," Maria told the dispatcher. "He's upstairs in the closet and he's not breathing."

"Is he conscious?"

"'Is he conscious?' No. No."

The nanny handed the phone to Jean, who had just come downstairs.

"He's dead," Jean told the dispatcher.

"All right. Well, why do you think he's dead?"

"Something's happened, and there's . . ."

"Is he cold? Is he stiff?"

"I hadn't touched him."

"Can I give you instructions on how to do CPR?"

But Jean knew there was no need for cardiopulmonary resuscitation.

The first policeman on the scene was Officer Albert Gordon, a nineteen-year veteran with the Metropolitan Nashville Police Department (MNPD). When he arrived, he saw Jean and Maria waiting on the front lawn. When Gordon went into the house, he was met by two paramedics, who were both walking down the stairs from the boys' bedroom. They stopped and briefed Gordon on the situation.

Gordon then went to the boys' bedroom and briefly looked into the closet. After seeing Jim's body, he notified his sergeant and the sector detectives responsible for investigating crime scenes. Then he went outside to keep everyone else—except the crime scene investigation (CSI) team—from entering.

While Gordon was inside, Jean asked Maria to call Kelley Cannon's mother, Diane Sanders. Maria spoke to Diane for a couple minutes; then she handed the phone to Jean. Diane asked Jean what was wrong. Not sure what to say, Jean blurted out that Jim was dead and told her to come to the house as soon as possible. Suddenly Jean went into a state of shock. She couldn't move. She couldn't speak. She didn't know how or why, but something Diane said convinced Jean that Kelley's mother already knew that Jim was dead.

Diane, who only lived about ten minutes away, arrived at the Cannon house shortly after she ended the call with Jean. By then, other investigators had arrived. Diane immediately asked one of the officers if her son-in-law was really dead, but the officer said she couldn't release that information. During her conversation with the officer, Diane asked about her grandchildren. She gave the police their names and ages and said they were probably with their mother—because that was the most logical place for them to be.

After speaking with the police Diane called her son Bobby, who was visiting a local university with his son, and asked him to meet her at Jim's. She also called Jim's work, as well as his divorce attorney, John Hollins, to tell them that Jim was dead. But she never called Kelley, nor did she drive over to her house to tell her the horrible news.

Hollins acknowledged that Kelley's mother called his office around noon on June 23.

"I'll never forget as long as I live," he said. "I had walked out of my office to go to lunch and I heard one of my legal assistants scream in the kitchen. I go running in there. She said, 'Jim is dead.' I asked, 'Jim who?' She said, 'Jim Cannon is dead. Kelley killed him. This is Diane on the phone.' I told her to put the call into my office. I run back to the office and pick up the phone. Diane says, 'Kelley killed him. She finally killed him.' That's the first thing she said. Then I heard, 'He's in the house.' She was talking to the Metro Police. Then one of the detectives got on the phone with me, because Diane had told him I represented Jim in the divorce. He asked me if I could bring him copies of the court orders. I had my legal assistant make copies of all the orders that the judge had entered in the divorce case. Kelley was not supposed to have contact with the kids. That day she had all three kids with her. They wanted to know what was going on. Jim's body was still in the house upstairs. I went over there and I met with the detectives downstairs."

When Metropolitan Nashville Police Department detectives Brad Putnam and William Stokes arrived at the Cannon house, they were briefed by other police on the scene. After speaking with Jean and Maria, they walked through the house, looking for potential evidence. They noticed that a window in the front of the house was partially opened.

They walked upstairs and into the boys' bedroom, where they found the body of Jim Cannon lying on his right side in the closet. He was naked, and it was obvious he had been dead for quite some time. He was cold to the touch and rigor mortis had set in. His body was positioned in such a way that his right arm was above his head and his left arm was hanging down, leading the detectives to believe that he had been dragged to the closet.

Blood and fluid were coming from his nose and mouth. There were marks on his neck that appeared to be parallel to each other, as if something had been wrapped around his neck a couple times. It appeared that he had been strangled. There was also a superficial scratch on the front left side of his chest. Police didn't see any other signs of trauma on Jim's body. They did notice a very strong odor of bleach emanating from inside the closet, as well as from Jim's body. Just to the left of Jim's head, Putnam and Stokes saw an open container of bleach. The lid was on the floor of the closet, close to the bottle. There was a small blue pillow in front of Jim's face, and children's clothing was underneath the lower part of his body. The clothes were discolored, as if someone had poured bleach on them.

Behind the door, which opened inward, there was a white latex glove near Jim's feet. And there was a fingertip of a latex glove on the floor outside the closet. A Motorola cell phone charger was also lying on the floor. Its cord had been ripped off. The detectives also saw several spots of blood on the floor in front of the bunk beds.

Putnam then walked down the hall to the master

bedroom. He saw a spot of blood on the floor next to the bed. He also noticed what appeared to be a blood spot on the dust ruffle.

Putnam went downstairs to talk to Jean. He wanted to know whether there were any latex gloves in the house. She said there were some in the pantry and showed him where they were. The box of American Red Cross gloves in the pantry was half empty. Putnam also asked if there were any bleach bottles. Jean explained that the bleach was kept in the laundry room, above the washer and dryer. In the laundry room Putnam saw one opened bottle of Clorox bleach on the back shelf. Jean said there had been a full bottle on the shelf when she left the previous Thursday.

Later that day, as part of the investigation, Brad Putnam went to talk to Amy Huston. Amy told Putnam that although Jim and Kelley had been having problems in their marriage for a number of years, Jim only started talking to his friends about those problems in the beginning of 2008.

Amy explained that until Kelley called her to meet at BrickTop's, the last time she had heard from Kelley was sometime in April, when she had been released from rehab. Kelley called Amy to ask if Jim knew about her affairs. That conversation was a short one, since Amy didn't have any information to give Kelley.

Although Amy had been friends with both Jim and Kelley, her friendship with Kelley soured when Kelley asked for her help getting out of rehab some months earlier and Amy had refused. She never talked to Kelley after that, until that call in April.

Amy told Detective Putnam that Kelley had called her the previous evening and was extremely distraught. However, she didn't tell her why she was so upset. Amy figured Kelley wanted to talk about the divorce, but she didn't elaborate. She just asked Amy to meet her at BrickTop's, and to bring other people if she could.

So Amy got up, put on shorts and a T-shirt, and then went to meet her. But because it was already after eight, Amy didn't try to contact their other friends. For one thing, she didn't know what shape Kelley was going to be in, and she didn't want to subject anyone else to an emotional scene. For another, it was Sunday night, and all of their friends had families and kids and jobs they had to go to the next day. She figured no one else would be willing to go, anyway.

Amy got to the restaurant before Kelley, so she sat down at a table and ordered a glass of wine. Kelley finally arrived at the restaurant about nine-thirty. The two women hugged and then sat down; they each ordered a glass of wine.

Amy told the detective that as the two women talked about Kelley's marital problems, Amy realized her friend wasn't so much distraught as angry.

Throughout their conversation, Kelley didn't ask Amy if she knew how the kids were or if they missed her. She just kept repeating that she was the primary caregiver, and Jim didn't even know the names of his own children.

Amy told Detective Putnam about the phone call

Kelley received at the restaurant, apparently from Jim. Amy explained she wasn't quite sure how Kelley's five-minute conversation with Jim ended, since Amy had received a call from another friend on her own cell phone.

The two women stayed at the restaurant for about ten or fifteen minutes after Kelley wrapped up her call with Jim. Then Amy paid the check and they left together, around eleven. As Amy left the parking lot and headed home, she drove by Kelley's still-parked car. Kelley was inside.

When MNPD officer Johnny Lawrence and his CSI team arrived at the Cannon house, they went right to work processing the crime scene. During his investigation Lawrence spent a lot of time in the boys' bedroom, where Jim's body had been discovered.

Lawrence walked into the closet where Jim's body was in order to determine if there was any blood there before the investigators started taking pictures. As he entered the closet, a strong odor of bleach hit him smack in the face. He noticed a bottle of Clorox bleach lying on its side on the carpet, and the carpet was a little damp. There was a coat hanger next to Jim's body. Lawrence stepped on it, trying not to disturb anything else. However, because his boot was slightly wet from the bleach, it left an impression on the hanger.

As he was working the scene, he also discovered a latex glove behind the door inside the closet near Jim's body. Lawrence collected the glove and bagged it as evidence. He also discovered the charger to a cell phone. The cord to the charger had been ripped off. He picked up the charger and saw what looked like blood on it, so he collected it as well.

The investigators also noticed some brownish stains on the carpet. They did a preliminary test at the scene that indicated the stain could have been blood, but it wasn't conclusive. So they cut out pieces of the carpet to send back to the lab for more extensive testing.

Lawrence and his team also tagged and bagged a video game controller that was in the boys' room. They weren't sure if it had anything to do with Jim's murder. However, they collected it because it looked out of place on the floor, rather than put up under the television set, where game controllers are normally kept.

The crime scene investigators also collected the bottle of bleach, some water bottles, a briefcase, a little white tablet (most likely, an aspirin), a pair of eyeglasses and a man's Rolex. After they bagged the evidence, they dusted the place for fingerprints. Then Alicia Primm, one of the civilian CSI investigators, took pictures of the inside of the house, while Johnny Lawrence photographed the outside. As he was taking pictures, Lawrence noticed a partially opened window. A cord, which appeared to be a satellite radio antenna, was hanging down in front of the window. The cord looked like it had been knocked out of place. After finishing with the photographs, the investigator processed the window for fingerprints.

Lawrence also processed the wineglass in the

sink for DNA and fingerprints. The team collected the handles of the bathroom faucets and took swabbings of the front of the bathroom cabinet to determine if the reddish stains on the items were, in fact, blood.

Lawrence and the investigators also collected a carpet that had some red stains on it from one of the bathrooms, but not the master bathroom. Those stains were not bloodstains. There were also some stains in the hallway leading from the master bedroom to one of the children's bedrooms that did test positive for blood.

The investigators also discovered—and collected as evidence—a white latex glove that had been tossed over the branch of a tree in the backyard and a similar glove draped over a nearby shrub, as well as an empty beer can in an empty planter pot in the front yard. Primm swabbed the mouth of the bottle for DNA; then she processed it for fingerprints.

Civilian crime scene technician Rhonda Evans also helped Officer Lawrence process the crime scene at Jim's house. When she arrived at the Cannon house, she met with Detective Putnam, who gave her a bag of clothing to take back to the property room at the police station so it could be documented and secured. In the bag were Kelley's white tank top, a pair of blue jeans, a pair of white high heels and one box of powder-free latex gloves in a Walgreens box.

While she was at the scene, Evans went to the second floor and helped the investigators lift fingerprints from the wall in the hallway, which were turned in to the police fingerprint examiners. When she finished collecting the fingerprints, Evans got a call from her sergeant, who instructed her to return to the lab.

CHAPTER 3

Metro Nashville Police Department officers Jeff Biggerstaff and Jeffrey Poole, who was being trained by Biggerstaff, were assigned to go to Kelley's apartment on Elmington Avenue, which was about half a mile from Jim's house. They had been instructed to check on Kelley and the well-being of her children and to call Brad Putnam, the detective heading up the investigation, once they had done that.

When the two officers knocked on the door, a woman wearing a silky top, black jeans and a dark-colored sweater answered. In response to their questions she identified herself as Kelley Cannon. Kelley allowed the police into her apartment. The officers noticed that the two boys were playing video games and little Sophie was wandering around the apartment. Neither the children nor Kelley seemed upset. So Biggerstaff called Putnam and stayed with Kelley until he arrived.

It was strange, though, that although the cops

told Kelley they were there to make sure she and the kids were okay, she never once asked them why.

A little while later, William Stokes and Lieutenant Nancy Fielder met Biggerstaff and Poole at Kelley's place. Stokes and Fielder took Kelley into her bedroom to ask her some questions.

Kelley told Detective Stokes and Lieutenant Fielder that she hadn't seen Jim since May 22.

"That's when all this started," she said.

"Oh, the separation and all that? Okay, where was that at?" Stokes asked.

"At my home."

"Okay, just an all-day kind of thing, or what?"

"No, he had a restraining order over me. I went to Cumberland Heights (a drug- and alcohol-treatment facility). . . . I'd been in the home for forty-five days, and he said he was going to hold the civil restraining order over my head for ninety days, and he came home," Kelley responded.

"When you said you'd been home for ninety days, you mean your home?" Stokes asked, a bit confused by Kelley's response.

"My home."

"Okay, I didn't know if you meant treatment facility, or what."

"No, I came home. He picked me up and I came home, and he said he was going to hold the restraining order over my head for ninety days."

Kelley again said she had only been home for forty-five days when Jim told her that, but she said the two didn't really have a fight.

"He just said he was going to do everything he could to keep me from the children and throw me in jail."

"This was on May twenty-second? He came home and started saying this stuff?"

"Yeah, he was supposed to already have an apartment for me, where I could go. And he threatened me and he shoved me, with the baby, and he said, 'This isn't working,' and 'I'm going to do everything I can to keep you from the children,' et cetera, et cetera. 'I'm calling 911.'"

"He pushed you physically, you said, on that night?" Stokes asked.

"Yeah, with the baby in my arms. And then I thought he had left, and I put the baby in my car to leave."

"Where were the little boys at this time?"

"They were in the front."

"Of the house?"

"Yeah. And they were scared to death of him, you know. I mean they weren't going to cross him."

"So you left with the baby?"

"Yeah, I tried to leave with the baby, but he blocked my car in."

"Oh, okay. That was the night that you got arrested."

"Yeah, I tried to leave and he had blocked my car in. And I was scared for the baby. And I bumped his car, 'cause I had the baby in the car, to get out of the driveway, and left. And about that time the police came—they just had the blue lights on. They didn't have the sirens on. And I moved down [the street] and just sped up because they were on my bumper and I thought that they were meaning for me to just leave—leave immediately. So I just hit the accelerator long enough to speed up to try to get completely out of there. I thought I was doing the right thing because he had a civil restraining order over me and he had been threatening me."

"A civil restraining order, like through the DA's office, just saying 'stay so far away from me' or 'don't have contact'?" Stokes asked.

"No, no, no, like no verbal abuse, no harassment."

"Okay, so it was not a 'stay away' order necessarily, just a 'get along' kind of order."

"Right. There was no altercation."

"For the forty-five days since you'd been back? He just came in and made a statement?"

"Yeah, yeah."

"Okay, he physically pushed you, too."

"Yeah, and then he got in his car, and I said, 'Come on, let's work this out.' And he got in his car, started up, started banging on the window. And at that point I thought he'd just left. But, apparently, he had parked his car—there's an alleyway on the side of our house and he had blocked in my car so that I couldn't leave. And I just bumped it enough to get out. And . . . he didn't even know where the baby was. And he was on the 911 call, sitting there [and] saying, 'She's got the baby,' but he didn't even know where the baby was. I was scared to death because he's the attorney."

"Okay, so that was the last time you saw him?" Stokes asked.

"Yeah."

"You didn't have any kind of court or anything together? Nothing like that, right? When's the last time you spoke with him on the phone, or anything like that?"

"Well, I went to jail and he filed an ex parte on me."

"On the twenty-second, right?"

"The twenty-third."

"Okay, you went to jail on the twenty-second or the twenty-third, right, because of the incident you were just telling me about, and he filed an order of protection with the commissioner."

"I thought I was doing the right thing . . . just getting her out of an unsafe situation and complying with what he had been threatening me with for ninety days."

"So let me ask you again, is that the last time you ever spoke with him or saw him?"

Kelley told the detectives that Jim had been calling her recently. In fact, the last time she spoke to him was the previous night while she was having dinner at BrickTop's with her friend Amy. She said he called on her cell phone to say that he wanted to reconcile with her and that he'd let her see the kids.

"He [said], 'I don't want to do this anymore. I know I filed that ex parte again, but I want you to see the children, and I can't do this by myself.'"

"How did he sound on the phone? Like normal? Had he been drinking? Was he upset?"

"Yeah, he'd been drinking."

"Did he actually say that, or you could just tell from the voice?"

"No, he would never tell me that he'd been drinking, but we've been married for about twelve years."

Stokes wanted to know if that was the extent of the conversation between the two.

"No, he said his lawyers were pushing to extend the ex parte for a year and [he] doesn't want to do it. He wants to drop it. He can't do it by himself, and he wants me to see the children, and he wanted to reconcile."

"Well, that's good," Stokes said. "Do you know why we're here?"

"Can I ask you something?" Fielder asked.

"Uh-huh."

"When did you pick the children up?"

"I got a call and he said he wanted me to see the children, and he couldn't do it anymore, and I couldn't find him there. . . ."

"What do you mean 'there'?" Stokes asked.

"What?"

"Did you go to the house last night?"

Kelley said she did go to the house, sometime before midnight, but she wasn't sure exactly what time it was. When she arrived, the baby was awake in her crib, but the boys were asleep in the master bedroom.

"The back door was open," she said.

"The back door—was it wide open or opened a little bit, or what?" Stokes asked.

"It was just open, unlocked."

"Was the front door locked, or do you know?"

"I have no idea."

Kelley said everything looked normal outside, but the house was a wreck inside. The lights were on in one main room, and there were beer cans in the family room. The kitchen was a wreck.

"Did you go in the back door? Is that how you went in?" Fielder asked.

"It was open. Nothing was locked, and the lights were on."

"Okay, so you went upstairs, right? Found the kids and—"

"I mean, I was scared of him again," Kelley said, not answering the previous question.

"Did you look all over the house for him?"

"Yes, and I called his name."

"So you obviously went into the master bedroom to get the boys. You obviously went in [Sophie's] room to get her. You went through the downstairs, because you said it was [a] mess, and you saw beer cans, correct? And you went in the other upstairs rooms, looking for him, right? The boys have their own room, but they sleep in the master bedroom. Is that [right]?"

"Yeah, they have a room."

"Did you [go] in that room?"

"Yeah, and it was totally askew."

"What did you see in there? Anything other than it just being messy? Anything out of place? Who'd you [go] over the house with?"

Kelley said she went to the house by herself and Amy had gone home.

"He didn't sound right on the telephone," Kelley said, even though Stokes did not ask her about the conversation.

"What do you mean?" Stokes asked.

"I mean, he just sounded desperate and he sounded scared."

"And you went home from the restaurant?"

"Uh-huh," Kelley said.

"'He sounded desperate'?" Stokes repeated Kelley's words. "When you say, 'He sounded desperate,' how do you mean? Just because of the little things you've told me about, or was he mentioning other things, other problems, or what?"

"He said that he'd been threatened."

"Did he say by who, by chance?" Stokes asked.

"No, no. But, you know, the bottom line, he didn't want to do this."

"He'd been threatened because of y'all's situation?" Stokes's comment was more of a question than a statement.

"Yes."

"But he didn't say who? You have no idea who might have done that?"

"No. What's going on? Where is he?"

This was the first time during the interview that Kelley asked Stokes about her husband.

"He's at home," Stokes said, not yet ready to tell Kelley that Jim was dead. "I need to know what you saw when you were at the house."

"I'm telling you what I saw."

"All right. Now, this statement here you say he told you, 'I've been threatened because of our marital status and our marital problems.' Is that a fair statement?"

"Yes, and he feels threatened. He felt threatened."

"By who? That's my question. I mean, even if he didn't tell you, do you have any idea who might have been doing [it] to him?"

"No, because I haven't really talked to him. Every time I talk to him, it's been about the legal system," Kelley said, becoming agitated.

"Okay. I might ask questions that might upset you, but it's just the way I have to do things, because I don't know you. I don't know him. I don't know your situation, so I have to ask these questions, trying to get a clear picture in my head about what's going on. That's why I'm asking these questions. Okay, so you picked up the kids and you went through the house, trying to find him, couldn't find him. The house just looked messy. Did it just look messy? Is that how you would describe it?"

"One of the boys' chest of drawers was, like, overturned, which really scared me."

"Do they have more than one?"

"Uh-huh."

"Which one was it, in particular?"

"It was the one on the left."

"It was, like, knocked over completely? As you go into the room, to the left, you said? What else did you see? 'Cause you noticed the dresser was knocked over. This is something a little bit new, so I'm hoping you're remembering more stuff. Can you think of anything else?"

Kelley said she just saw a bunch of bottles on the floor in the boys' bedroom and Jim's briefcase.

"And that kind of stuff is not normally in the boys' room, I take it from [what] you're telling me."

"No."

Kelley told Stokes that she hadn't had much sleep since she picked up the kids at Jim's house because she was worried about [their relationship]. She said she was also worried sick about the children and that fact that she couldn't find Jim when she was at the house.

"When you couldn't find him last night, where did you think he was?" Stokes asked.

Kelley said she had no idea.

"Would he have just left the children there?"

"No. I mean, I haven't been back to the house, so I don't know his normal schedule anymore. I don't know what he's doing."

"But since you've been married for twelve years, would you consider it unusual for him to leave the children like that?"

"Yes."

"Did you think to call anybody last night, looking for him?" Fielder asked.

"I was frantic."

"You just thought he had left the house and left them there?" Fielder questioned.

"The fact that I couldn't find him," Kelley said, not quite answering the question, and not quite finishing her sentence.

"Was his car in the driveway when you got there?" Stokes asked.

Kelley said both of Jim's cars were in the driveway.

"So what did you think?" Fielder asked. "You've been married to him for twelve years. What did you think about the children in there by themselves?"

"I freaked out. I freaked out. I didn't know what to think."

Kelley told the detectives that Jim had never left the kids alone before; but then again, they'd never before been in such a situation.

"He's quite desperate," she added.

In response to their questions Kelley told the detectives that Jim had arranged for her to move into her current apartment.

"I've been moved four times," she said. "That's why everything's so discombobulated."

As they were talking with Kelley, Stokes noticed Sophie was putting a short white straw, about two inches long, in her mouth. When he told Kelley about it, she snatched the straw out of the child's hand and tried to hide it. When Stokes asked what it was, Kelley said it was a Juicy Juice straw. But Stokes wasn't buying it. The straw Kelley was trying to conceal was no Juicy Juice straw.

"Was he seeing anybody else that you know of?" Stokes asked.

"Yeah, he had been seeing other people."

"What about you?"

"No. Absolutely not."

Kelley then told Stokes and Fielder the name of the woman Jim had been seeing—someone he had known since his days in boarding school. Kelley said Jim started seeing her in August 2007, but she believed the affair was over. Kelley said despite his indiscretion, she took him back. But she said she still had suspicions that he was still seeing the woman, even though he said he had ended the affair.

Stokes then asked Kelley about Jim's drinking habits. She said he preferred whiskey over beer. The conversation then moved on to Kelley's prescription drug use. She said she had become addicted to the painkillers she was taking after she had broken her back about three years earlier. Then, almost as an afterthought, she told the detectives that Jim was also taking her pain meds.

"Any ones in particular that you were addicted to and he was using also?" Stokes asked.

"OxyContin and Percocet."

"So he took your meds? He did not go out and get them off the street, or anything like that, that you know of?"

"No."

"He just took them out of your bottle?"

"Uh-huh."

Kelley said that one of the Cannons' maids, Esther, was supplying him with pot on a pretty regular basis.

"And then when all this started, he would accuse me of being an addict. And I've lost thirty pounds [from] grieving over the affair," she said. "I got pneumonia, and it's all documented. And he started saying, 'No, you're a narcotics addict.'"

Kelley said she lost the weight because of the affair and because she got sick, not because she was a narcotics addict. She said she was so sick that her weight dropped to ninety-seven pounds.

Kelley continued to talk, although she didn't seem to make much sense.

"I told him I wanted a separation, and he, being the smart lawyer that he is—"

"Is this when you came back from rehab or while you were in rehab?" Stokes asked.

"No, this is before," she said. "I told him I wanted a separation, and then what he did was . . . Well, I hadn't driven in two weeks, that's how sick I was. I was dizzy from the pneumonia. I told him I wanted a separation. He left the house. He went and filed for divorce. He picked my boys up from [day care] to have physical custody, because I hadn't filed any divorce on him. The next day he called an ambulance to come to my house, telling them I was an addict and I could be violent, and all this kind of stuff. I was compliant with them, knowing full well that I had just gotten out of the hospital. I still hadn't gained any weight back and I still had a fever from the [pneumonia]."

"Is this when you were still taking pain medication, too?" Stokes asked.

"No, I wasn't taking any pain medications at this point."

After some questioning by Stokes, Kelley finally admitted she was still refilling the prescriptions, but it was only because Jim was taking them. Kelley said after Jim got temporary custody of the children, he dragged them from hotel to hotel without any of their things. She said that when she returned home after being released from the hospital, Jim and the kids were gone. She was frantic because she had no idea where they were, and the police wouldn't help because he had temporary custody.

"Then he put me up at the [Loews Vanderbilt Hotel Nashville], and I hadn't seen my kids [in a few days]. I had also taken a voluntary drug screen at the insistence of my attorneys on March sixth, and it was clean," Kelley said, jumping from one topic to another.

Kelley said she was so desperate to see her children, and she was in such bad physical shape because of the pneumonia, that she admitted herself to Cumberland Heights on the advice of her therapist. She claimed that although Jim said she could see the children, he "jerked her around" about seeing them. When she finally got out, she called Bobby Jackson, one of her divorce attorneys, and explained that Jim was holding the divorce papers over her head—forcing her to live in a hostage situation. Kelley claimed that Jim had manipulated Jackson to the point that he had withdrawn as her attorney. She said she was now represented by Worrick Robinson, a criminal attorney.

"He's a good attorney," Stokes said. "Do you remember anything else about last night that you can think of? Anything else pop into your head?"

"No, I was just frantic."

"How long were you in the house?"

"Long enough to get the children and get diapers, get wipes. I really didn't stay long enough to get enough of the boys' clothes that I needed."

"Fifteen, twenty [or] thirty minutes, less?"

"Maybe twenty, I don't know. Long enough to try and get enough functional things for the children."

"So all the stuff you brought from the house is just relating to the kids, or did you bring anything else, like some of your stuff or anything like that? Just [the] kids' stuff. Certainly none of his stuff, I would imagine, right?"

After asking Kelley a couple questions about her rental car, Stokes asked her for the full names and birth dates of the children. After gathering that information, he summarized all the information Kelley had given him regarding her activities the previous evening.

"Let me ask you something," Fielder said. "When you said he had called you and he was being threatened, did he tell you what kinds of threats?"

"No, he said he thought he wanted us to get back together. I'm still stunned at this whole situation, to tell you the truth."

"Okay, like your mom and dad, they wouldn't get upset enough to do something like that, and his parents wouldn't be upset enough to do something like that?" Stokes asked.

"No."

"You get along with your mom and dad, and does he get along with his?"

"My dad, he's in Santa Fe."

"What about your mom?" Fielder asked.

"My mom is here."

"Do you get along with her okay?" Stokes asked.

"Oh, yeah."

"Is there anything else you can remember about last night?"

"No, except for that I was frantic for the children's safety."

"Did you think about calling the police when he wasn't there and he left the kids unattended?" Fielder asked. "Maybe something happened to him. That enter your mind at all?"

"I just wanted to get the kids out of the house. I mean, I wanted to get them safe. And you know I was going to [call] on the officers today."

"And what were you going to tell them today?" Stokes asked.

"Exactly what I told you."

"You were going to file a missing person report, or something?"

"Whatever they suggested, I was going to do."

"You just wanted to tell them about the situation?"

"Yeah."

"Are the boys on the couch?" Stokes asked.

"Yeah."

"They can't hear me, right?"

"No."

"Your husband was found dead today. In the house. And that's why we're here."

"Where was he?" Kelley asked.

"I don't want to tell you that right now. I'm not the lead detective," Stokes said. "I will let you speak to the lead detective, okay? But that's why we're here, because you have the children and we think you might have been the last person maybe to have talked to him or seen him. I'm sorry."

"He was found dead?"

"Yes, ma'am. Are you sure there's nothing else you can remember?"

"How did he die?" Kelley finally asked.

"Don't know. I don't know. That's what we're trying to figure out," Stokes said. "That's why we're here asking questions. That's why we're asking everybody questions that had any contact with him."

"Have you made any calls this morning since the officers have been here?" Fielder asked.

"No."

"And, of course, it's just me, but I [would] find it unusual if the police came to my house and stayed with me for hours. I'd be calling somebody, asking why, what was going on," Fielder said.

"I have been scared to death. I mean, I've been scared to death."

"Because they were here?" Fielder asked.

"Because who was here?"

"Because the police were here."

"No, because I couldn't find him anywhere last night."

"Did you try to call him this morning?" Fielder asked.

"Yes, I did."

"What time did you try to call him this morning?"

"I don't know, couple hours ago."

"Did anyone answer the phone?"

"No."

Fielder then asked Kelley what time the cleaning lady came in and if she would have answered the phone. Kelley said she would have answered the phone. Fielder apologized for having to question Kelley, but she explained that it was part of the investigation.

"I couldn't tell you on the front end, because I have to have a credible story from you," Stokes said. "And if I would have told you on the front end that [he was found dead], it would contaminate [the interview]. Is there someone you can call to come here and stay with you?"

"My mother," Kelley said, giving Stokes her mother's name and telephone number.

"Who found him?"

"The housekeeper."

"How long have you been there?" Kelley asked.

"I don't know," Stokes said. "I'm not the lead investigator. I'm just assisting, and I left to come over here and [talk to you]."

"He's just laying there dead by himself?"

"I don't know any details, ma'am. I'm sorry. If I knew them, I would tell you what I could," Stokes said. "You understand why I had to ask the questions I asked? And then, why I was stressing certain things trying to find out what happened? Because it's the only way I'm going to figure this out, and I could really use your help. Mrs. Cannon, later on, not necessarily today or anything, but would you be willing to come in for a more formal interview, just to make sure we have everything down correctly?"

"Yeah, absolutely."

"The lead detective is Brad Putnam, so he might be calling you," he said. "Meanwhile, your mother's who you want us to contact to come stay with you? Is there another person in case we can't get hold of her?"

"Are you sure he's dead?"

"I wouldn't be here, otherwise. And I'm not in the habit of telling people that, if it's not what I saw. I wouldn't do that to anybody."

Stokes again asked Kelley if there was anything else she remembered and if she was sure no one else was in the house when she got the kids. Kelley said she didn't remember anything else and there was no one else in the house.

"He's dead," Kelley said. "I don't see how he can be dead. I just can't conceive his death."

"Do you think that's something he would've done to himself? Was there ever any indication of that?"

"I don't know. Things were so bad between us."

"But my understanding is that he was a fairly stable individual, whereas that kind of stuff was concerned—in your opinion, being married to him for twelve years."

"No, he wasn't stable. I mean, he was a bad drinker."

"Okay, that's what we're trying to find out—why this happened and what the circumstances were."

While Stokes was speaking with Kelley, he noticed several medicine bottles on the nightstand in the bedroom. One was a prescription for clonazepam.

When they finished talking, Kelley went into the bathroom and began washing her hands slowly and thoroughly. In plain view on the sink counter was a rectangular box with SEROQUEL printed on it. The interior packaging was protruding from the box and several doses of the drug were missing.

Just about then, Brad Putnam showed up at Kelley's place. He introduced himself to Kelley and asked if they could go into her bedroom to talk. Once inside, he asked her about the last time she saw or spoke to her husband. Odd, she didn't seem at all upset about his death. Odder still was the question she asked Putnam: "Do I need an attorney?"

Putnam said she wasn't under arrest. He just wanted to find out when she had seen Jim or talked to Jim last, and if there was someone who wanted to harm him. Kelley told Putnam about the call she received from Jim the previous evening when she was with Amy. She said he was frantic because someone had threatened him, but he never mentioned a name.

CHAPTER 4

After Kelley Cannon finished her story, Detective Putnam asked if she would sign a consent form so the detectives could search her apartment and her car. She signed willingly. He also asked her what she had been wearing the previous evening when she went to dinner with Amy Huston and when she went to get the children from Jim's. At first, she said she had been wearing jeans and a white tank top, but she later said she had been wearing a dress when she met Amy at the restaurant.

During the search Putnam collected a pair of white Candie's sandals. There was a red spatter on the left side of the heel of the left shoe. The detective thought it might be significant. Earlier that day Putnam had spoken to Amy Huston, who had described the clothes Kelley was wearing—including white Candie's sandals—when they met for dinner the previous evening. Putnam collected the pair of size-one Mossimo blue jeans and the white tank top. He also took a box of Walgreens latex gloves, which were in a brown paper bag in the living room. A piece of the box had been ripped off.

While the police were conducting the search, Kelley's attorney, Worrick Robinson, telephoned. He advised Kelley not to answer any more questions. He asked to speak with Putnam, who explained that Kelley had signed a consent form so police could search her apartment and her car. Putnam said he had not yet started to search the car, but he was having it towed to the station. Robinson asked him not to search the car. Putnam agreed, but he said he'd get a search warrant if necessary. Putnam had already looked in the vehicle and noticed part of the corner of the box of Walgreens latex gloves, matching what he had found in the living room. Before he left Kelley's apartment, Putnam made arrangements for Jim's sister to take the Cannon children. Kelley had violated the custody agreement when she took the kids from Jim's house.

As Putnam was getting ready to leave Kelley's, Robinson arrived to speak with Kelley. He told Putnam he'd be in touch about Kelley's car. Putnam then took the items he had collected from Kelley's apartment, brought them back to Jim Cannon's house and gave them to one of the crime scene investigators.

A little while later, Robinson went to Jim's house and told police they could search Kelley's rented car. But he asked if she could use one of Jim's cars because otherwise she wouldn't have transportation. The detectives decided to release Jim's black GMC Yukon after they were done examining it.

But one of the detectives told Robinson that Kelley wasn't allowed on the property, so she would have to make arrangements to pick up the car, which she did.

Brad Putnam finished up at the scene; then he went back to his office to prepare a search warrant so he could do a more thorough search of Kelley's apartment.

After police received permission to search Kelley's rented Pontiac, civilian CSI Rhonda Evans was assigned the task. The first thing Evans did was to photograph the outside and the inside of the vehicle, including all the items in the car, as well as in the trunk. Then she dusted the outside and inside of the Pontiac for fingerprints.

When that was done, she began collecting potential evidence from the vehicle. She gathered up a piece of a box of latex gloves, a portion of a Band-Aid wrapper from the front seat of the Pontiac, as well as the sticky adhesive part of a Band-Aid, and some gauze, with what looked like blood on it.

After she collected the items, she packaged them up and took them to the property room to be logged in as evidence.

Rick Greene met Kelley Cannon through her mother, Diane. Sometime in the evening of June 23, Rick received a call at work from a friend.

"Did you see the five o'clock news?" Rick's friend asked.

"No."

"Kelley killed her husband."

Rick sent Kelley a text message that very same night, at ten or ten-fifteen, asking if she was okay. Kelley called Rick back and asked him to come to her apartment, which he did.

The first question Rick asked her was what happened to her husband. Kelley said she had been out with a friend at a restaurant and that Jim had called her and was upset. And she said, when she got to the house, the door was open. She told Rick she could hear the baby crying, so she went upstairs and looked around and didn't see Jim. She got the kids and left the house.

The pair spent time together—they had been in a relationship since Memorial Day of that year— then Rick left. But he never asked Kelley point-blank if she had killed her husband.

William Stokes and Brad Putnam went back to Kelley's with a search warrant. When they arrived, at about twenty minutes to eleven, nobody was home. So the cops waited in the parking lot. Within the hour Kelley arrived, driving the Yukon; she was followed close behind by a man driving a Dodge pickup truck. After Kelley and the man parked their vehicles, he got out of the truck, walked over to Kelley's car and leaned into the driver's-side window.

At the same time Stokes and Putnam got out of their car and walked toward Kelley and the man. As soon as they reached Kelley's car, the man backed away from the window, but he didn't say anything. Putnam started talking to Kelley and told her about the search warrant. She got out of her car and walked to her apartment with the two officers. Her visitor, who had heard Putnam say the words "search warrant," took that as his cue to get the hell out of there.

Accompanied by Kelley, the detectives walked to her apartment. Once inside, they noticed there was a pornographic movie playing on the television. Kelley was still wearing the black denim pants she had been wearing earlier that day. Putnam told her he needed to take the pants back to the station with him, so she went into her bedroom to change. When she came out of her room, she gave the pants to Putnam, telling him she had urinated on them. Putnam also collected an empty carton of Virginia Slims cigarettes and a size-small blue dress.

As the police were leaving, Kelley said she was concerned for her safety and was afraid of staying by herself. The detectives told her to call 911 if she thought there was someone prowling around her apartment.

The next night Rick Greene went back to Kelley Cannon's place. When he arrived, Kelley was sitting on the floor, going through papers that were in a fireproof box about the size of a suitcase—a box that Rick had never seen before. When Rick asked what the papers were, she said they were the kids' Social Security numbers, their birth certificates, her marriage certificate, insurance policies and things like that.

But there was something else in the box as well—cash. Lots of cash. Over $2,000 in twenties.

As Kelley started counting the money, Rick asked where she got it. She said she had taken out an advance on her credit card. But until that day Kelley's financial situation had seemed pretty dire. And Rick was under the impression that she had either maxed out her credit cards or Jim had cut them off. Right then, Rick stopped asking questions . . . at least for the moment.

A little while later, they were sitting in the living room. Once again he started asking her questions about Jim's death. But this time he got right to the point.

"Look me in the eye and tell me that you didn't know his body was in the closet when you left that house," Rick said.

Without answering, Kelley got up and walked into the kitchen. When she came back, she said, "Rick, I can't tell you anything, because I don't want you to have to lie."

Late in the evening of June 25, Brad Putnam contacted Lieutenant Matthew Pylkas, of the MNPD, to ask him to pick Kelley up on three outstanding warrants for violating Jim's order of protection prohibiting her from having the three children. Putnam had gone to Kelley's apartment but she wasn't home so he put out a BOLO (be on the lookout) call for Kelley.

Putnam gave Pylkas a specific description of the Yukon that Kelley was most likely driving and its license plate number. The lieutenant went to White Bridge Road and Harding Pike, because he knew that was near where she lived. Pylkas's training told him the best place to find someone is a very large, heavily traveled intersection approximately within five minutes' driving time of that person's home or a place you know they frequent.

So Pylkas waited in a parking lot at that intersection; and not a few minutes later, Kelley drove by. Pylkas turned on his lights and sirens and followed her at a very low rate of speed for about three-tenths of a mile. Kelley didn't pull over and stop, even though there were plenty of places to do so. But finally she pulled into the parking lot of Walgreens at Harding Pike and Kenner, across from Saint Thomas Hospital.

Pylkas called for backup; then he walked up to Kelley's car. The first thing he noticed was that her hands were shaking uncontrollably and she was acting very nervous. He peered into the car and noticed that it was packed full of merchandise from a local store, and it all appeared to have been recently purchased.

When MNPD sergeant Twana Chick heard Pylkas call for backup over the radio, she immediately headed to the scene. After Pylkas briefed her, he asked her to photograph Kelley's car. Pylkas and Chick were also trying to figure out who should come and pick up the vehicle. They wanted to be sure the car was removed from the parking lot. However, contacting someone to get the car was easier said than done.

Kelley couldn't decide if she wanted police to

impound the Yukon, so it would be in a safe location, or have her brother pick it up. Finally she asked the officers to call her brother, Bobby, who was at a local university. They ultimately reached Bobby, who agreed to take Kelley's car.

While the police waited for Bobby, Chick took some pictures of the Yukon and its contents, including a bunch of shopping bags in the backseat and a large amount of cash that Kelley had with her. When Kelley's brother arrived, Pylkas turned the Yukon and everything in it over to him.

The police then took Kelley back to the station, where she was charged with three counts of criminal contempt for violating the order of protection. Chick was then assigned to take pictures of Kelley. As she did, she noticed an old bruise and a cut on her left wrist. She also noted a dark area on Kelley's wrist, almost as if she had pulled off some type of bandage.

After they obtained a search warrant, police took a DNA sample from Kelley. She was booked through Metro Nashville night court around midnight and was released on a $45,000 bond, shortly after nine in the morning, on Thursday, June 26. A court date was set for the following Tuesday for Kelley to answer for violating the order of protection. At that point the police had not named Kelley as a suspect in her husband's death—although her attorney Peter Strianse told the local media that investigators were calling her "a person of interest."

Strianse said Kelley absolutely denied having anything to do with Jim's death, and even defended the fact that she took the children in violation of a court order. He said he knew the reasons she ended up with the children, but he wasn't at liberty to talk about them.

CHAPTER 5

Jim Cannon's body was taken to the Metro Nashville Medical Examiner's Office to be autopsied. Dr. Thomas Deering, a forensic pathologist, was the medical examiner (ME) on duty the day Jim's body arrived. Deering worked for Forensic Medical Management Services, which had been contracted by Metro Nashville to provide forensic-pathology autopsy services. Before that, he was an assistant professor of pathology at the University of Tennessee Department of Pathology in Memphis. He was also an assistant medical examiner for part of that time. As the ME, Deering's job was to find out why Jim died, as well as how he died.

Deering started Jim's autopsy at eleven in the morning on June 24. The first thing Deering and his associates did was to photograph Jim's body, which had arrived unclothed. Then they weighed and measured Jim's body—he weighed 163 pounds and was five feet six inches tall—then they started looking for any injuries, as well as any signs of illness.

They cleaned him up and took additional photos of his injuries, as well as X-rays. Deering made diagrams of the things that he saw—measuring, annotating and illustrating his findings.

During Jim's autopsy Deering and his team discovered that his neck was scraped and bruised—many of the bruises were long and thin. Jim also had a bruise on his left cheek, a number of scrapes around his nose and below his right ear, as well as a purple bruise on his upper left arm. There was a brown mark on the back of Jim's right shoulder, which he had received after he was dead. It looked as if he had been dragged across something coarse and the top layer of his skin had been scraped off. Deering could even see a sort of weave pattern on Jim's skin, which could have come from a rug.

The doctor also noted that the blood vessels in both Jim's eyes had hemorrhaged. In fact, when Deering pulled Jim's eyelids apart, he noticed that there had been so much bleeding he could hardly see any of the white of his right eye. The bleeding in Jim's left eye was more splotchy and some of the white was still visible. The splotches were the result of a cluster of petechiae, tiny red dots the size of pinpoints caused when the capillaries in Jim's eyes burst.

The presence of petechiae, particularly to the degree that Deering found in Jim's eyes, indicated that there had been a lot of pressure on the blood vessels in his eye, so they burst and then bled. That suggested to Deering that Jim had been asphyxiated, meaning there was not enough blood and oxygen going to his cells.

There are a number of ways a person can be asphyxiated. For example, a small child could be asphyxiated by inadvertently locking himself in a refrigerator and running out of oxygen. Or someone in a house fire could be overcome by carbon monoxide and be asphyxiated. Someone can be asphyxiated if he chokes on a large piece of meat, can't breathe and dies.

Strangulation is a form of asphyxia because the blood vessels and/or the airway is cut off. You can strangle someone with your hands, or you can do it with a ligature or some kind of rope or cord or something that lets you put pressure on the neck. And because the petechiae were so obvious in Jim's eyes, taken in conjunction with the lines of bruises and abrasions around Jim's neck, Deering was sure Jim had been strangled—most likely with a ligature of some sort.

In the case of ligature strangulation, a person's internal jugular veins are cut off. If the jugular veins are cut off for about six to ten seconds, that person will pass out. Holding the ligature longer than that, maybe a couple minutes, will cut off the oxygen to the victim's brain, causing brain death. Then the person's heart and lungs will stop and he will die.

The fact that Jim's face was beet red was further evidence that he had been strangled with a ligature. His face was red because the pressure caused the blood to be trapped in his head; and since the pressure applied while he was being strangled closed off his veins, the blood pooled in his head because it had nowhere else to go.

Deering didn't think Jim had been strangled

with someone's bare hands, because the bruising on his neck wasn't consistent with manual strangulation. There were no bruises or abrasions that looked like they had been made by someone's fingertips or fingernails—bruises that would look more splotchy or round.

During Jim's autopsy Deering also found that there were numerous bruises on Jim's scalp. There was a small bruise on the left side of his scalp and several larger bruises on the right. He didn't have a skull fracture, but there was some kind of blunt-force trauma to the side of his head—in more than one spot—meaning he had been hit on the head with something. Most of the bruises had been caused when Jim was still alive.

The thing that really stood out for Deering was the number of bruises on Jim's tongue. As part of every autopsy Deering examined the deceased's tongue—in part by cutting it lengthwise, looking for bite hemorrhages. People who have seizures or suffer blows to the head often bite their tongues.

When Deering looked at Jim's tongue, he was surprised by the number of bruises in the inside of Jim's tongue. What was even more remarkable was that the bruises went all the way to the back of his tongue—a very unusual occurrence for bite hemorrhages because a person can only stick his tongue out so far.

One of the ways Jim's tongue could have been bruised was if someone had aggressively shoved something in his mouth, like a gag, and he was trying to shove it back out with his tongue. And at that point he wouldn't have been able to cry or scream out for help.

There was a lot of bruising around Jim's right eye. He had a black eye, as well as a pattern of very discrete dark red or purple abrasions alongside his eye and his nose. His nose actually appeared kind of bruised. His face, in general, was rather pink, but his nose, in particular, was much redder. Knowing that Jim's tongue was all bruised, Deering thought the bruises on Jim's face had been made by the tips of someone's fingers.

If Deering was right and someone did shove something in Jim's mouth causing the bruising to his tongue, that person may have been holding it in place with his or her hand.

As part of the autopsy, Deering also dissected Jim's neck. He cut through each thin layer of muscle and removed the skin so he could fold them back, one at a time, and look for injuries inside the neck—particularly bruises in the case of a strangulation victim.

Deering cut his way to Jim's thyroid gland, examined it and removed it. Then he examined Jim's larynx, or voice box, his hyoid bone, which is a U-shaped bone that sits above the level of the voice box, and his trachea, or windpipe. So layer by layer the doctor cut through Jim's neck, looking for injuries. He also removed the voice box to look for injuries behind it where the esophagus, or food tube, sits. The voice box consists of several pieces of cartilage tied together by ligaments.

When Deering took apart Jim's voice box, he found squeezing-type injuries and hemorrhaging in the ligaments inside, which indicated the person who killed him used a lot of force.

Deering had rarely seen the type of injuries he

discovered when he dissected Jim's neck. Typically, a forensic neck dissection was a very subtle examination because it didn't necessarily take a lot of pressure to strangle someone. Deering usually looked for just a few bruises or some hemorrhage behind the voice box to indicate that there had been some pressure applied to the neck.

But when Deering dissected Jim's neck, he found that there were bruises everywhere. There were so many injuries that he knew immediately that Jim had been strangled. Deering discovered numerous injuries that were caused when Jim's murderer put pressure on his voice box and jammed it up against his backbone—a very hard thing to do.

As part of the autopsy, Deering examined Jim's hands, neither of which was bruised, then clipped and collected the ends of each fingernail so they could be tested for any foreign DNA. Toxicology tests indicated that Jim's blood alcohol was .15, twice the legal limit to drive.

About a month after Jim's death, Detective Brad Putnam brought Deering a black cell phone adapter. After measuring the width of its cord, Deering told Putnam it was consistent with the width of the ligature that had been used to strangle Jim.

Jim Cannon's family had made plans to have his body cremated on Friday, June 27, but Kelley filed a motion to stop it that morning. Alison Greer, Jim's sister, wanted him cremated. Alison had control of what was done with her brother's remains due to a court decision. Alison's attorney filed the

motion giving Alison control over her brother's remains because they had no idea where Kelley was.

"The thing that is most urgent is putting a stop to the cremation scheduled for this morning," said Kelley's attorney Andrew Cate during a hearing on the matter. "There's no reason why that has to take place today."

Cate argued how Kelley hadn't been allowed to visit Jim in the funeral home, nor had she been able to see his body. The judge ruled that Alison should retain control of her brother's remains, and he awarded Kelley ninety minutes to visit his body.

Another matter addressed in court that day was the custody of the Cannon children, who were staying with Jim's sister. Kelley's attorney told the judge that Jim's will named Kelley's brother as their guardian in the event that something happened to him. The judge did not rule on that issue at the hearing.

Kelley Cannon viewed Jim's body shortly after two in the afternoon on Friday. The funeral director said Jim's remains were cremated soon after she visited.

The next day, Saturday, a member of Jim's family called police to Jim's Bowling Avenue home because a locksmith was changing the locks under Kelley's lawyer's supervision. Police arrived at the scene to prevent a confrontation between Jim's relatives and Kelley's attorney. Police told those involved to resolve their disagreement or to take it to civil court, because it was not a criminal matter.

Cate said because the house had been in Kelley's

name since 2005, he had recommended that she change the locks so Jim's family couldn't take anything else out of the house. Cate claimed that sometime after Jim died, his relatives went to the house and took his Mercedes, as well as things from inside the home.

CHAPTER 6

Kelley Sanders Cannon had always lived the good life. A Nashville debutante, she was raised by her father, Stan, a successful plastic surgeon and her mother, Diane, who stayed at home to raise her three children—two boys and a beautiful little girl. Like the heroine in Bob Dylan's song "Like a Rolling Stone," Kelley went to Tennessee's finest schools. She was a cheerleader and prom queen at Harpeth Hall, an exclusive prep school for girls in Nashville that also boasts such famous alumni as actress Reese Witherspoon and country singer Amy Grant. To hear her friends tell it, Kelley was a real lady, beloved by all who knew her.

After high school, Kelley headed off for college, where she joined a sorority. After all, isn't that what all Nashville debs did? After college—it was early 1989—Kelley applied for a writing position in the PR department at NASA's Marshall Space Flight Center in Huntsville, Alabama.

Pamela Brady, an administrative assistant at Management Services Inc., a NASA contractor, was the liaison between the manager of the PR department and the various applicants. The two women met when Kelley was hired to write informational brochures for exhibits to promote the space program. They really hit it off and became fast friends. To Pam, Kelley was just as sweet, charming and as polite as could be.

Kelley worked for NASA for two years; then around 1991, she decided to go home to Nashville. She and Pam stayed in touch, however, and remained friends. They exchanged cards and letters and even visited each other. Once back in Nashville, Kelley got a job as deputy press secretary for former Tennessee governor Ned Ray McWherter. She left that job to enroll in premed courses at Lipscomb University. Her dream was to follow in her father's footsteps and pursue a career in medicine.

Kelley started dating Jim Cannon, a young attorney, while she was in medical school. They were both in their twenties. However, the two had met years earlier when Kelley and Jim's sister became friends when they were both at Harpeth Hall. Although Jim's friends welcomed Kelley, her parents were not quite so enamored of him. They were from different worlds. Jim's mother and father had divorced when he was just a boy, and he wasn't talking to his sister. To make matters worse, Jim had money problems. In fact, he had filed for bankruptcy shortly before Kelley told her parents they were getting married.

Even though her parents weren't thrilled with that prospect, they still gave Kelley and Jim a once-in-a-lifetime wedding that they'd never forget. Kelley and Jim got married in 1996—Pam Brady was the maid of honor. After the marriage Kelley

left medical school to focus on having a family.
Their first son, Tim, was born in 1998, followed by
another son, Henry, in 2000.

As luck would have it, Jim's career took a turn
for the better. He stopped practicing law, founded
Medical Reimbursements of America (MRA), a
firm that collected bad debts for hospitals, and
became a multimillionaire—much to the surprise of
Kelley's mom. However, Jim made enemies along
the way, including an ex-partner who said Jim had
cheated him out of about $250,000. And for some
reason Kelley seemed to believe the partner and
was concerned about the bad blood between them.

They bought a big house—a big house that
needed a lot of work—but a big house nonetheless.
Then in 2003, while Kelley was working on fixing
up that big house, she fell and hurt her back. Her
doctor prescribed some pain pills—very powerful
pain pills.

Problem was, Kelley liked the way they made her
feel—a lot. So much so, in 2003, she entered a
treatment program. And it appeared to work—for
a while. But she still had trouble with drugs and alcohol until 2006, when daughter Sophie was born.
But things went from bad to worse. In the summer
of 2007, Kelley was convinced that her husband was
having an affair with someone at his office. She
confronted him about it. At first, he denied it; later,
he admitted to it—at least that's what Kelley said.

Kelley's life just seemed to get rockier; once
again she needed a crutch—or two. She went to see
a psychiatrist, who prescribed medication for depression. However, that made her drowsy and all
she wanted to do was sleep. As a result she downed

Coke after Coke, hoping the caffeine would help her stay awake.

John Hollins Jr. and Jim Cannon had known each other for about twenty years. The two men had had mutual friends and socialized together a bit when they were young lawyers. But Hollins hadn't seen Jim for about fifteen years, before Jim started talking divorce. Hollins, a partner at Hollins, Raybin & Weissman, primarily handled divorce, child custody and domestic-relations cases.

In an interview Hollins said he had met Jim when they were both out of law school and in their twenties. That was the late 1980s, early 1990s. They met socially through some friends of friends. For about two years the friends were running around with the same crowd of girls.

"We went out partying and I got to know him pretty well," Hollins said. "We'd go to bars; we did that a lot. We did a lot of barhopping and a lot of dancing. We'd go to each other's houses. We had a lot of fun. Jim loved that. He was very social. He enjoyed cocktail parties and getting to know new people."

Jim was the kind of guy who never met a stranger. They were just friends waiting to be made.

"I've never heard anybody say anything bad about him. He liked to take a drink—we all did back in that time. We drank a lot, and partied a lot. He had a great sense of humor," Hollins said. "He was a little guy. He was five-foot-seven and one hundred forty pounds. He was the life of the party. Nobody ever said anything negative about him.

Everybody who knew him really liked him. He was very personable."

But then Jim got married and John got married—to people outside their circle of friends—and the men lost contact. But Jim's first marriage was short-lived. And then he met Kelley.

Hollins didn't see Jim again until he called him in late February 2008 to talk to him about divorcing Kelley. Jim wanted John to represent him. The men met and Jim filled Hollins in about all the sordid details of his marriage.

"We met and he told me the whole history about Kelley's inpatient treatment and drug and psychiatric programs, and he told me about the time when she had come after him with a butcher knife. She was on pills or on drugs, or something. They were in an argument [and] she pulled a butcher knife on him. She didn't stab him. He was on the phone with 911. They heard him say, 'Kelley, put the knife down. Kelley, put the knife down.' She was charged with aggravated assault. Later, I think they got it worked out, which was a pattern. I don't know how many times. She just got belligerent when the police were involved. They took her to jail several times because of that. That's what Jim told me."

The day after that meeting, February 29, John filed the paperwork in the Eighth Circuit Court that would set Jim's divorce, as well as his untimely death, into motion.

But even though Kelley put Jim through hell, Hollins said, Jim didn't really want a divorce. He just wanted her to get help for her drug and alcohol addiction.

"The original petition we filed, we got a court

order where he got custody of the children," Hollins said. "And the court gave him exclusive possession of the house, where he was killed. She couldn't harass him or the kids. That was late February or early March 2008. At this point she is spiraling out of control. Her weight is about ninety pounds. Sometime in March, she goes to Cumberland Heights, drug- and alcohol-treatment facility, and she stays there for thirty days. When she got out, Jim wanted her to come home. He wanted to give her another chance. He didn't want the divorce. He wanted her to get better."

In the divorce complaint Hollins asked Judge Carol Solomon to grant Jim temporary custody of the three children. And he asked the judge for a restraining order to prevent Kelley from harassing, threatening or harming Jim or intimidating the kids. Judge Solomon granted both orders on March 3. She also ordered Kelley to stay off the booze and pain meds.

Hollins had also petitioned the judge to grant Jim exclusive possession of the Cannon house, something she decided against because of the wording of Hollins's request. After redoing his pleading Hollins resubmitted it to the judge, who agreed that Jim should be given the house. The judge then ordered Jim and Kelley to appear before her within ten days to testify about the allegations of abuse. After the hearing the judge made a decision to extend the order of protection to keep Kelley away from Jim.

In the divorce papers Jim claimed that he and the children weren't safe around Kelley because of her behavior. According to Jim, Kelley used narcotics and smoked cigarettes in front of him and the kids. Jim also alleged that Kelley physically assaulted him more than once. In 2002 or 2003, she tried to kill herself, slashing her arms with a razor blade. And during their eleven-year marriage, she had been arrested and charged with both simple and aggravated assault against him.

Jim couldn't handle her, so he was forced to have her committed to inpatient and outpatient rehab facilities to deal with her addiction to alcohol and narcotics.

Although Kelley was diagnosed with a form of psychosis and prescribed an antipsychotic drug, some of her psychotic episodes were still so scary that Jim was forced to call police on numerous occasions. Kelley took her medicine regularly for two or three years, but she continued to abuse alcohol. During that time period she was arrested for throwing a lead crystal glass at her husband during one of her drunken and psychotic episodes.

Before one admission to the addiction facility at a local treatment center, Kelley was screaming and so combative with Metro Police officers and paramedics that she had to be restrained physically. She was taken directly to the drug treatment center, where she was kept in "physical lockdown" for seven days.

In 2005, Kelley started doctor shopping to get prescriptions for Lortab, Percocet, and OxyContin for alleged back pain. To avoid suspicion, Kelley had her prescriptions filled at small drugstores in the area. Since Kelley had never had back surgery or back pain, Jim couldn't understand why she needed the medications. All he knew was that she downed ninety to one hundred 10-milligram pills a month.

On February 27, 2008, Kelley told Jim she was hearing voices in the house and when she was talking on the telephone. Trying to avoid a confrontation, Jim offered to leave the house, but Kelley stopped him from going by hiding his briefcase, which contained his wallet. Jim begged her to give it back so he could check in to a hotel for the night. After three hours of pleading with her, Jim was forced to call the Metropolitan Nashville Police Department for help.

When they arrived, Jim went outside to meet them. As soon as he shut the door, Kelley locked it, preventing Jim and the police from entering the house. For about ten minutes the police knocked repeatedly on the door; Kelley finally opened it and handed them the briefcase. After talking to Jim about Kelley's behavior, the police decided that someone should spend the night with her and the children if Jim went to a hotel.

Jim called the nanny and she and her roommate agreed to babysit Kelley and the kids. Jim left the house and headed to a nearby hotel at about half past midnight. He had only been gone about two hours when he received a call from the nanny and Kelley, who were using the speakerphone. For the next hour and forty-five minutes, Kelley complained of hearing voices. Then the call ended.

The next morning the nanny called Jim. She was worried because Kelley was verbally abusing the couple's youngest son. She was accusing him of colluding with the voices against her. The nanny told

Jim the young boy started crying. She said she drove him to school and he cried all the way there.

Fed up with Kelley's antics, Jim filed divorce papers on March 1. A couple days later, a Davidson County judge gave Jim temporary custody of the three children. He also issued restraining orders and an injunction that would prevent Kelley from coming into contact with Jim or the children.

But Jim really wanted Kelley to get better and be his wife and the mother of their children. So the couple agreed that Kelley could live in their house if she went for drug and alcohol treatment. Kelley went to Cumberland Heights around March 6, 2008. While she was there, Kelley wrote to her attorney, asking him to stop the divorce proceedings because she and Jim were trying to get back together.

She was released in early April 2008 and welcomed back home. The plan was for her to continue to receive outpatient treatment. Even though the restraining orders were in place at the time she returned home, the lawyers for both sides just decided to leave everything in place for sixty days before making any final decisions.

But Hollins didn't like it, because he didn't think it would work. And he was right.

"Then she starts drinking and drugging shortly thereafter," Hollins said. "I think it was around May eighteenth or twenty-first—she was screwed up. She gets into the car with the young child and tries to grab the other kids and tries to take off. She runs over the bicycle. She tried to run over Jim. She leaves and she's going seventy in a thirty-mile-per-hour area. The police pull in as she pulls out. They don't chase her 'cause they don't want her to kill the kid. Through the OnStar, they find her at a hotel in Brentwood, which is a suburb south of town."

John Hollins was referring to the argument that Jim and Kelley Cannon had outside on the driveway. Kelley was acting so crazy that Jim called 911.

"She's having a psychotic break," Jim told the dispatcher. "She attacked me and hit the car. It's so pitiful, so friggin' pitiful. Now she's got the baby. Now she's trying to leave. Don't leave, Kelley. She's threatening me right now. . . . She's a lunatic. She's putting the baby in [the] car. Henry and Tim, move away. Do not get in the car. Absolutely not. Get away from me, Kelley, get away."

But Kelley didn't listen. Instead, she grabbed Sophie and put her in her car in the backseat. She backed up over one of the boys' bicycles and rammed Jim's car. Then she took off down the road, speeding up to about seventy miles an hour through a residential neighborhood.

Officer George Ward was dispatched to the scene. As he drove, he received information from Jim relayed through dispatch. He responded to the scene with lights flashing and sirens blaring, because whatever was happening was deemed to be an immediate emergency because Kelley Cannon had taken one of the couple's three children and was driving erratically. In fact, she had pushed Jim's car out of the way with her own car. Ward said he was going to the Cannons' house to make sure everyone was safe. As he got close to the house, he turned his siren off.

As Ward was driving up Bowling Avenue, he saw a black GMC Yukon driven by Kelley coming up to the end of the driveway. Kelley looked right at Ward, who made eye contact with her. He was heading right at her, but then she turned left out of the driveway onto Bowling and left again onto Hampton Avenue. She then went in the other direction. Ward turned his siren back on when he saw Kelley pulling away. He was right behind her and he kept accelerating, trying to catch her. When the cars hit about seventy miles an hour, Ward backed off. He didn't want her to end up wrecking out, with a child in the car.

Ward turned around and went back to the Cannons' house to talk to Jim. When he got out of his cruiser to approach Jim, Ward noticed the man's short-sleeved shirt was ripped and there was a grass stain on it. He also had a bruise on his right bicep. Ward also observed that the rear bumper of Jim's car had been damaged.

Jim told Ward that Kelley's car was equipped with OnStar, so they'd be able to figure out where she was going. As soon as the other officers arrived at Jim's house, one of them contacted OnStar. With Jim's permission the company tracked Kelley down. Ward took out a warrant on Kelley for domestic assault, as well as a warrant for reckless endangerment and evading arrest. One of the other detectives helped Jim with an order of protection against his wife.

They arrested Kelley and charged her with felony evading arrest, felony child endangerment and assault against her husband. Her court date was set for August 18. This time, as far as Jim was concerned, Kelley had gone too far. This time the children had been involved. So he e-mailed John Hollins and told him to go ahead with the divorce. But that wasn't quite all. Because of Kelley's addictions and alleged erratic behavior, Hollins was able to convince a judge that she might be a danger to her family. The judge also issued an order banning Kelley from going back to the house and prohibiting her from seeing the children.

After that Kelley lived in a variety of places. In fact, for a week or two, no one had a clue where she was staying because she was moving around from one hotel to another. While Jim was at home taking care of the kids, Kelley was trying to make a new life for herself. She even met a couple guys who were attracted to her.

Jim finally located Kelley and arranged to get her into the apartment on Elmington. She lived there for a few weeks before Jim was murdered.

CHAPTER 7

On Tuesday, July 1, 2008, Kelley Cannon appeared in a Nashville courtroom to answer the charges that she violated an order of protection that prohibited her from having contact with her three children. The charges stemmed from the night before Jim's body was found when she took the children from his house and brought them to her apartment.

Kelley had hired two attorneys to help her move through the legal system: criminal attorney Peter Strianse and Andrew Cate, who would represent her in custody hearings and in matters regarding Jim's will, among other things.

Both of Kelley's attorneys viewed Jim's divorce filings as one-sided. Cate considered a lot of the allegations in the divorce petition to be unfounded. In fact, Cate cited that Kelley didn't file a response to Jim's divorce petition because she always wanted to get back together with him. And according to Cate, Jim called Kelley almost every day to discuss their future and possibly reconciling. Cate said Jim even named Kelley the executor of his will. Kelley's mother, Diane, was the alternate executor.

Although police had not yet identified Kelley Cannon as a suspect in the case, her attorney Peter Strianse said investigators were calling her a "person of interest." Strianse said, whenever you have a husband or a wife who dies under suspicious circumstances, police will always consider the other spouse a person of interest. However, Strianse said, Kelley said she *did not* murder her husband.

As Kelley was leaving the hearing, she told reporters she was "devastated" by everything that was happening.

The attorneys told the press that Kelley intended to fight for full custody of her children. Strianse said she was "obviously devastated" to be away from her children and to have lost her husband, and she was trying to take care of everything.

After Jim's death Kelley was so distraught that she couldn't even function. She was shunned by his family and friends who considered her the main suspect in his death because of her drug addiction, her bizarre behavior and her part in the troubled marriage. Kelley, though, denied that she was anything but a good mother and a loyal and dedicated wife.

Although Kelley didn't speak to the media after her arrest, she did talk extensively to the *Nashville Scene*, an alternative weekly in Nashville, just days before she was arrested for murdering her husband.

To hear Kelley tell it, it was Jim who was the drug addict. It was Jim who was emotionally unstable. It was Jim who begged her to violate the orders of protection he took out against her.

Kelley told the *Nashville Scene* about the call she

received from Jim the night she was out with Amy Huston. According to Kelley, Jim was pretty scared the night he died—and he was very rarely afraid. Kelley said that during that call Jim said he was afraid and that he loved her. He told her that he wanted her to go over to the house.

"He said, 'I'm just telling you, things have spun out of control . . . [things] that I can't even talk about. I feel threatened, and I'm afraid,'" Kelley told the *Nashville Scene*.

Kelley said after she "paced and paced and paced," she drove to the house around midnight. Her plan was to peek inside through the windows to ensure that there were no problems. But her plans changed when she drove into the driveway and noticed that the back door to the house was open.

Kelley described what she saw when she went into the house. All the downstairs lights were on and some of the furniture had been turned over. Everything was in disarray. There were even towels thrown around on the floor. She called out for Jim, but he didn't answer. Kelley said she went upstairs to the children's rooms.

Kelley rounded up the kids, starting with Sophie. The boys were sleeping in the master bedroom. She looked for Jim in his office, where she said he typically slept. It was empty. She also looked in the boys' bedroom, but it was empty. Although there was no one in the boys' bedroom, Kelley said she knew Jim had been sleeping there because his briefcase and glasses were in the room. Kelley told the *Nashville Scene* she never saw Jim at all.

"I kept calling for him, and I didn't hear him," she told the *Nashville Scene*. "And then I thought,

'Oh, I've got to get the kids out of here. Whoever did this has got to be in the house and may be watching the house.'"

Kelley said even though she figured something was wrong, and she was afraid, she still packed a bag with Sophie's things. She said she didn't call the police, despite being afraid, choosing instead just to take the kids to her place.

Kelley was asked to respond to claims Jim had made in his divorce papers that she told him she was hearing voices in the house, as well as when she was talking on the phone. According to Kelley, Jim made up that story to cover up the fact that he was having an affair—one of several, she said, he had had over the years.

Kelley said what really happened was that she called home when she was out with the boys, and a woman answered the phone. When she got home, she asked Jim who the woman was. Kelley claimed that Jim became so enraged that he kicked the family's takeout chicken dinner across the floor. According to Kelley, Jim's reaction was typical. When contacted by the *Nashville Scene,* John Hollins said he had no reason to think Jim was having an affair.

Kelley offered her own theories as to who could have murdered her husband—the assailant ranged from his former colleagues to the alleged mistress, whom Kelley described as a stalker.

Still, Kelley never called Jim on his infidelities because she loved him. "I loved him with all my life," she told the *Nashville Scene.* "I wouldn't have married a man and stuck with him through bankruptcy. There's too many things that show my heart and the truth of my devotion and dedication to him."

But according to the *Nashville Scene,* as Kelley talked about her marriage and how Jim wronged her, it became clear that in her eyes Jim was the liar. In Kelley's mind Jim was covering up his jealousies, rage and the fact that he was so controlling by putting the blame on her. Kelley said she never said anything, even right after Jim's murder, because she didn't want to "sully his name."

However, Kelley said at one point she did want a separation from Jim—only because she said she caught him going through her purse looking for bills. According to Jim, Kelley was addicted to pain medication. Kelley told the *Nashville Scene* that a doctor had prescribed the pain pills because she had fallen and injured her back in their home. Although Kelley claimed Jim watched her fall, he always said she had never hurt her back.

"He had convinced my mother that I was a total drug addict. . . . I had to hide the pain pills from him," she told the alternative weekly. "I had lost so much weight with basically grieving myself sick over his . . . He never really came back to the marriage after he had the affairs."

Kelley said she asked her husband to stop drinking and to go to marriage counseling, but he refused. She claimed that was okay because at least the family was together. She said she was trying to keep things as normal as possible for the sake of the kids.

Then Jim filed for divorce and petitioned the court for injunctions to keep Kelley away. But, according to Kelley, Jim really wanted her back, even going so far as to ask her to violate the orders of protection so she could stay with him and the children.

Kelley claimed it was John Hollins who was pushing Jim to move forward with the divorce.

Kelley told the paper that when she talked to Jim the night he died, Jim said he "couldn't get Hollins under control." According to Kelley, Jim told her everything had spiraled out of control and that he still loved her.

John Hollins declined to comment to the *Nashville Scene* regarding Kelley's characterization of him. But Hollins did say that Jim never once mentioned reconciling with Kelley.

When Kelley finally gave in and went back home, she said Jim got on her about any little thing that went wrong, telling her he was going to kick her out.

Kelley said that the May 21 incident when she put Sophie in the car and tried to leave, ramming into Jim's car in the process, did not go down the way Jim said it did. She said Jim was angry at her because she had called his psychiatrist to tell the doctor that Jim was addicted to sedatives.

The psychiatrist told Jim to find another therapist, she said, forcing Jim to locate a new doctor to prescribe those sedatives. Kelley said Jim was so furious that while they were in the kitchen he shoved her and Sophie.

Afraid for herself and her children, she tried to flee, bumping Jim's car in the process. She claimed Jim said he'd do everything in his power to make sure she was locked up in jail so she wouldn't be near the children. But Kelley told the weekly paper that she and Jim agreed that she'd tell the police it was all her fault so he wouldn't lose his license to practice law.

Kelley did admit that she entered a drug rehabilitation facility, but she didn't quite take responsibility for the actions that landed her there. One time, she said, Jim tricked her into going to rehab. He told her that once she got home, he'd go in himself.

Though Jim said Kelley's weight dropped to just ninety pounds because she was using drugs, she said the weight loss was due to pneumonia, as well as the emotional strain of not being with her children—when she was living outside the home—not to mention the stress from her husband's affairs.

One time, Kelley said, she collapsed in her room, weakened because she had not been able to keep any food or liquid down. She called an ambulance to take her to the hospital, but a counselor convinced her it would be best if she went to Cumberland Heights to "get her sea legs." Kelley said she made her problems out to be worse than they were because she wanted to be admitted to the treatment facility so she could have a comfortable place to stay.

During her interview with the *Nashville Scene,* Kelley portrayed Jim as an unfeeling and uncaring man who was never around as a husband or as a father. Even so, she stayed with him for the simple reason that she loved him and she wanted her kids to have a father.

What was particularly odd was that Kelley didn't seem to understand why anyone would consider her a suspect in the murder of her husband. After all, she was the person who helped Jim become successful.

"I was the prom queen. I grew up here. I married this guy when he had just gone through a divorce and went bankrupt my first year and supported him.

I took him back after the affairs and without ado—there was no separation, there was nothing. . . . And that was okay. I didn't care—whatever," Kelley told the *Nashville Scene*.

Shortly after Kelley's interview with the weekly, Ellen, a nanny who worked for the Cannons, gave her own interview to the newspaper to refute Kelley's story. Ellen, who had worked at the Cannon home from early March 2008 until she was fired in May of that year, had a different tale to tell.

Ellen was recommended to the Cannons by her roommate, who had worked for Kelley and Jim for a short time but was moving on to another job. The roommate told Ellen that Jim and the kids were great. But the mom, not so much. In fact, at that point, the roommate said, Kelley was in rehab. Something to do with drugs.

Ellen's roommate told her to be careful working for the Cannons. And it wasn't long before she figured out why. Before Ellen's first official night working for the family, Jim let Ellen know what was going on with Kelley. He told her at that time that Kelley was in rehab for pills—OxyContin, to be exact—and she'd lost thirty pounds.

Jim told Ellen that sometimes Kelley was so "whacked-out" she had a hard time just standing up. Needless to say, Ellen was really concerned. But the fact that he was honest with her was a plus. She also liked the way he was when around the children. Despite her misgivings, Ellen agreed to work for the Cannons. Her shift started early in the morning and ended when Jim got home from work in the afternoon.

One of the first things Jim asked Ellen to do was help him find all the places where Kelley hid her drugs. Jim told Ellen that Kelley had filled sandwich bags with crushed OxyContin and cutoff straws she used to snort the drugs and stashed the plastic bags around the house. Ellen told the *Nashville Scene* that she and Jim discovered Baggies all over the house— in the boys' closets, in the kitchen cupboards and even in baby Sophie's sock drawer.

Ellen's first couple weeks at the Cannons were pretty routine. Packing school lunches for the boys, driving them to and from school, doing laundry. Then came the Sunday when Jim asked Ellen to go with him to family day to see Kelley at Cumberland Heights. Kelley was almost done with her month-long stay at the facility. The kids were particularly rambunctious that morning. They let their dad know, in no uncertain terms, that they didn't want to go. But, of course, they went.

When they arrived, Ellen, who was holding Sophie, took the kids to a room so they could see Kelley. Ellen said hello and introduced herself to Kelley. Kelley, however, didn't say any greeting in return. She just got on Ellen for putting a coat on Sophie that she thought was dirty. After a few minutes of listening to Kelley, the boys asked Ellen if she'd take them to the playground.

Try as she might, Kelley just couldn't get the boys to talk. And that gave Ellen a bad feeling. It seemed that the kids wanted to be with her more than their own mother. She later told Jim she was kind of nervous because she felt like she was taking Kelley's place.

A week later, Kelley came home. She was only supposed to be there for a short while because Jim had made plans for her to spend ninety days in a treatment facility in Arizona. That, however, never happened. And soon life at the Cannons' went horribly wrong.

Then every day was a nightmare. All Kelley really had to do was pick the boys up from school. But Ellen said that each afternoon at three-thirty, Jim would call to ensure that Kelley had picked them up. Ellen told the *Nashville Scene* that Kelley was right—Jim was a "control freak," but only because he was worried about what could happen to the boys when Kelley was taking care of them.

Jim had good reason to be concerned. When Kelley was home, one of Ellen's responsibilities was to keep a supply of grape cough syrup on hand. She said Kelley always kept a bottle of the medicine and a pack of cigarettes in the pocket of her housecoat.

One morning when Ellen arrived at the Cannon house, she discovered the television was blaring and the dishes were piled high in the kitchen sink. But no one was around. So she checked around to see if anyone was home. When she got to the master bedroom, Ellen found Sophie sitting on the edge of the bed, with a red marker in her hand. Kelley was passed out, faceup, lying next to a huge red circle that the baby had drawn on the bed.

Despite everything, Ellen told the newspaper that Jim stayed with Kelley. He knew she needed help, but he loved her and he wasn't leaving.

Then one Saturday night, about five weeks before Jim was murdered, he asked Ellen to help out at the house. Everything seemed to be okay. Jim and the kids were just home watching television. But things aren't always as they seem. The next day Kelley called Ellen and fired her.

Needless to say, Ellen was stunned. She still had a year to go on her contract. And Jim had asked her to go with the family on their summer vacation. Ellen tried calling Jim, but Kelley wouldn't let Jim take the call.

Although Ellen kept in touch with the Cannons' housekeeper after she was terminated, Ellen only found out that Jim had been murdered when she saw it on the news.

Ellen told the *Nashville Scene* that the only thing that ran through her mind was an immediate judgment about Kelley Cannon: "She did it. She did it."

CHAPTER 8

On Thursday morning, July 10, 2008, Kelley was arrested without incident at her mom's house in West Nashville. She was arrested for strangling Jim Cannon to death. An analysis done on evidence collected by the Tennessee Bureau of Investigation (TBI) linked Kelley to Jim's murder. Kelley's mother, of course, said there was no way her daughter could have killed her husband.

Kelley appeared on closed-circuit television that evening from the Davidson County Jail before the Metropolitan Nashville & Davidson County Court night commissioner to be charged with killing Jim Cannon.

Kelley's mother told the local media that she and Kelley were in bed sleeping when police showed up at the door. Kelley had moved in with Diane two weeks earlier after finishing up treatment for substance abuse. Diane said that she was in absolute shock that Kelley had been arrested and charged with murdering her husband.

She said her daughter was "devastated" by Jim's

death and it was "absurd" to think there was any way she could have strangled him to death. After all, Kelley only weighed ninety pounds, while Jim weighed in at 190. And Jim could have overpowered her in a few seconds.

But the police, as well as Jim's family and friends, including attorney John Hollins, knew the right person was behind bars—for the moment at least. All they wanted to do at that point was take care of the Cannons' three children. Although Tim, Henry and Sophie had been living with Jim's sister, Kelley was trying to wrest them away from a loving home to be with her. In fact, she had a custody hearing scheduled the morning she was arrested.

Although Kelley's mother, Diane Sanders, declined to be interviewed for this book unless she was paid, she did speak to the *Nashville Scene* the morning Kelley was arrested.

Diane told the *Nashville Scene* that her daughter just got mixed up with the wrong man, but she didn't think Kelley murdered him. During Diane's interview she disclosed details about Jim's murder that she shouldn't have known, considering police had been tight-lipped regarding the details of his death and his autopsy results hadn't even been released.

"Physically, I know the details of the murder and everything," she told the weekly. "I can't divulge what I know."

Diane told the newspaper that Jim's body had been stuffed into a closet in the boys' bedroom. "There was a chest of drawers knocked over that weighs about three hundred pounds, because it's solid wood, against the door of the closet—like blocking the door so he couldn't get out," she said. According to the *Nashville Scene*, two other sources close to the investigation confirmed that detail. However, the housekeeper and the nanny who first found Jim could have given Diane that information.

"There's no way a little ninety-pound girl like her could've done all that was done to him in the manner in which he was killed. And knocked over a three-hundred-pound chest and all that kind of stuff," Diane said. "Physically she couldn't have done it. I don't know how you drag a one-hundred-ninety-pound man across the floor, you know, and put him in a closet—a deadweight. Deadweight."

At one point, Diane said, police were investigating whether Kelley had an accomplice. But, she said, Kelley didn't have any money to hire someone to kill Jim, adding that her daughter didn't have any boyfriends, either.

Speculating about a possible motive, Diane said it didn't make sense for Kelley to kill Jim, since he was her only source of income.

"Why would you murder somebody when that's your source of income? It wouldn't be for the insurance or anything—that's stupid," Diane told the newspaper.

Diane said in the days and weeks after Jim's murder, Kelley, who had been staying with her mother until she was arrested, was a basket case.

"She's just been like a zombie—absolutely changed. Can't think, can't eat, can't sleep. Her brain is just fried. She doesn't hardly even know where she is," Diane told the *Nashville Scene*.

Even though Kelley never admitted to having a

drug problem, Diane said that Kelley was, in fact, addicted to drugs. That's why Kelley ended up in rehab at Cumberland Heights.

"She started with popping the pills to ease her mental pain and stuff, and got in trouble . . . ," Sanders said, which was precisely why Jim wanted a divorce.

Trying to find logic in an illogical situation, Diane said if Kelley was guilty, she would have left town after she murdered her husband. She wouldn't go back to her apartment and just wait for the police to track her down. And if she had killed him, she certainly wouldn't have put up such a fight to stop Jim's family from cremating his remains.

In an article in the *Nashville Scene,* Diane Sanders commented, "Anyway, she's already been convicted in the media. What's this—the O.J. Simpson case of Nashville?"

Kelley Cannon's preliminary hearing on murder charges was held the following Wednesday morning, July 16, at the Birch Building in downtown Nashville. When Kelley walked into the courtroom, she was wearing a bright yellow jail-issued jumpsuit and handcuffs on her wrists.

At the hearing Detective Brad Putnam testified that Jim's body was found in the closet of his sons' bedroom, where he often slept.

Putnam testified that the autopsy results indicated Jim had been strangled. Putnam said that a blood-spattered phone charger was also found in the room, but police never found the cord for the phone charger.

Putnam also said there were bruises on Jim's body indicating he had struggled with his assailant.

He told the judge that from the very beginning the evidence pointed to Kelley Cannon.

He also testified that latex gloves—as well as just the tip of one glove—found at the scene had Jim's DNA on the outside and Kelley's DNA on the inside. Putnam testified that Kelley was caught on surveillance video stealing latex gloves from the Walgreens located at White Bridge Road and Charlotte Pike in West Nashville.

"The front camera shows her walking out the front door past the registers with the box of latex gloves still under her right arm," Putnam said in court. Putnam testified that when the detectives searched Kelley's apartment, they found an opened box of latex gloves.

The detective said that Kelley Cannon's mother provided information that led to her daughter being named a suspect. But Diane told reporters that Putnam "misconstrued" everything she said to build a case against her daughter.

The detective also told the court about the conversation Kelley had with Jim the night she was out with Amy Huston—the night before Jim was killed. Putnam said that Kelley admitted to being in the house the night before his body was discovered. He then explained Kelley's version of what happened when she was in the house, as well as what happened when police interviewed her at her apartment.

Kelley's criminal attorney, Peter Strianse, tried to counter the testimony against his client, saying the hearing was just preliminary and the investigation into Jim's murder really hadn't been completed at that point.

After the judge heard all the testimony, he decided there was enough probable cause to send the case to the grand jury. Diane, who was in the courtroom for the hearing, told the media that Kelley's arrest was devastating and broke her heart.

Strianse filed a motion for a reduction in Kelley's $500,000 bond, but he later withdrew the motion, saying he would refile it the next week.

Kelley was scheduled to return to court on August 18, but not for her husband's murder. The hearing was in regard to the three counts of criminal contempt for violating the order of protection preventing her from seeing her three children. At the hearing the judge dismissed the criminal contempt charges against Kelley.

The following Monday, Kelley appeared in court. This time she was wearing blue prison garb. She waived her hearing on reckless endangerment and evading arrest charges stemming from the incident in May when she rammed into Jim's car, tried to leave with Sophie in the car and led police on a wild chase through the neighborhood streets. So general sessions court judge Gale Robinson sent the case to the grand jury.

At the hearing the judge dropped the charges against Kelley for violating the order of protection. In a motion Strianse had argued that the protection order prevented Kelley from coming into contact with Jim, not the children.

After a bond hearing on Wednesday morning, Kelley posted the $500,000 bail, then went to her mother's house in Green Hills. As part of the conditions of her bail, Kelley was required to wear a monitoring device and she was ordered to stay away from her children. The restraining order to keep Kelley away from her kids alleged that she had abused them physically and mentally.

Shortly after being released on bail, Kelley Cannon told reporters that the criminal case against her was absurd.

"I think the whole investigation is botched and sloppy and ridiculous," Kelley told a television news reporter. "It was ridiculous. It's compromised. It's contaminated."

Kelley told the media that she'd been in shock.

"I haven't been able to grieve my husband, my children. I'm a nervous wreck," she said. "It makes me furious. It makes me furious."

Kelley was asked if she could have strangled her husband. Her response: "Absolutely not. There's no way."

When asked why she couldn't have done it, Kelley said, "Physically I couldn't have done it, and morally I couldn't have done it. He was my best friend."

According to Kelley, Jim was angry because she had asked for a separation, and that was the reason he filed for divorce. Reporters asked Kelley about the tip of a latex glove that investigators found at the crime scene with her DNA on the inside and Jim's DNA on the outside. They also asked her about the other latex gloves that police had found outside. Kelley said she had no idea who used the gloves or why.

All Kelley would say was that she was glad to be out of jail because she was innocent—a fact, she said, she would prove in court.

"There are some things going to come out about Jim that I didn't even know about Jim. I can't say anything else," she told the media.

For the moment Kelley was going to focus on her defense while trying to gain custody of Tim, Henry and Sophie, who were living with Jim's sister. She believed that as their sole living parent, it was only right that she should have custody of them.

"It's been extremely hard on her to be separated from the children. That's been the hardest thing for her," her attorney said at the time.

Kelley told the media that it made her sick that her children were living with her sister-in-law. She said she was working on getting them back.

"I've been in jail and my husband's murdered. I haven't seen my children. How would you feel?" she asked a local reporter. "I'm lost."

A former prosecutor for the juvenile court told the media that it was doubtful that Kelley would be getting her kids back.

"Obviously, the courts want to discourage people from murdering their spouses to get their kids back," he said.

Jim's family was concerned, so they began taking measures to ensure that they were safe. In fact, they filed for an order of protection to keep her away from her children, as well as from Jim's sister and her three children. Because of Kelley's unstable behavior and drug abuse, her in-laws were concerned that she might just show up to take the kids.

"We're dealing with human life and threat of

losing a life, so they're taking it very seriously," circuit court clerk Ricky Rooker told the local media. And that meant Kelley would be arrested if she violated the order. Kelley challenged the order of protection during a circuit court hearing the next week, and a custody hearing was set for November.

Kelley Cannon was arraigned for Jim's murder on September 17, 2008. She didn't speak, but her attorney Peter Strianse entered a not guilty plea on her behalf. He said he hoped the court would set a trial date by the end of the year. After the arraignment Strianse told the media that Kelley was doing as well as could be expected, and was living with her mother.

Kelley couldn't believe that she had been charged with murder. He said she was upset, frustrated, scared and intimidated by the process, but she was focused on getting back custody of the kids.

That afternoon Kelley, who said she was having financial problems, appeared in probate court to ask the judge to release Jim's assets, which had been frozen and put into a trust.

Then at the beginning of October, police released reports revealing some of the evidence that they had collected against Kelley. Her mother told a local television station that Kelley was distraught over Jim's murder and the fact that she wasn't able to see her children. And Diane expressed surprise about the evidence the police had against Kelley.

According to the reports that were released, police said they found spots of blood on the carpet and the walls in the bedroom where Jim's body was found. They smelled bleach and discovered an empty one-gallon jug of Clorox bleach next to Jim's body. Kelley's oldest son, Tim, told police he saw his mom cleaning the walls. Tim said she told him she was "cleaning Kool-Aid." Tim said that as Kelley rounded up the three kids before she left Jim's home, he called out, "Dad, where are you?" But there was no answer.

In the reports police also mentioned a videotape of several of the district attorney's (DA) assistants, who were about Kelley's size, moving furniture in the room where Jim's body had been found. According to these released reports, the videotapes claimed to show the female assistants easily moving the chest of drawers in front of the closet—where it had been found the day Jim's body was discovered.

Medical Reimbursements of America, the health care collections firm headed up by Jim Cannon, reached an agreement later that month with the administrator of his estate to purchase the equity in the company for $5.2 million. Jim, who had co-founded Medical Reimbursements of America in 1999, had also secured venture capital backing from Clayton Associates, based in Franklin, Tennessee.

The operating agreement of MRA, which was a limited-liability company (LLC), included terms that allowed the company to buy the shares of a deceased member. Stuart McWhorter, of Clayton Associates, invoked those terms when he sent a letter to court-appointed estate administrator Mike Castellarin on behalf of MRA about a month after Jim was murdered. In his letter McWhorter said that in May 2008 MRA had revenues of almost $1.7 million and he projected that the company's annual revenues for 2008 would be $20.1 million.

At that time Jim's 25 percent equity interest in the firm was said to be worth $4.8 million. To reach that figure, Castellarin had relied on the terms in the operating agreement that called for an outside firm to reach an appraisal that would set the value of the stock. Castellarin then hired two local accountants to give him two separate estimates of the worth of Jim's shares.

One of those firms estimated Jim's shares were worth $5.6 million. His projection of the company's future earnings was based on its growth over the previous five years. Using four different methods to value Jim's shares, the outside firm estimated their value between $5.1 million and $5.4 million. Taking both those estimates into consideration, Castellarin set the value of Jim's shares at $5.2 million. Under the terms of the buyout, $1 million would be paid up front; the balance would be paid over the next four years.

In addition to the value of Jim's shares in MRA, his other assets totaled nearly $1.9 million. If Kelley was convicted of murdering her husband, she would be prohibited under state law from inheriting any of his property.

The Cannon estate case, however, was not a simple matter. Jim's sister had been named custodian of the Cannons' three children; an attorney from Springfield, Tennessee was the court-appointed guardian of the children; and a public guardian for

Davidson County had been named as the guardian of the children's property interests.

To make matters more complicated, Kelley Cannon had petitioned the court to disqualify a Nashville attorney from representing Jim's sister. Kelley claimed that because the attorney had once represented Jim, he was ineligible to represent the deceased's sister.

In March 2009, Kelley went back to jail because she had cut off the ankle bracelet she was required to wear while out on bond and disappeared for two hours. For some reason no one was alerted to the fact that the electronic device had been removed until the two hours had passed. Kelley tried to tape it back on, but that didn't quite work. Kelley's attorneys told the judge she had a rash and took it off while she went to the drugstore. The authorities, however, weren't buying it.

That was the second time Kelley had gotten in trouble since she was released on bond. In February, she was arrested for harassment because she called one of Jim's former business partners on his cell phone four times in a fifteen-minute time period on January 18. The man, who knew that she had been charged with murdering Jim, was alarmed by the calls. Davidson County Criminal Court judge Cheryl Blackburn said Kelley Cannon should stay in custody until the court decided what should happen to her.

But the judge first decided to send Kelley to a private facility for an evaluation and treatment of mental-health issues. After the evaluation she went back to jail to await the judge's decision on her future before the trial.

At a hearing in April, Kelley's bondsman told the judge he didn't want anything more to do with her. He said he had never had so much trouble with anyone in his sixteen years in the business. In fact, he had never had anyone tamper with an ankle bracelet in defiance of a court order. The judge decided in favor of the bonding company, ruling it was no longer responsible for Kelley.

Court administrator Larry Stephenson said a computer glitch had caused the mess. For some reason the monitoring system was alerted to the fact that Kelley's bracelet had been tampered with, but the computer didn't notify the appropriate officer. The glitch was only discovered during a routine meeting on March 24 when an officer noticed Kelley's ankle bracelet had been taped. Apparently, a software upgrade was in progress at the precise time Kelley had taken off her bracelet. Although the problem had been fixed, authorities still had no idea where Kelley was for six days.

At that point Kelley had to stay in jail. There was a possibility that she could once again get bail if another bonding company decided to represent her, but that didn't happen. She remained in jail until her trial.

In May, Kelley's attorney Andrew Cate asked the Davidson County Probate Court to approve a payment from Jim's estate to cover the $243,000 in fees and expenses Cate had accrued since he started representing her in matters related to Jim's estate. The costs were not related to her defense for killing her husband. Kelley also wanted to borrow another $132,000 from the estate. This issue wouldn't be settled until after Kelley's trial.

Kelley's first-degree murder trial began late in the afternoon on Monday, April 26, 2010. A twelve-member jury—as well as four alternates—was selected from a pool of seventy-six Davidson County residents and seated just before three-thirty.

CHAPTER 9

After the jury was seated and everyone was settled, the judge asked the prosecutor if she wanted to make an opening statement.

Assistant District Attorney General (ADAG) Katrin "Katy" Miller began by telling the jury that the case revolved around a married couple, Kelley Cannon and her husband, James, who had been married for about twelve years. They had three children: Tim, who was nine at the time, Henry, who was seven, and an eighteen-month-old toddler, Sophie.

In February 2008, Jim Cannon filed for divorce against his wife, Kelley.

"They were back and forth," Miller said. "Mrs. Cannon had some issues with drugs that caused her to go into rehab, and Mr. Cannon was hopeful that by her seeking treatment, that would save their marriage. It was not to be."

Miller then explained to the story about all the problems Jim and Kelley had had in their marriage. She also told the jury about the witnesses they would be hearing from during the trial and the information they would be providing that would prove Kelley murdered her husband.

"I submit to you that after you hear every single bit of evidence in this case, that every piece of evidence will point to Kelley Cannon as the person who strangled her husband, and absolutely nobody else," Miller said. "And I submit to you that based on her actions, her intentions by her words, that she was not going to let her husband take her children, that she planned to murder him and that she did, and that you will find her guilty of first-degree murder."

Next up was Kelley Cannon's attorney, Peter Strianse.

Strianse began his comments by telling the jury that Miller's opening statement was like getting on a vacation tour bus with the guy on the microphone who drives everybody around and shows them the town.

"And everybody sort of sits there like a lump in a very passive way. And you only get to see what the tour guide in the bus wants to show you," he said. "And the state wants you all to be passive tourists this week as you hear the proof. The state wants you to get on their bus this week. They want to grab the microphone, and they want to show you just what they want to show you, ladies and gentlemen."

However, Strianse said, each juror was going to have to be another kind of tourist—the kind of tourist who doesn't get on a tour bus, but rather looks at the sights himself and draws his own conclusions.

Strianse said on the state's tour there were going to be certain sites that were off-limits. And there were certain inconvenient truths that were not going to be visited during the state's tour.

Kelley's attorney told the jury members that the state wanted them to believe what it was selling during the trial, which was that Kelley decided on a "bare-knuckle violent confrontation with her husband," someone who was much larger, much stronger and physically superior to her. But that just wasn't the case. He explained that the witnesses would testify to that fact.

"Solving this crime, ladies and gentlemen, means finding out, I guess, who done it," he said. "But in this case to solve the crime you'll need to determine who physically done it. Not who was just merely present there at the scene."

Strianse told the jurors what troubled him most about the state's case was that it was obviously physically impossible for Kelley, who was battling anorexia and who was in terrible shape, to murder her husband in that violent, confrontational manner.

He also told jurors that police failed to consider any other suspects, including the two men who were romantically interested in Kelley—Paul Breeding and Rick Greene. Strianse told the members of the jury that at the end of the state's case, something and someone were going to be missing. The something, he said, was proof beyond a reasonable doubt, as well as the inability to exclude other reasonable theories of who could have killed James Cannon—who could have had the physical wherewithal to kill James Cannon.

"Because Kelley Cannon certainly did not have the physical wherewithal to do it," he said. "And not only is that something missing, but that someone is missing. And that someone is the person who had the physical wherewithal to kill James Cannon on either the late hours of June twenty-second or the early-morning hours of June 23, 2008. And, ladies and gentlemen, it will be your duty to acquit Kelley Cannon after you hear all of the evidence in this case."

CHAPTER 10

After opening statements the state called its first witness—Tim Cannon. After Tim was sworn in, the judge explained that the attorneys were going to ask him some questions. If he didn't understand them, he should ask to have them repeated.

Assistant District Attorney General Sharon Reddick began by asking Tim to state his name and then spell it. After asking the perfunctory questions, including his age and date of birth, as well as the names and ages of his siblings, Reddick asked him who he was living with at that time. Tim said he and his brother and sister had been living with his uncle Robert Greer and his aunt Alison Greer and their children for the past couple years.

Reddick then talked to Tim about where everybody slept when his mom stopped living with his dad and his siblings.

"Well, sometimes we would switch beds, and sometimes I would sleep in my mom and dad's room. And sometimes my dad would sleep in my room," Tim said, adding that he and his brother shared one room and his sister had her own room.

"And how many beds were in the room that you are calling your mom and dad's room?"

"There was one, I think, king-sized bed."

"So it was a big bed. And you and your brother would sleep in that?"

"Uh-huh."

"Where would your dad sleep?"

"Sometimes my dad would sleep in his office," Tim said. "And sometimes—most of the time he would sleep in our room . . . on the bottom bunk."

Reddick showed Tim a picture of his bed; then she put it on a screen so the jurors could see it.

"You've already told us that he slept on this bottom bunk. Is that right?"

"Yes."

"Now point on there where your dad's head would usually—"

"Yeah, it's right there," Tim said, pointing it out on the screen.

"That's where your dad's head would be when he would sleep?" Reddick asked. "That's the pillow. So his feet were down at that other end?"

"Yes, right down here. That's where his feet were," Tim said, again pointing it out.

"Okay. So he would kind of be facing the TV if he wanted to watch TV, or whatever?"

"Yes."

"And that's how he slept?"

At that point Reddick began asking Tim about the night before his dad died.

Tim explained that he and his brother fell asleep in his dad's king-sized bed; his sister slept in her room, and his dad slept in the boys' room. This was something he had been doing for several weeks.

"Did something unusual happen later on that night after you fell asleep?"

"Yes. My mom woke me up and I asked why. And she said, 'We just have to go.' And I said, 'Can I go get a pillow?' And she said no. And so my brother was ready to go just with her . . . and she had Sophie."

"So when you asked your mom, 'Can I go get a pillow,' where were you?"

"I was in my mom and dad's room."

"And where was the pillow?"

"The pillow was in my dad's room."

"The room where your dad was asleep?"

"Yes."

"Okay, so the room where your dad was asleep was the room where all your clothes and stuff were. Is that right?"

"Yes."

Reddick asked Tim what time his mom had come to the house. Tim said he thought it was around one or two in the morning.

"Do you remember what your mom said when she woke you up there in the middle of the night?" Reddick asked.

"She said, 'Let's go.' And that's all she . . . and she said, 'No.' That was to the question I asked her," Tim said.

"So you asked her if you could go down to your bedroom to get a pillow?"

"Yes."

"And she said no?"

"Yes."

"And then after that, what did you do? Where did you go when you left your mom and dad's bedroom?"

"We went down the front stairs, instead of the stairs where my room was, so . . ."

"Can you kind of describe a little bit what you're talking about there? Are there two sets of stairs in your house?"

"Yes, there are."

"And the top of the stairs at the back of the house—what bedroom is closest to those stairs?"

"My dad's room."

"The room that your dad was sleeping in?"

"Yes."

"Which is really your room?"

"Yeah."

"I know, it's confusing. And at the top of the stairs in the front of the house, what bedroom is closest to those stairs?"

"That's where my mom and dad's room is closest to."

"And the stairs at the back of the house, they go down into the kitchen, kind of, don't they? Is that right?"

"Yeah."

"And out into the garage and out into the back part of the house, right?"

"Yes."

"And the stairs at the front of the house go down into the foyer and the front door?"

"Yes."

"Okay. You went down the front stairs?"

"Yes."

Tim told the jurors that his mom never allowed him or his brother, Henry, to go down to his bedroom to get their clothes, toys, pillow or anything else, for that matter. He added that after he and his siblings, as well as his mom, went down the stairs, they went to the front door and then they went outside.

"After you woke up and you were still in the house, did you see or hear your dad at all?"

"No."

"Did your mom say anything to you about 'Where's Dad?' or anything about your dad?"

"No."

Tim said he felt scared when his mother woke him up in the middle of the night. And it left him wondering why she was even in the house. Kelley never told him why, either. Tim told the court that after they left his house, his mom took the children to the place where she was living, which was about a mile or two away. On the drive to her apartment, Kelley never said a word to the kids.

Once they got to his mom's place, they just went to sleep. He and Henry slept with her in a queen-sized bed, while the baby slept in a crib. Sophie had been to the apartment on other occasions, but the boys had never been there. When the boys woke up the next morning, they asked their mother how to turn on the TV so they could watch cartoons, which they did for an hour or two.

"Then I heard a knock on the door," Tim said, "and she went to answer, and it was the police. I saw them at the front door. I thought they were there because my dad was trying to, like, find us, or something like that."

"And do you know what happened after the police got there?"

"Well, they came in to talk to her, and then we went in the police car."

"And it was sometime after that, that you found out your dad had died. Is that right?"

"Yes."

Reddick asked Tim why he said he was scared when his mother woke him and his siblings up in the middle of the night.

Tim said it was because he thought she was trying to take them away, somewhere really far, so his dad could never find them.

"Had something happened that made you think she might try to take you away?"

"Well, this one time when she was still living with us, my mom and dad got in a big fight. They went outside. . . . He went outside with his phone, and my mom came out with a knife. [She] pushed him down, trying to undo his phone battery so he couldn't call the police, like pushed him down on the ground. He was, like, fighting, trying to get her off. And she was trying to undo the battery from his phone. And she did that, but—but he had already called the police."

"So you saw her push him all the way down to the ground. Did you see her get the phone away from him?"

"Well, the battery came out. And then he tried to put it back in, but it was, like, broken. Then she went in, got Sophie, smashed into the back of my dad's car, and then drove, like, beside it and then went into the road. And then the police, like, came and chased after her."

"And was that kind of scary?"

"That was really scary."

"But after that, Sophie came back to live with you-all. And that was a little while before the night that you've already told us about, when she woke you up in the middle of the night?"

"Yes."

"Was that something you were worried might happen again, that she would—"

"Yes."

Reddick again questioned Tim about the night Kelley took the children from Jim's house.

"You've already told us she wouldn't let you go into your bedroom?"

"Yes."

"Could you see into your bedroom at all from where you were?"

Tim told the jurors that he tried to look down the hall to see into his room, but he couldn't see anything because all the lights were off.

"Okay. That's all," Reddick said.

Peter Strianse then began his cross-examination of Tim Cannon by explaining that he was trying to help the boy's mother.

"I'm sorry that you have to be here today," he said. "Let me just ask you a few questions. You said that your dad liked to sleep in your bedroom. Is that right?"

"Yes."

"Now, your dad really liked to sleep in the office, didn't he?"

"Not a lot. Sometimes he would sleep in there, but he really liked to sleep in our room because he said it helped his back."

"Didn't he like to sleep in the office because he could keep it completely dark in the office?"

"Yes."

"And your mom had set up some special drapes in that office so he could go in there and sleep. Is that right?"

"I don't believe so. . . ."

"Did your mom ever call that room 'the cave'?"

"Yes."

"Okay. And that's where he would generally like to sleep. Is that right?"

"Some—He didn't really like to sleep there, because he liked to hear us and make sure we were safe."

Although Tim was doing his best to remember and answer Strianse's questions, it was obvious that he was getting flustered.

Strianse asked Tim if he remembered being interviewed by a social worker and a police officer shortly after his dad died. Tim said he didn't remember that, nor did he remember giving police a statement at that time.

"Okay. You met recently with the district attorney's office. Is that right?"

"Yes."

"Okay. And was that on Friday of this week?"

"Yes, it was."

Strianse then told Tim he had a copy of the statement that Tim had given to the police or to a social worker. He told Tim that in the statement he never mentioned anything about wanting to get a pillow and that his mom wouldn't let him go into his room. He asked Tim if he remembered talking to a nice lady who was a social worker.

"I don't—What do you mean by 'social worker'?"

"Well, I don't know. She identified herself as a social worker. Do you remember Mr. Putnam, the police officer that came to the apartment on June twenty-third?"

"I don't remember his name, but I knew a police officer came there."

"He was one of the ones that came to the apartment to interview your mom on June twenty-third, and he would have been at this meeting with this lady."

"Okay."

"Are you remembering that at all?"

Tim said he didn't remember it.

Not getting anywhere with that line of questioning, Strianse moved on.

"Now, do you remember saying anything about being refused access to that room, that you couldn't go into the room by your mom at any time, before you spoke to the DA on Friday?"

"She said I could not go in that room."

"Okay. You're remembering what happened back then?"

"Yes."

"Okay. But you're not remembering giving a statement about that?"

Tim again told the jury what happened the night his dad was killed. He didn't seem to understand what the defense attorney was asking him. Strianse tried one more time.

"Do you remember telling Detective Putnam, the police officer, that you walked through your bedroom and saw a couch that was pushed up against the closet?"

"I don't remember that."

"You don't remember telling them that? And that you went down the back stairs?"

Tim said he didn't remember saying that to the detective or the DA.

"Okay. And it was just on Friday that you told the district attorney you went down the front stairs?"

"Yeah, I remember going down the front stairs, but I don't remember saying anything about going down the carpeted stairs."

"So if you had told somebody, there was a couch that was up against the closet, and you saw that on the way out, that would have been a mistake?"

"I don't—I don't remember that."

"Okay. You don't remember saying that?"

"No, I don't."

"And you thought that your dad had gone to sleep that night in your bedroom. Is that right?"

"Yes."

"But I think you also told us you went to sleep before he did. Is that right?"

"Yes."

"So you wouldn't have seen him where he slept, did you?"

"No, but he said he was going to sleep in that room."

"Okay. He told you he was going to go to sleep in that bedroom?"

"Yes."

"And then when your mom came, you said you thought it was one or two o'clock?"

Tim said he guessed that was the time, but he didn't look at a clock.

"Okay. Now, you said that your mom looked nervous and jumpy?"

"Yes."

Strianse then asked Tim if before he spoke with the district attorney, he had ever told anyone his mom looked nervous and jumpy.

Tim said he had mentioned it because she "was on drugs and stuff." The boy also told the jurors he was afraid of his mom when she whisked the children away to her apartment.

Strianse, however, wanted the jury to know that maybe Tim wasn't as afraid of his mother as the prosecution would have them believe.

"Now, do you remember going over to her apartment, over at the Grove? You know the little apartment she had on Elmington?"

"Yes."

"And do you remember jumping up and down on the bed with your brother, Henry?"

"No."

"Do you remember you guys getting in bed and watching *Terminator 2* before you fell asleep?"

"No."

"You don't remember that at all?"

Tim once again said he didn't remember much about that night because he was really scared.

Strianse then asked Tim about the day his mom and dad were struggling over the phone. He wanted to know when Tim told that story for the first time.

"Was that this Friday, when you spoke to the DA?"

"No, I believe I told the police officer that."

"Okay. Which police officer did you tell that?"

"I don't remember any faces or any names."

After Peter Strianse finished with Tim Cannon, the prosecutor had some additional questions she wanted to ask him.

"Tim, on Friday, when we met, was that the first time you had ever met me?" Reddick asked.

"I believe so."

"We had never talked before?"

"Yes."

"And we talked about on Friday how you talked to a social worker and a police officer two years ago. And you didn't remember doing that, right?"

"Yeah."

"And we also talked about how some things that happened two years ago you just don't remember at all?"

"Yeah."

"Are you doing your best to remember as much as you can?"

"I'm trying really hard."

"Okay. Thank you, Tim."

CHAPTER 11

The next witness called to the stand was Jean Armstrong. While she was approaching the bench, the judge told Peter Strianse to instruct Kelley Cannon not to nod or shake her head if she agreed or disagreed with the testimony of a witness. The judge had noticed her doing that when Tim was on the stand.

"She's a very emotional person, but I don't—you know, I didn't want to interrupt him. But she's got to stop that," Judge Cheryl Blackburn said.

After Jean was sworn in, Katrin Miller began her direct examination. Jean told the jurors that she had been the Cannons' housekeeper at the house on Bowling Avenue. She said she had been hired by Kelley about a month and a half before Jim was murdered. However, shortly after Jean was hired, Kelley moved out of the house and she never saw her again.

Jean told the jurors that after Kelley left, she typically began work at eight-thirty in the morning and worked about six and a half hours. She said Jim had also hired two nannies to watch the children.

"Now, specifically directing your attention to June twenty-third, do you remember that day?" Miller asked.

"Yes."

Jean said she had gone to work at Jim's, as she usually did, that Monday morning.

"Do you remember telling me that you had not worked that previous Friday, and something about the house?"

"Oh, yes. It was funky. I'm sorry."

"I know you're nervous. Had you been off that Friday?"

"Yeah."

Jean said she knew she had arrived at work at eight-thirty that Monday morning, because she had looked at the time on her cell phone as she was walking through the front door.

"Okay. And did you normally go in the front door or the back door?"

"Always the front."

"And did you have a key to the house?"

"Yes."

"Did you have to use your key to open the front door that day?"

Jean said she didn't have to use her key because the door was unlocked, which was unusual. She also noticed some other things that were unusual. For one thing, the back door was opened and the house appeared to be empty. However, both cars were in the driveway. But that wasn't really unusual because Jim Cannon typically left for work shortly after nine. Jean told the members of the jury that the children were usually up by the time Jim came downstairs, around nine. But that morning the cars were there, but the family wasn't.

"What did you do then, once you arrived there and noticed these things?"

"I just done what—I just did my work."

Jean said she started the laundry, picked up the trash and began doing the dishes. Then Maria, one of the nannies, arrived just before nine. Just about that time, she said, she went upstairs because she knew Sophie should have been up by then. She explained that when she went upstairs, she didn't see anyone.

"Did you notice anything out of place when you initially went upstairs?"

"Yes—just a lot of things."

Jean recalled that there was a wineglass, as well as a toppled-over trash can, in the master bathroom and a bloody towel beside the bed in the master bedroom. She took the wineglass down to the kitchen sink and put the bloody towel in the washing machine with the rest of the dirty clothes.

"It was—The place was just destroyed. It wasn't normal. They hadn't picked up after themselves at all," she said, adding she didn't see her boss or the children.

Jean explained that she and the nanny speculated on what might have happened. They thought maybe one of the children had been badly hurt and had been taken to the hospital in an ambulance, which would explain why both cars were still at the house. Then she said she asked the nanny to go back upstairs with her to help her move the chest of drawers that was up against the closet in the boys' bedroom. Once they moved the chest, Jean opened the closet door and was shocked to find her boss inside.

"Can you describe what he looked like?" Miller asked.

"He was just—The color of his skin, it was not normal. It was dark," Jean said, visibly shaken as she recalled the horrific sight. "The first thing I seen was the palm of his hand, and it was like the color of charcoal."

"What did you do when you saw him in there?"

"I immediately slammed the door back."

"And did you ask Ms. Cross to do anything?"

"I think at that point I just looked at her. And she asked me what was wrong, and I told her that Jim was in the closet."

Jean told the jurors that before she let Maria call 911, she checked Jim again to make sure he hadn't just passed out. When she realized he was dead, she told the nanny to make the call.

"And in the closet did you notice or smell anything out of the ordinary, other than his body being there?"

"There was bleach. There was the smell of bleach."

"And did you see a bleach bottle in there?"

"Yes, laying on the floor."

Jean then told the jurors that she also had Maria call Kelley's mother, Diane Sanders. Then Maria handed Jean the phone.

"What did you tell her?"

"I told her about Jim."

"What did you say, if you can remember?"

"Well, she asked me what was wrong, and I sort of thought that maybe Maria had already told her.

I didn't mean to, but I blurted out that Jim was dead."

"And what was your reaction to Ms. Sanders's response to you?"

Before Jean could answer, Peter Strianse objected to the question.

"Overruled," the judge said. "The question was reaction—her reaction to the response."

"It's obviously grounded in some hearsay statement," Strianse said, not willing to concede.

"Well, overruled."

"What was your reaction to Ms. Sanders's response when you told her that Jim was dead?"

"I immediately just went into a state of shock. I couldn't—I couldn't move. I couldn't speak. I couldn't do anything."

"Why is that?" Miller asked.

"She—"

"Without saying what she said," the judge explained.

"Without saying what she said, why were you suddenly in a state of shock?"

"Because I knew that she already knew that he was dead, and that's why."

Miller then showed Jean some photos of the outside and inside of the Cannon house and asked her if they represented what she saw the morning she found Jim Cannon's body. She said they did.

Miller also showed Jean a photo of some latex gloves and asked if they were in the house when she worked there. She was trying to get the jury to distinguish between those gloves and the tip of the latex glove that police had discovered at the crime scene.

"And who brought the gloves to the house?" Miller asked.

"I did."

"And what was your reason for bringing the gloves into the house?"

"To clean with. I wore them when I cleaned."

"And why is it that you brought your own gloves, instead of having the Cannons purchase some gloves for you?"

"Well, they did, but they purchased the kind you just use once. And they was way too big for me, so I brought these."

"And are these the only gloves you're aware of in the house?"

"Yes."

"And what would you use them [for], as far as cleaning around the house? What things would you be doing with those gloves?"

"The shower to keep the chemicals off my hands, even wash the dishes with them, just any and everything really."

Next Miller showed Jean pictures of the closet where she found Jim's body, the dresser that was placed in front of the closet and finally a picture of Jim's body.

"This is Exhibit 5D. What does that photograph show, Ms. Armstrong?"

"Jim Cannon."

"Is that the way he looked when you opened the door and saw him?"

"Yes."

* * *

After asking Jean Armstrong a couple more questions about her work at the Cannons', Katrin Miller told the judge she was done with the witness.

"Those are all the questions I have, Your Honor."

The judge wished the jurors a pleasant evening and sent them on their way. The next morning, after the jurors were brought in, the prosecution called John Hollins Jr., because Jean had not yet arrived. She arrived in the middle of Hollins's testimony.

CHAPTER 12

John Hollins was a lawyer with the law firm of Hollins, Raybin & Weissman. He was a practicing attorney for twenty-three years, and his practice was mainly devoted to domestic relations, divorce, child custody and similar types of issues.

Hollins had known Jim Cannon for about twenty years. They worked together when they were just starting out. They had mutual friends and sometimes socialized together. Hollins said he hadn't seen Jim for fifteen years before he was hired to represent him in the divorce. Hollins had also petitioned to get Jim custody of his three children.

"I specifically requested that Mr. Cannon have temporary custody of the parties' three children. That was granted. I also requested that Mrs. Cannon be restrained from threatening him, harassing him or harming him in any way. The judge granted that order," Hollins told the jury. "I also requested that Mrs. Cannon be restrained from threatening, harming, intimidating the parties' three children.

That was granted. And also I requested that Mrs. Cannon be restrained and enjoined from using or abusing any narcotic medication, alcohol or drugs in any way. That was also granted. There was one other request that I made that the judge did not grant at that time. I asked for exclusive possession of the parties' home on Bowling Avenue. And that means that Mr. Cannon and the children would live in that home by themselves. Mrs. Cannon would not be allowed to live in the home or come to the home. That was not granted by the judge at that time."

"Did you go back into court to try to get exclusive custody of the house for Mr. Cannon, when the judge didn't do it in that order that we just made an exhibit?" Katrin Miller asked.

"I did. I think the day the judge signed the order was March 3, 2008," Hollins said. "I found out the day she signed it that she did not grant Mr. Cannon exclusive possession of his house, and she had written on the order she couldn't do it the way I had filed my pleadings. So I filed a motion for temporary injunction that day, March 3, 2008. I put additional information about the history of events that occurred between the parties in the petition. And I believe the next day, on March 4, 2008, that Judge Solomon did grant my request at that time for Mr. Cannon to have exclusive possession of the house, and that Mrs. Cannon could not come to the house and she could not interfere with Mr. Cannon's basically [sole] possession of the house."

"And at the time of Mr. Cannon's death, on June twenty-third, were those orders in effect?"

"They were."

"At some point, Mr. Hollins, did Mr. Cannon seek an ex parte order of protection?"

"He did."

"Can you explain to the jury what that is?"

"I can. An order of protection is a court order that is granted typically in cases where domestic violence is involved. And it's very similar to these temporary orders I just discussed," Hollins explained. "The order of protection, original granting or not granting, is based on allegations made by one party. So what usually happens is the party who has been the alleged victim of domestic violence will fill out a petition that alleges all the circumstances and facts that the court may conclude that, yes, they were a victim of domestic or another kind of violence. And I did receive a phone call from Mr. Cannon, I believe, on May 22, 2008, about an incident of domestic violence that occurred the night before. He asked me what did I recommend, how should he proceed from there."

"Your Honor, I would object to anything Mr. Cannon would have told him," Peter Strianse said.

"Sustained."

"Based on that conversation, did you give Mr. Cannon some advice about how to proceed with an order of protection?" Miller asked.

Hollins said that he told Jim he would have to go to the criminal court clerk's office and fill out an application detailing how he was a victim of domestic violence, which would then be presented to a judge. The judge would determine whether to grant an order of protection or not. If the initial order of protection was granted, it would be good for a period of up to ten days. And then there would be a full hearing for the court to hear all the evidence to determine whether that order of protection would be extended for up to one year.

Miller asked Hollins if he knew whether the hearing had been held within ten days. He said the original hearing had been scheduled for June 11, 2008. It had to be postponed to June 18 because one of Kelley's attorneys had a conflict.

"Do you recall if a hearing was held on June eighteenth?" Miller asked.

Hollins said the hearing had been postponed until July twenty-third.

"So at the time of Mr. Cannon's death, the ex parte order was still in effect. You just hadn't had the final hearing due to circumstances of attorneys."

"That is correct. I think the court orders reflected that the order of protection would remain in force until a full hearing was held."

Hollins told the jury that he and Jim, who was calmer than he had been in a while, talked for about forty-five minutes on the Friday before he died. During that conversation Hollins told Jim he would do everything he could to get the divorce finalized before the children went back to school.

"And I told him it was going to be okay, he would be okay," an emotional Hollins told the members of the jury. "He was killed on Monday."

"Mr. Hollins, how did you learn of Mr. Cannon's death on Monday, the twenty-third of June?"

"It was about twelve-thirty on Monday, and I was

getting ready to go to lunch. I was at my office. I was out by the elevator—"

Before Hollins could finish his statement, Strianse asked the judge if the attorneys could approach the bench. The judge agreed.

"I don't know where this is going, but I remember reading in the *Nashville Scene* that he claims that Diane Sanders, Kelley's mother, had called and said that Kelley had killed Jim," Strianse said. "So I hope that's not where you're going."

"I'm trying not to go there," Miller said.

"What is the purpose in going even anywhere near it?" he asked.

"She did call him and told him Jim was dead," Miller responded. "And a police officer got on the phone and asked him to bring the court documents out to the scene, which we've already talked about in your opening statement. I can lead him."

"Just don't get into what Diane Sanders said," the judge said.

"He knows that, but I'll lead him," Miller told the judge.

"Mr. Hollins, without stating what was told to you in the conversation, did you receive a phone call, or did somebody call your office on June twenty-third?" Miller asked.

"Yes, ma'am."

"And who was that person?"

"That was Diane Sanders, Kelley Cannon's mother."

In response to Miller's questions, Hollins told the jury he had first met Diane Sanders at a hearing on March 5, 2008, and they had exchanged telephone numbers.

"Okay. And who told you that Jim Cannon was dead?"

"She did."

"Okay. And while you were speaking to her on the phone, did a police officer get on the phone?"

"He did."

Hollins told the jury that the police officer asked him to bring all the court documents pertaining to Jim and Kelley's divorce.

With that, Miller finished her direct examination of Hollins.

Peter Strianse began his cross-examination. Strianse wanted the members of the jury to think that Kelley Cannon was not upset about Jim divorcing her because she had already been planning to seek a divorce. He also wanted them to realize that she was not physically capable of murdering her husband.

Strianse asked Hollins if he knew that Kelley had talked to an attorney about divorcing Jim, as early as October 2007. Hollins said he didn't know until that very minute that Kelley had consulted with an attorney.

"You were not aware that there were allegations of marital infidelity on the part of Jim Cannon before he filed his action?"

"Later, Jim and I did discuss that."

"When you filed the emergency motion for temporary injunction that was filed at four oh-four P.M. on March third you were aware that he had possession—physical possession—or custody of the two boys at that point?"

"Yes."

"But he did not have custody of Sophie at that point in time. Is that right?"

"I thought he had temporary possession of all the children."

"And among the things that you say is that as of the date of this filing that Mrs. Cannon weighed approximately ninety pounds. Is that right?"

"That's correct."

"And that she needed IV fluids and had to be transported to Saint Thomas Hospital?"

"That's correct."

"So as of March 2008, it was your understanding that she weighed about ninety pounds? And was obviously in poor physical condition if she's being rushed to the hospital and in need of IV fluids?"

"She was at that time. That's right."

Strianse then asked Hollins about a letter he wrote to Kelley's divorce lawyer, Bobby Jackson.

"Now, you're writing this letter on March 6, 2008. And you're referring to a phone call that you had with Mr. Jackson earlier in the day, where you write, 'As we discussed by phone on March 6, 2008, Mrs. Cannon collapsed in the lobby of the Loews Vanderbilt Hotel Nashville this afternoon. She was then rushed by ambulance to Baptist Hospital's emergency room.' Do you remember writing that letter?"

"I don't, but I did write it. That's my signature."

"So if you wrote it, that would have been your understanding of the state of her physical health as of March 6, 2008?"

"Yes, I do remember that."

Strianse also asked Hollins about the agreement between Jim and Kelley that would allow her to live in their house if she went for drug and alcohol treatment. Hollins said after Kelley was released from the rehab facility, she would live with Jim and the kids and continue outpatient treatment. He said he talked to Kelley's attorneys about modifying the court order granting Jim the exclusive use of the house, but they decided to wait until she had completed the inpatient treatment.

Hollins also told the members of the jury that it seemed as if Jim and Kelley might try to get back together. He said Jim didn't want a divorce; he just wanted his wife to get better.

"At that point I think if she was willing to go back to treatment, he was willing to hang in there once again. You know, he wanted her to get better," he told the jurors. "He wanted her to be the mother of his children and wanted her to be his wife. He struggled terribly with the divorce. He told me to put everything on hold and see how she's going to do. And I said, 'That's fine. If she can get help and y'all stay together, that's great in my book. I don't want y'all to get divorced.' And so he wanted her to have another chance, so hopefully the treatment would take and she could function as their mother and as his wife."

So Kelley went to Cumberland Heights around March 6, 2008. She was released in early April 2008 and welcomed back home, Hollins said.

Strianse then showed Hollins a letter Kelley had written to her lawyers when she was in rehab, asking her attorneys to stop the divorce proceedings because she and Jim were trying to get back together. Hollins had also received a copy of the letter at that time. He said that even though the restraining orders were in place at the time she returned home, the lawyers for both sides just decided to leave everything in place for sixty days before making any final decisions.

However, Jim petitioned the court for an order of protection against Kelley on May 21, 2008, and Kelley left their home.

Wrapping up his cross-examination, Strianse asked Hollins if he had filed a wrongful-death suit against Kelley in June 2009, seeking a total of $40 million in damages. Hollins confirmed that he had filed the lawsuit.

When Peter Strianse was finished, Katrin Miller asked John Hollins who had asked him to file the lawsuit for wrongful death against Kelley. He said he had filed it on behalf of the Cannon children.

Miller then asked him whether Kelley Cannon actually received any outpatient treatment when she got out of rehab. Hollins said he didn't think she had.

After Hollins was excused, Judge Blackburn recalled Jean Armstrong to the witness stand to continue her testimony from the previous day. The judge reminded Jean she was still under oath.

Strianse then began his cross-examination.

The first thing Peter Strianse asked was whether she remembered meeting with Detective Brad Putnam a few days after June 23, 2008, and giving him a written statement of what had happened that day.

After Jean said she remembered, Strianse showed her a copy of the letter, which was dated June 24, 2008. Then he asked her some questions about it.

"Obviously, the events of June twenty-third would have been fresh on your mind when you sat down to write this out. Is that right?"

"Yes. I started it on the day after. I think I finished it, like, three days later."

"I'm not going to read it to you. I just want to take you through parts of it, okay?"

"Okay."

"You got there at eight-thirty. Is that right?"

"Right."

"And the front door was closed but unlocked. Is that right?"

"Yes."

"You walked straight to the kitchen? And you found the back door wide open. Is that right?"

"Yes."

"And you went to the patio to see if Mr. Cannon was out there. Is that correct?"

"Yes."

"And you didn't see him out there. Is that right?"

"No."

"And then you immediately started your usual routine is what you wrote. Is that accurate?"

"That's correct."

"At first, you gathered all the dirty clothes from downstairs?"

"Yes."

"And you put what you characterize as the first—"

Before he could finish his statement, Judge Blackburn called him to the bench to find out exactly where he was going with his line of questions.

She wanted to know why he was going over Jean Armstrong's statement—unless something in it was inconsistent. Strianse said it was inconsistent.

"Well, get to the points that are inconsistent," the judge said, giving the attorney a lesson in how to do his job.

"I'm trying to get some context to it," Strianse said.

"Well, that's not the way you do inconsistent statements to get context. Ask her, did she say this or not. I mean, how long is this?"

"There's only several highlighted areas I want to get to."

"Well, get down to those. But you don't read the whole thing. That's not the way you do prior inconsistent statements."

Strianse continued questioning Jean.

"Ms. Armstrong, in your statement you talked about seeing some unusual things in the house that morning. Is that right?"

"That's correct."

"You saw clothes piled up on the kitchen floor, which was unusual."

"Yes."

Strianse then asked Jean what the rest of the house looked like. She said it was "not in normal condition" and detailed the things that were out of order, like the half-smoked cigar on the ottoman, a beer can in the backyard and about seven liquor bottles in a brown paper bag near the downstairs bar. Jean told the jurors she put the alcohol away and tossed the bag.

"And what did you think when you saw those six or seven bottles of alcohol that were in the bag?"

"I didn't know why they were purchased, because there was already plenty of alcohol in the home."

"Do you remember telling Detective Putnam that you thought that Jim had been highly intoxicated the night before or—"

"Yes, maybe the entire weekend."

"Okay. So you had been there almost two months at that point? Had you come to know the habits of the Cannon family, if you will, the children and Mr. Cannon?"

"Yes."

"And did you conclude that Mr. Cannon drank from time to time? In fact, drank a lot?"

"I wouldn't say 'a lot.' He drank every day. But I never seen him drink over one drink."

"But you were concerned that this weekend he may have been intoxicated?"

"Yes."

"Now, you started next in the kitchen, is that right, after you put these liquor bottles up?" Strianse asked.

"Yes."

"And that was around nine o'clock? And it's about that time that Ms. Cross comes in. Is that correct?"

"Yes."

"And do you remember telling the officer that it's about nine twenty-seven that you and Ms. Cross are in the kitchen talking?"

"Yes."

"And that you thought it was unusual that nobody was up. Is that right?"

"That's right."

Jean said she figured her boss had been drinking

the previous evening and was sleeping in. But then, right around that time—9:27—she started feeling that something was wrong because Sophie wasn't up. And she was always up before Jim came downstairs at nine.

"But it's your testimony that you didn't venture upstairs to check on her. Is that right?"

"No, I did not."

"And you had been there an hour by that point in time?"

"Uh-huh."

"Okay. You found a wineglass—you told us yesterday and it's in your statement—that was upstairs. Is that right?"

"That's right."

"And where was that found upstairs?"

Jean said she found it on the vanity in the master bathroom. She brought the glass downstairs, but she didn't have a chance to wash it. Ultimately the police took the wineglass as evidence.

"Now, when you were upstairs collecting the wineglass is when you found the towel that had blood on it. Is that right?"

"Yes."

"And then you took that downstairs and threw it in the washing machine?"

"Uh-huh."

"Now, do you remember telling the officers that when you were upstairs retrieving the wineglass and retrieving this towel is when you saw the chest of drawers?"

"Yes."

"Okay. Did you look for the children at that point

in time?" Strianse asked, finally getting to the inconsistency in Jean's statement.

"I had already looked for them prior to that."

"Okay. But I thought that was your first trip."

"No, not when I . . . The first trip upstairs was on Sophie. When I got concerned about her, I left the kitchen, went upstairs, checked on her and then came—came back down. I didn't start gathering up anything until after I realized no one was upstairs at all."

Strianse then asked Jean to read her statement to herself to see if it refreshed her memory about the sequence of events.

"I have it written as it was," she said after reading it.

"Okay. Isn't it written where you don't go upstairs until Maria gets there, at about nine twenty-seven, and you-all start comparing notes about things being strange?"

"I didn't go upstairs until quite a bit after Maria arrived."

"Okay. Anywhere in your statement does it say that you went upstairs before Maria arrived?"

"No."

"Okay. So you really don't go upstairs until about nine twenty-seven or nine-thirty. Is that fair?"

"Approximately, yeah."

"Okay. And you wrote this the day after the events of June twenty-third. Is that right?"

"Started on it. Yes, sir."

Strianse asked Jean about the dresser that was turned over in the bedroom.

"Did you think Mr. Cannon had knocked over the dresser?"

"I didn't know who had knocked it over."

"But didn't you write that to the police, that you thought he might have been upset with the children and knocked the dresser over?" Strianse asked, highlighting another inconsistency in Jean's story.

"Yes, yes, yes."

"You thought he might have been drinking, got upset and turned it over?"

"Yes, yes."

"You also told the officers that you didn't think that Mr. Cannon had been sleeping in that bed in the boys' room. Is that right?"

Jean said his things were moved in there, but she didn't see any evidence that he actually went to bed as usual. That was because when he went to bed, he usually took the lamps off the dresser and actually put them down in the bunk bed with him.

"And you didn't see those lamps in the bunk bed. Is that right?"

"No."

"And you concluded that he had not been in the bed. Is that right?"

"Yes."

"When you first saw the body of Mr. Cannon in the closet, you thought he had passed out. Is that right?"

"I didn't know."

"And Maria wanted to call 911 immediately. And you said, 'Well, hold up. Let me check on him. I don't want to embarrass him if he just happens to be intoxicated and passed out in the closet.'"

"That is correct."

That was exactly what Strianse wanted the jurors to believe.

The attorney then turned his questioning to the latex gloves Jean said she brought to clean the Cannon house—gloves that did not match the tip of the glove found at the crime scene. He also asked her about Sugar, the family's little dog. He wanted to know if Sugar ever used the closet to do her business—an event that might explain the piece of the glove police discovered near the closet.

Jean, however, said the dog never made a mess in the closet or anywhere in the house, for that matter.

When Peter Strianse finished his cross-examination of Jean Armstrong, the prosecutor had a follow-up question for the witness.

"Ms. Armstrong, had you ever seen Mr. Cannon intoxicated?"

"No."

"And you testified that he only had one drink a day. How do you know that?"

"I mean, that's all I ever seen him drink. That's what I'm saying."

"Okay. You had just seen him drink one drink. Is that your testimony?"

"One. Maybe once I might have seen him drink a couple. No more than that."

Both attorneys said they had finished with the witness, so the judge excused Jean Armstrong.

The judge then warned Kelley Cannon not to shake or nod her head in agreement or disagreement with the witnesses' testimony. Apparently, mentioning that issue to her attorney hadn't done much good.

"You will have the appropriate time to testify, if you want to," the judge said. "But that is a comment on the evidence, and you need to stop it, okay? Do you understand that? You don't shake your head one way or another. If you need to say something to your attorney, write it down and give it to him if he's busy."

With that, the court was recessed.

CHAPTER 13

The next witness was Kelley's mother, Diane Sanders. As soon as she was sworn in, the judge said she wanted to talk to her before the jury returned. The judge wanted to be sure Diane knew how to respond to the attorney's questions. The judge actually held a mock direct examination with the jury out of the room.

"Ms. Sanders, we're having sort of a short hearing outside the presence of the jury to make sure we understand the rules that you're going to have to follow here in the courtroom," Judge Blackburn said. "So Ms. Miller is going to be asking you some questions. Mr. Strianse may be asking you some questions. When you answer the question, make sure you answer just the question, okay? Don't elaborate, most particularly about what people might have said to you other than perhaps Mrs. Cannon, okay? So let's kind of go through the questions we're going to be asking you, and let's go from there."

After both attorneys had had the chance to run

through their questions with Diane, the judge had a few final words for the witness and stressed again what she expected from Diane on the stand.

"Ms. Sanders, when we bring the jury in, we'll swear you again and go through the same thing. But remember to pay attention to the question and answer the question, and especially don't say what people told you, okay? Do you understand that?"

Diane nodded her head.

"I just want to make sure we do the same thing we just did."

"Okay."

"Bring the jury in," the judge said.

After the jury members had been seated, and Diane was sworn in again, the prosecutor began her direct examination by asking Diane her name and if she was Kelley Cannon's mother. She also asked how many children she had, what their names were and where they lived. Diane said she had three children, Kelley Cannon, Thomas, who lived in Louisiana, and Bobby, who lived in Tennessee.

Katrin Miller then directed Diane's attention to the night Jim was murdered. Responding to the prosecutor's questions, Diane said at that time she was living off Hobbs Road in Nashville. She said Kelley was living in an apartment on Elmington. Diane said her house was about ten minutes away from Kelley's apartment, as well as about ten minutes from Jim's house. Diane said Kelley had been living in her new apartment for about a week before Jim was murdered, but she had never been there.

"Now, the morning that your son-in-law was

found murdered, June twenty-third, how did you find out about his murder?"

"Well, his housekeeper called me at my home."

"Do you remember about what time it was?"

"It was probably around eight or eight-thirty, around that."

"Okay. And when you got that phone call, what did you do?"

"She had told me what had happened, and I didn't believe her. And she said I needed to come quickly. And I said, 'Okay, I'll be right there.'"

"Okay. Did you go over to the house on Bowling?"

"Yes, I did."

"And were the police already there?"

"Yes."

"Did you talk to the police when you got there?"

"I asked them, because I didn't believe that Jim was dead. And I said, 'Is he dead?' And she (a member of law enforcement) said she couldn't release that information to me."

"My question was 'Did you talk to the police?'" Miller repeated. "Your answer is yes. Is that right?"

"Yes."

Diane told the members of the jury that her three grandchildren weren't home when she arrived. She said she told the police at the scene they were probably with their mother.

"And why did you tell the police you thought they were with their mother?"

"It was just the most logical place they could be."

"Had you talked to your daughter that morning?"

"No."

"Did you call any other family members and tell them about your son-in-law's murder?"

"I called my son who was in Nashville with his son."

"Which son was that?"

"Bobby."

"And did he come to the scene?"

"Yes."

"Did you call anybody else from the scene?"

Diane said she called John Hollins and then called Jim's work and told them.

"And do you remember your cell phone number at the time?"

"Yeah."

"What was it?"

Diane rattled off her cell phone number and also confirmed the number of her home phone for the prosecutor.

"So you called several people there while you were there on the scene. Is that right?"

"That's correct."

"Did you call your daughter, Kelley Cannon, and tell her what had happened?"

"No, no."

"Did you call her to see if the children were over there and safe?"

"No. I don't think I had her cell phone number at the time."

"Okay. Do you recall speaking with your daughter the day before?"

"No, I don't recall that."

"Is it possible you could have spoken with her and had a lengthy conversation?"

"Well, anything is possible."

"Okay. Do you recall her cell phone number being —?" He named a number.

"No."

"You don't remember that?"

"Uh-uh."

"Did you ask your son Bobby to go over to your daughter's house and tell her what had happened?"

"No, I did not."

"Did you go over to your daughter's house and tell her what had happened?"

"No, I stayed right there."

"Why didn't you go over to your daughter's house? You said it was very close."

"Because I really—I really didn't know where it was. I knew it was in one of those complexes, but I didn't know, you know, the apartment number or anything."

"But you told the police where it was with the children?"

"Yeah, I said it was one of those over there, you know."

"Those are all the questions I have," Miller told the judge.

Peter Strianse then began his cross-examination of Diane Sanders. He wanted the jury to understand why Diane hadn't gone to her daughter's apartment to tell her Jim was dead.

"You told us you never visited your daughter, Kelley, over at this apartment on Elmington. Is that right?"

"That's correct."

"She had only been over there about a week or so at the time of her husband's death."

"I think that's correct."

"And it was located at some complex?"

"Yes."

"You didn't know the number?"

"No."

"And had never visited there?"

"Never."

Diane admitted that she and Kelley had been somewhat estranged at that time. However, they would talk from time to time.

"And you would fill her in on how the kids were doing and that sort of thing?"

"Well, I had no idea how the kids were doing."

"Had you not visited the grandkids at that point?"

"No. Well, I . . . let's see. We're talking about June—I had seen the children that Sunday."

"And had you seen the children with any regularity before that Sunday, June twenty-second?"

"Yes. I saw them pretty regularly."

"And when you would infrequently talk to your daughter, would you sort of bring her up to date on how the kids were doing, and that sort of thing?"

"Yeah."

Diane said she talked to Jim on Sunday, June 22. She said he liked to cook catfish outdoors and had called her to invite her over to eat catfish. But he kept changing his mind about what he wanted to do and ultimately just decided to take the kids to a local swim and tennis club. Diane said she offered to take the kids to the movies or do something if he didn't want to go to the club, but he said that was where he was going.

"And I said, that's fine with me, whatever you want to do. It was a beautiful day."

"So you never ended up over at [their house on] Bowling?"

"No. And then it got to be late, and he said to call him that evening. And he called me up, he said they were going to eat—"

Judge Blackburn interrupted Diane to remind her only to answer the questions that she was being asked.

After Peter Strianse finished questioning the witness, Katrin Miller said she had a few more questions for her.

"Now that Mr. Strianse has kind of refreshed your memory about . . . You remember very well about your conversations with your son-in-law?"

"Yes, I do."

"Okay, you had several phone calls with him."

"Yes."

"Cooking catfish, going to the pool, back and forth. Do you now remember talking to your daughter, Kelley Cannon, that afternoon for nearly an hour on the telephone?"

Diane said maybe she did and maybe she didn't. But she really couldn't remember.

"It's possible you did?"

"It could be a possibility, but I don't really recollect listening to—"

"Even though you remember all the other phone calls with your son-in-law?"

"With my son-in-law, right."

At that point neither attorney had any more questions, so Diane Sanders was excused. The prosecutor then called Albert Gordon to the stand.

CHAPTER 14

Albert Gordon had been a police officer with the Metropolitan Nashville Police Department for nineteen years. On June 23, 2008, he received a call to respond to a home on Bowling Avenue for a potential homicide. Gordon arrived at a little before ten in the morning. He was the first Metro Police officer on the scene. He saw two ladies, later identified as the housekeeper and the nanny, standing outside in front of the house. When he went into the house, he saw two paramedics walking down the stairs.

"Did you have a conversation with them? You don't need to tell me what they said, but did you talk to them?" Katrin Miller asked.

"Yes."

"At that point, when you talked to them, they weren't coming down with a body they were going to resuscitate, were they?"

"No."

"Did you go up in the bedroom where the body was?"

"I went to the bedroom, yes. To the closet, rather."

"Did you spend much time in there or just glance at it very briefly?"

"Briefly. Yes."

"And at that point what did you do? What was your job to do?"

"I set up what we call an incident command, and I start notifying the people that needed to come out to start the crime scene investigation."

"And who would that be?"

"That would be my sergeant. It would also be the detectives from West Sector."

"And did you do anything as far as securing the crime scene?"

"Yes, that's my job to be sure that no one reenters the home, unless they were an official police personnel or medical personnel."

"At some point did a civilian arrive other than emergency personnel? A lady?"

"Yes."

"And who was that lady identified to you to be?"

"The mother-in-law of Jim. I didn't know who Jim was at the time, but later I found out it to be Mr. Cannon."

Gordon said he talked to Diane briefly; then she started talking on her cell phone.

"And when you went in the house after the para-medics had left, was there anybody else in the house?"

"No."

"How long did it take for the detectives to arrive and your sergeant?"

"I think they started arriving maybe ten minutes after that."

"And other than securing the crime scene, did you have any other involvement with this case?"

"No."

"Those are all the questions I have, Your Honor," Miller said.

After greeting Officer Gordon, Kelley's attorney asked Gordon if Officer Mike Swoner had been at the Cannon house when he arrived. Gordon said he had not been there.

"At some point in time did you sort of hand the baton to Officer Swoner?" Peter Strianse inquired.

Gordon said Officer Swoner relieved him at the scene and became the incident commander. He again reiterated that the only official people on the scene when he arrived were the two paramedics, who had already gone up and looked in the closet and determined that Jim Cannon was dead. After they left, there was no one else in the house, so he secured the scene and didn't let anyone else enter. He also told the jury that although he didn't search the entire house, he went upstairs, looked in the closet, then went back downstairs.

"You didn't go into all the rooms of the house to do a walk-through or a protective sweep or anything like that?"

"No. I protected it from the outside and wouldn't allow anyone back in."

Albert Gordon was then excused, and Jeffrey "Jeff" Biggerstaff, a seventeen-year veteran of the MNPD, was called to the stand and sworn in. Biggerstaff told the jury that he and another officer, who were working patrol, were called to the Cannon home on June 23 to assist the detectives with the investigation of a dead body. They got there around ten o'clock or a little later in the morning. When they arrived, the detectives asked them to go to Kelley's apartment to find her and to see if her children were with her.

A woman answered the door and the officers asked to speak with Kelley Cannon. The woman then identified herself as Kelley. Biggerstaff asked if they could go in and Kelley allowed them inside her apartment. When they walked in, Biggerstaff told the members of the jury, they noticed that the children were playing video games and appeared to be calm. Kelley also seemed to be calm at that point.

Biggerstaff then notified the detectives who were at Jim Cannon's house that they had located Kelley and the kids. The two officers were asked to stay with Kelley until detectives arrived.

"Now, on that day, Officer Biggerstaff, what were you wearing?" Katrin Miller asked.

"I was wearing a Metro Police Department uniform."

"And what kind of car were you driving?"

"It was a Chevy Impala with police logos on it."

"And when you located Mrs. Cannon, did she ask you why you were there?"

"No, she didn't. I just told her that we were there to check the welfare of her and her kids. Once we did that, we notified detectives and stood by until they got there."

"Did you tell her anything about her husband?"

"No, ma'am."

"And did you remain there until the detectives got there?"

"Yes, ma'am."

"And did you stay there while the detectives were there talking to Mrs. Cannon?"

"Yes, ma'am."

Prosecutor Miller said she was finished with the witness.

Peter Strianse now began his cross-examination of the officer.

"When you arrived over at Elmington, it seemed to be a normal scene over there. Is that right?"

"Yes, sir."

"The boys were playing video games?"

"Yes, sir."

"Do you remember there being a toddler, an eighteen-month-old girl?"

"I vaguely remember that."

"Wandering around the apartment?"

"I vaguely remember there were three kids in the apartment. I don't know the ages exactly."

"Had you informed Mrs. Cannon, when you got there, why you were there?"

"We did not inform her of that."

"You [had] been instructed by detectives at the scene not to tell her that her husband was dead?"

"We were instructed to check the welfare of her and the kids and then to notify them if we made contact with her."

Strianse continued this line of questioning, which made it appear that the police had already concluded

Kelley had murdered her husband, without even considering other suspects.

"How was the decision made that Officer Biggerstaff, that day, was not going to tell Kelley Cannon that her husband had been found dead?"

"We were just instructed by detectives, who were investigating the case, to notify them when we made contact. At that point we did. And once they got there, they handled the investigation at that point."

"But there was a conscious decision made that they sent you over there with instructions not to tell her that her husband had been found dead?"

"No, sir. They did not tell me not to tell her. As soon as we made contact with Mrs. Cannon and the kids, and I verified that their welfare was good, I contacted the detectives to let them know that I had located her and the kids. And they just instructed us to stand by until they got there."

"So you made that decision on your own. Is that right?"

"Yes, sir."

"And at that point in time, you were a field-training officer. Is that right?"

"Yes, sir."

"You're in patrol?"

"Yes, sir."

"You're certainly not the lead investigator in the case?"

"No, sir."

"But you took it on yourself that you were going to keep the death of her husband a secret from her. Is that right?"

"I didn't know the details of the whole case. We

were just instructed by detectives to go try to locate and check the welfare of her and her kids."

"And she asked what you-all were doing there, didn't she?"

"She never said anything to me."

"Well, I thought you told us a few minutes ago that she asked why you-all were there."

"I just instructed her that we were there to check her welfare and her kids."

Strianse told the judge he had no other questions for Jeff Biggerstaff.

Since Katrin Miller had no follow-up questions, Detective William Stokes, who had been with the Metro Nashville Police Department for nineteen years, was called to the witness stand. The morning Jim's body was found, Detective Stokes and Detective Brad Putnam were dispatched to the Cannon home to handle the investigation. When they arrived at about ten fifty-five, they were briefed as to the situation by their supervisor, Lieutenant Nancy Fielder. They later did a walk-through of the house. When the call came in from Officer Biggerstaff, Stokes, Putnam and Fielder went to meet him at Kelley Cannon's apartment.

When they got there, Kelley answered the door. She was wearing a silky top with a sweater over it and dark jeans. When they went in, they noticed that the two boys were watching television and Sophie was just wandering around.

"Did she ask you why you were there?" prosecutor Miller asked.

"I believe we just went ahead and . . . I don't

think she asked. I think we just told her that we would like to speak with her and talk to her."

"Okay. And who gave you your instructions, as far as going to that location and talking to Mrs. Cannon?"

"Detective Putnam and Lieutenant Fielder."

"Okay. And at that point who was the lead investigator on the case?"

"Detective Putnam."

"And Lieutenant Fielder would have been also Detective Putnam's supervisor, as far as being a lieutenant?"

"Yes, ma'am."

"But as far as calling the shots on how the investigation progressed, that would be Detective Putnam's call?"

"Yes."

"And when you went in the apartment, did you have a tape recorder with you?"

"I did."

"And were you planning on getting a statement from Mrs. Cannon?"

"Yes. I was directed to go speak with her by Detective Putnam."

"And did you, in fact, talk to Mrs. Cannon and get a statement from her?"

"I did."

"And did you tape-record it?"

"I did."

After entering a recording on a CD and the transcript of Detective Stokes's interview with Kelley Cannon into evidence, Katrin Miller played it for the jury. She also gave the members of the jury, as well as the judge, court reporter and Kelley's attorney, a copy of the transcript. The judge then instructed the jury on the admissibility of the statements they were about to hear.

When the CD finished playing, the state's attorney Miller said she had just a couple more questions for Detective Stokes.

"Where did the interview [among] yourself and Mrs. Cannon and Lieutenant Fielder take place inside this apartment?"

"In the bedroom."

"Okay. It was away from the children, and it was about the only other room in the apartment. Obviously, the toddler, the eighteen-month-old child, was there present in the room. Is that correct?"

"Yes, ma'am."

"And where did you have the tape recorder? There's a lot of static that we can hear on the tape."

"It was a small bedroom. We were sitting on a bed. The dresser had stuff on it. I was holding a leather-bound notebook, with a clipboard. I was holding the recorder in my left hand and the clipboard while I was writing stuff down."

"So Mrs. Cannon could tell that you were recording her statement?"

"I didn't try to hide the recorder."

"Did you stay there at that apartment until Detective Putnam got there?"

"I was outside when he arrived."

"And when he got there, did you give him the tape recorder you had been using?"

"I did. I switched the recording folder so it would be fresh in a different folder on the recording for him."

"And that's digital recording. Is that correct?"

"Yes."

"That's all the questions I have, Your Honor."

Before dismissing the jury for lunch, Judge Blackburn gave them some instructions about what they could consider as evidence. Then she reminded them not to form an opinion and not to discuss the case with anyone. After the jury left, the judge also reminded Stokes that he was in the middle of his examination and he, too, was not allowed to discuss the case with anyone, including the attorneys.

After the lunch break, Kelley's attorney began his cross-examination of Detective Stokes. He wanted the jury to believe that Kelley Cannon knew William Stokes was recording the interview but had nothing to hide. She answered all his questions and even volunteered information.

"We just heard the interview that you did of Mrs. Cannon on June 23, 2008. That interview lasts about an hour. Is that a fair assessment of the time?" Peter Strianse asked.

"Yes, sir. Approximately, I believe."

"And she answered all the questions that you put to her during that interview. Is that right?"

"Yes, sir, she did."

"And she even pointed out for you where the rental car was out in the parking lot. Is that right?"

"Yes, sir."

"And I think you told us that although you didn't tell her explicitly, 'Mrs. Cannon, I'm recording this interview,' anybody with walking-around sense would have seen you with a digital recorder in your hand. And you certainly made no effort to hide the fact that you were recording anything?"

"No, sir."

"So she would have known—as she was imparting this information—she knew that it was probably being recorded and you were a law enforcement officer. Is that right?"

"If she had seen the recorder in my hand, yes, sir, she would have realized it was being recorded and that I was law enforcement, since I did tell her who I was."

"And toward the end of the interview—I don't know if you remember this, you may have the transcript in front of you—you asked her if it would be okay at some other point for her to come in and have another interview. Do you remember that question?"

"Yes, sir."

"And she said, I think, 'absolutely' that she would. Is that right?"

"I believe 'absolutely' was the word she used. Yes, sir."

Strianse then asked Stokes to read to himself the portion of the interview where he introduces himself to Kelley.

"That's where you're introducing yourself as Detective Stokes and you appreciate her talking with you. And then you say 'about this'?"

"Yes, sir."

"Now, at that point in time, there's really no definition as to what 'this' was, was there?"

"No, not between me and Mrs. Cannon. No, sir."

"Because you had basically gone over to the

apartment to see if she was there and the children were there. Is that right?"

"I had already been told that she was there with the children. And I was directed to go there and speak with her."

"But she didn't know why you were there at that point?"

"I didn't tell her why I was there at that point. No, sir."

"You only said that you were there 'about this.'"

"Yes, sir."

Strianse then asked Stokes to look at another line in the transcript. The defense attorney's contention was that the detectives didn't seem to be working together, because just as Stokes was about to tell Kelley about her husband, Nancy Fielder interrupts him. Then she decides to speak to Kelley herself.

"It was sort of like you-all were two ships passing in the night, where you say, 'Do you know why we're here?' And then Nancy Fielder cuts in and says, 'Can I ask something?' Is that right?"

"Yes, sir."

"So you-all never really get to the bottom of why you-all were there, at that point in the conversation?"

"I was going to tell her at that point, but then Lieutenant Fielder started asking questions."

"Now, at that point in the interview, were you prepared to tell her that her husband had been found—"

"That was my intention. Yes, sir."

"Then Mrs. Cannon asks, 'What's going on? Where is he?' And then you make the decision at that point in time just to say, 'He's at home'?"

"Yes, sir."

"Which was sort of a half-a-loaf kind of answer, wasn't it?"

"Yes, sir."

"He was at home but—So what happened from your intention to wanting to tell her that her husband was there at home, and he was deceased, to you getting a little cagey with her just a couple of minutes later?"

Stokes said it was just the flow of the questions and the flow of her answers. He said at that point Kelley was still cooperating, and his job was to gather as much information as possible. He said sometimes when you tell people a family member had died, they become too upset to continue talking.

"And we saw that later in the conversation, when you finally got around to telling her, which was about fifty minutes into the interview, that she got very emotional?"

"She did get upset. Yes, sir."

"And even started hyperventilating. I think I have heard you tell her to breathe in through her nose and mouth because it might help her?"

"Yes, sir."

"So that was the reason why you didn't want to approach the subject earlier?"

"Like I said, I was trying to gather as much information as possible."

Detective Stokes explained that he and Detective Putnam went back to Kelley's apartment about ten-forty at night with a search warrant. Earlier that day, he said, he had helped Putnam put the search warrant together to present it to a judicial officer to be signed.

"And then, if I understand the timing, at about ten-forty, you assisted Detective Putnam in what the officers call 'the execution of the search warrant,' or actually going out there and serving the warrant and seizing whatever the items are that you're looking for. Is that right?"

"That is correct, sir."

"And did you, in fact, go out to the apartment there at the Grove at about ten-forty or so?"

"Yes, sir."

"And you approach the apartment and knock on the door, and nobody is there. Is that correct?"

"That is correct."

"And then you wait to see if Mrs. Cannon is going to return?"

"Yes, sir."

"And I think, according to your report, within a matter of minutes Mrs. Cannon drives back into the apartment complex. Is that right?"

"I'm not sure how long we waited, but it wasn't extremely long. But, yes, she drove back in the black Yukon."

"And that was a vehicle that she had made arrangements to get from the home at Bowling. Is that right?"

"That was my understanding. I wasn't present when it was taken from there."

"But the attorney that was representing her in that May incident made those arrangements. Is that your understanding?" Strianse asked.

"I'm not sure who made the arrangements, but I would assume that's who did it."

"But you did see her drive into the apartment complex in the Yukon. And following behind her is

James Cannon: millionaire, businessman, successful attorney, father of three, and murder victim. *(Courtesy of the Cumberland School of Law, Sam Henry University)*

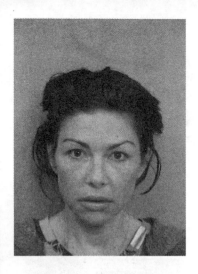

Kelley Cannon: former debutante, wife, mother of three, and cold-blooded killer. *(Courtesy of the Metropolitan Nashville Police Department)*

The Cannons lived in an upscale section of Nashville with a household staff that included a nanny and a housekeeper.
(Courtesy of the Metropolitan Nashville Police Department)

Detectives found the back door to the house open.
(Courtesy of the Metropolitan Nashville Police Department)

The kitchen window was also open. *(Courtesy of the Metropolitan Nashville Police Department)*

Police discovered a beer can in the yard. *(Courtesy of the Metropolitan Nashville Police Department)*

Police tested the wineglass found in the kitchen for possible DNA. *(Courtesy of the Metropolitan Nashville Police Department)*

Jim Cannon's order of protection against Kelley lay on the kitchen counter. *(Courtesy of the Metropolitan Nashville Police Department)*

Upstairs, police found Tim's and Henry's bedroom in disarray. Jim often slept on the bottom bunk. *(Courtesy of the Metropolitan Nashville Police Department)*

Jim's briefcase, water bottles, beer bottle, and glasses were found in the boys' bedroom. *(Courtesy of the Metropolitan Nashville Police Department)*

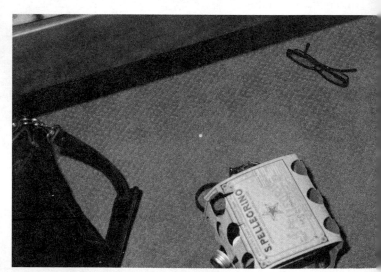

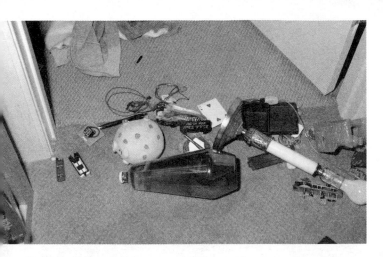

Items that had been on top of the chest in the boys' room.
(Courtesy of the Metropolitan Nashville Police Department)

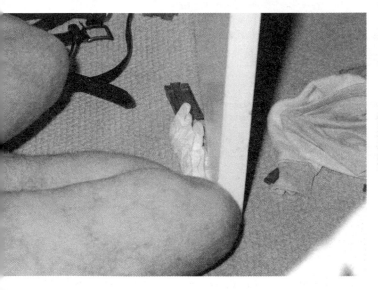

The murderer left a latex glove in the closet next to Jim
Cannon's knee. *(Courtesy of the Metropolitan Nashville Police Department)*

The boys' bedroom, with the tip of a latex glove the murderer discarded on the floor. *(Courtesy of the Metropolitan Nashville Police Department)*

Close up of the tip of the latex glove found in Tim's and Henry's bedroom. *(Courtesy of the Metropolitan Nashville Police Department)*

Police examined the Motorola cell phone charger with blood on it. Kelly used the charger to strangle her husband.
(Courtesy of the Metropolitan Nashville Police Department)

Police found latex gloves in the bushes and on a tree behind the Cannon house. *(Courtesy of the Metropolitan Nashville Police Department)*

Detectives found a portion of a Band-Aid wrapper and a piece of cardboard ripped from a box of latex gloves in Kelley's 2008 Pontiac sedan. *(Courtesy of the Metropolitan Nashville Police Department)*

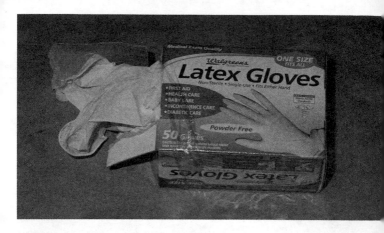

Police confiscated an opened box of Walgreens latex gloves from Kelley Cannon's apartment. *(Courtesy of the Metropolitan Nashville Police Department)*

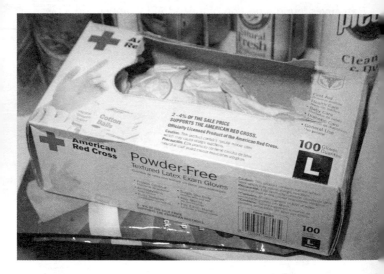

The American Red Cross gloves police found in the laundry room in the Cannon home. *(Courtesy of the Metropolitan Nashville Police Department)*

Lead investigator Det. Brad Putnam. *(Courtesy of the Metropolitan Nashville Police Department)*

Investigator Lt. Nancy Fielder. *(Courtesy of the Metropolitan Nashville Police Department)*

Assistant District
Attorney Katy Miller.
*(Courtesy of District Attorney
General Victor S. "Torry"
Johnson's Office)*

Assistant District
Attorney Sharon Reddick.
*(Courtesy of District Attorney
General Victor S. "Torry"
Johnson's Office)*

an individual driving a Dodge pickup truck. Is that right?"

"Yes, sir."

"And did you get a good look at the Dodge pickup truck?"

"It was dark, and at night, and with the time elapsed since then—If you're asking me to describe it, I don't really think I could."

"But you know it's a Dodge?"

"From what I wrote in my supplement, yes, sir."

"But you never got the tag number of that Dodge truck that evening?"

"No, sir, I don't think I did. I probably would have put that in my supplement if I had."

"But I think you observed the person driving the Dodge pickup truck following the Yukon?"

Stokes said he and Putnam saw the man get out of the pickup truck and lean into the window of the Yukon. But he did not get the man's license plate number or interview him at the time.

Strianse then asked Stokes what items police took from Kelley's apartment during the execution of the search warrant. Stokes said they took the dark pair of jeans she was wearing, a carton of Virginia Slims—although he didn't remember if there were cigarettes in the carton—and a dress.

"I don't want to be indelicate here," Strianse said. "But when she took off the pants and handed them over to you, did she tell you that she had urinated in those jeans?"

"Yes, sir. She went into the bathroom to take them off for us. When she came back out, I believe she was in a bathrobe. Before handing them over to

Detective Putnam, she informed us that, yes, she had, in fact, urinated in the pants."

"Do you remember if this dark pair of jeans was a Paper Denim and Cloth–brand pair of jeans?"

"All I remember is they were dark-colored, sir."

"You don't remember the size? Size zero?"

"No. They were fitting her, so whatever her size was. I didn't read the label."

"And when you left the apartment, did she tell you she was concerned for her safety?"

"Yes, sir, she did."

"And you gave her some advice that she needed to call the police if she felt like she was being threatened?"

"If she felt concerned or threatened, yes, sir."

On redirect Katrin Miller asked Detective Stokes some questions to let the jury understand that the man who was following Kelley in the pickup truck was not threatening her, nor was she really afraid for her safety.

"Detective Stokes, you and Detective Putnam went back to her apartment about ten-forty that night, the twenty-third—the same day that the body was found. Is that correct?" the prosecutor questioned.

"Yes, ma'am."

"Do you know whether or not the front door was locked or unlocked?"

"I think all I did was knock. I might have turned the handle and pushed, but I don't remember if it was locked or unlocked."

"Did you make any kind of notation in your supplement about that? Do you want to just scan that real quickly?"

"I might have. I simply said, when we arrived, I knocked on the door, but it appeared no one was in the apartment and that Detective Putnam and I had waited in the parking lot a short time later."

"Do you know how long it was before Mrs. Cannon came in the black Yukon, followed by the Dodge pickup truck?"

"Not the exact time, but it was probably well within an hour."

"And you said that the man got out of the pickup truck and then leaned into the window of the Yukon. Is that correct?"

"Yes, ma'am, as if he was speaking to Mrs. Cannon."

"Leaned into the driver's-side window then?"

"Yes, leaned into the driver's side."

"So he got out of his truck and walked over to the Yukon and leaned in and appeared to be speaking to Mrs. Cannon. Is that right?"

"Yes, ma'am."

"How long did it appear that he was speaking with Mrs. Cannon?"

"Oh, just a few minutes. Because as soon as they had parked, Detective Putnam exited the vehicle and started walking over toward them."

"And the man that was talking to Mrs. Cannon, did he introduce himself, or what did he do?"

"He just kind of stood back, and I believe Detective Putnam started talking to Mrs. Cannon. I don't remember him giving his name or anything else to us."

"Did he come in the apartment with you and Detective Putnam and Mrs. Cannon?"

"No, ma'am."

"Did you notice at one point if he even left?"

"He left as we were walking with Mrs. Cannon back over toward the apartment."

"And you told Mr. Strianse that Mrs. Cannon commented one of the last things was that she was concerned for her safety. Did she elaborate on what she was afraid of, or what concerns she had?"

"Well, she told me she was concerned for her safety and was nervous staying by herself. I advised her to call police if she thought someone was prowling around her apartment. So as best as I can remember, she was concerned about people outside of her apartment."

"But she had been living there by herself prior to that day, correct?"

"I think she told me during the interview since the Monday before."

When Katrin Miller finished up, Peter Strianse told the judge he had a couple follow-up questions as well. His aim was to counteract the effect of the prosecutor's redirect.

"After you saw the Yukon pull in and see this man leaning into the driver's-side window, you and Detective Putnam get out of the car and start walking toward the Yukon. Is that right?"

"Yes, sir."

"And as you walk toward the Yukon, Detective

Putnam advises Mrs. Cannon that there's a search warrant for the apartment. Is that right?"

"I believe we had walked up to the truck and then he advised her."

"And that would have been within earshot of this man, who had been leaning into the window?"

"Oh, yes, sir. I believe so."

"And after he learns that you're the police and there's a search warrant, he gets in his truck and leaves. Is that right?"

"Yes, sir."

CHAPTER 15

The next witness to take the stand was MNPD officer Johnny Lawrence, of the Technical Investigations Division, identification section. Lawrence had joined the Metro Nashville Police Department on January 12, 1981.

Members of the identification section go to crime scenes, take photographs, lift fingerprints, collect evidence and examine the scenes to find additional evidence. In addition to his extensive experience as a police officer, Lawrence also had specialized training in the area of crime scene investigation, as well as reconstructing the scenes of shootings and interpreting the patterns of bloodstains.

Lawrence and his CSI unit worked just about any type of case and call, from burglaries, graffiti, shootings and robberies. A patrol officer at the scene of a crime would determine whether the CSI unit was needed. If so, Lawrence and his colleagues would be dispatched to the location to assist the detectives.

Lawrence told the jury he was one of several

crime scene investigators called to the scene after Jim's body had been discovered.

"Who were the others?" asked prosecutor Sharon Reddick, who questioned Lawrence.

"It was myself and we have civilian employees also. We call them 'investigators.' It was Investigator Alicia Primm at the time, but she married since. Later on, Sergeant Daniel Orr came to the scene, and then Investigator Rhonda Evans became involved."

"Is it fair to say you have probably, by far, the most experience in crime scene investigation of that group? Correct?"

Lawrence said he was responsible for a large amount of evidence. He said he documented and collected the evidence and processed the scene.

Reddick then showed Lawrence some diagrams of the scene, including the yard and the house, and asked if he recognized them. He said they were diagrams he and Sergeant Orr had completed at the scene. She then put the diagrams on a monitor so the jury could also see them.

Reddick showed the diagrams to the jury and asked Lawrence to point out everything that was in each of them.

Lawrence then gave the jury members a tour of the Cannon house via the diagrams, pointing out the dining area, the laundry room and the stairs leading upstairs. He told the jury that when you walked in the front door, there was a staircase that went up and to the left. He added that there were two or three ways to get upstairs. Next he pointed out the backyard and the area where the Cannon vehicles were usually parked and the back door, which led out to the patio.

On another diagram Lawrence pointed out various features of the upstairs, including locations of the master bedroom, the hallway, the office, the bathroom and the boys' bedroom.

"And what's significant about this closet area?"

"That's the closet from the bedroom. It's a large closet, and that's the location that the victim was located in."

"During the investigation you spent a good bit of time in the boys'—what we're calling the boys' bedroom or playroom area. Is that correct?" Reddick asked. She then showed him a photograph of the bedroom and asked him to explain to the jury what was in the photograph.

The next photograph Reddick showed Lawrence was of the hallway leading to the opposite end of the house, where the master bedroom was located.

"So this door here is the hallway door. Is that correct?"

"Right. It's just an opening and going downstairs."

"And then immediately to the right as we look at it would be the closet door. Is that correct?"

"Yes, ma'am."

"Orient us to this photograph and tell us what is depicted in that photograph."

"You're back in the same location of the first one you saw. The stairway is in this location," Lawrence said, pointing it out. "The closet is straight ahead, and to the left. The bunk beds are over to the right. And to the back is the hallway leading to the master bedroom."

"And what is this item here?"

"That is a tip out of a latex glove, a fingertip."

"And was that item present there in that location when you arrived at the scene?"

"Yes, it was."

"This is another photograph generally of that same area, but from a longer view. Can you point out where that tip is in that photograph?"

Lawrence pointed it out to the jury.

"Now, did you personally collect that item, that tip of the glove that we just saw in the photograph?"

"Yes, ma'am."

"And how is it that you go about collecting items that you consider of evidentiary value at a scene like this?"

Lawrence explained that before any evidence was collected, it was photographed numerous times, identified with numbered markers, then measured for inclusion in the diagram. Then the crime scene investigators, who would all be wearing gloves, would pick it up, place it in a paper bag, then label and seal the bag.

The next photograph Reddick showed Lawrence was the closet and the latex glove that was behind the door, inside the closet. The photograph also included the body of Jim Cannon stuffed inside the closet.

"So to orient the jury to what you're looking for, where is that glove located in relation to where Mr. Cannon's body was?"

"With the position he was in, it was down at his knees."

"And did you collect that glove using the same

procedures that you've previously described to the jury?"

"Yes. Each piece of evidence is sealed separately."

Reddick then showed Lawrence a picture of the bedroom where the closet was and asked him to identify its contents. He said there was a chair and table backed up against the wall that was across the room from the closet.

"And did you notice anything at that point significant about that charger?" she asked, pointing to the cell phone charger in the photo.

"I noticed the cord was pulled off of it, and there was what appeared to be blood on the charger."

"And I'm going to show you another photograph and ask if you recognize it."

"That's the same one. It's close-up, and you can see here the damage done from where it was pulled. The possible bloodstain that I observed is actually on the other side. Once I picked it up, I observed it. You see the stain here, which was possible blood. And, again, you can see a close-up picture showing the wires that are pulled."

"And based on what you could physically observe about that charger, did you determine that it was potentially of evidentiary value and needed to be collected?"

"Yes, ma'am."

Lawrence said he photographed the charger; then he collected it as evidence. He also collected some evidence from the carpet.

"Did you specifically notice some things about the carpet in that bedroom that you thought might be of evidentiary value?"

"Several different locations."

"And tell us what you noticed."

"There were stains throughout the carpet typical of a child's playroom, with some different colors. The last picture you saw there was a yellow stain next to the charger. We also saw some red stains and some brownish-color stains. We did not know if it was blood or not. You usually do not, until you test it. We did do a preliminary test. It showed some slight indications, but we were not sure. To be on the safe side, we collected everything that appeared to look like blood. So we cut the carpet pieces out of the carpet."

"Then you made the determination based on some slight indication that they might be of evidentiary value to actually collect pieces of that carpet. Is that correct?"

"Right. We had some slight indications. Just to be on the safe side. We don't like to do a lot of testing because sometimes it can damage the evidence. So we try to limit that."

"I'm going to show you two more photographs. I'll ask if you recognize what's in those photographs. And I'm going to show you what I've previously marked with an *A* and ask if you recognize what's in that photograph."

"That is deep inside the closet area to the top, toward the front-door wall."

"When you walked into that closet initially, was there anything else—other than Mr. Cannon's deceased body—that you immediately noticed about that closet area?"

Lawrence said there was a strong odor of bleach.

The next picture Reddick showed Lawrence was a close-up of Jim Cannon's body. Lawrence pointed out a coat hanger and told the jury he saw it next to the body. He said he stepped on it, so he wouldn't disturb anything. However, he told them, his wet boot made an impression on the hanger.

Lawrence also pointed out other things in the picture that he had collected as evidence, including Jim's briefcase.

"Were you able to determine whether or not Mr. Cannon's wallet, ID or money was in that briefcase?"

"No, it was not."

"Did you and other officers there on the scene make attempts to locate Mr. Cannon's wallet, identification, money?"

Despite a pretty extensive search of the house, Lawrence said no one was ever able to find those items. (As part of Kelley's defense, her attorney, Peter Strianse, was trying to make the jury believe Jim's death was the result of a robbery gone bad.)

"Now, in addition to collecting certain evidence, did you also process certain items there at the scene for fingerprints?"

"Yes, ma'am."

Before she showed Lawrence any additional photographs, she asked him to describe how he processed a crime scene for fingerprints.

"On this particular incident, when I arrived on the scene, Investigator Primm was with me. I instructed her to start taking interior photographs of the area, and I would do the exterior. And what we normally try to do is show windows and doors to show any possible point of entry or any damage," he said. "So I started taking exterior pictures, and I came across a window that was partially opened.

So once I located that and I finished taking my pictures, I processed that window to see if we could locate any latents."

"And when you say 'process' a window or 'process' anything for fingerprints, what do you physically do?" Reddick asked.

"There's numerous ways to develop a latent fingerprint. On this particular window I used what we called 'magnetic powder' to process it and try to develop any latent print."

"And explain to the jury how it is—in addition to just looking to see if there are points of entry— explain to the jury how it is that you make a determination of whether or not something is worth trying to process for fingerprints?"

Lawrence said everything is different and the investigators really can't just tell by looking whether or not they can get a print off any particular surface.

"Sometimes wood you can, sometimes you can't. Glass is pretty consistent. The window looked kind of disturbed in the area," he explained. "There was a cord that looked like a satellite radio antenna. If anybody has got a satellite radio, you know you've got an antenna at your residence. The cord was partially across the front of the window, but hanging down like it had been knocked off. So that was the reason I processed that window."

"So it drew your attention and you decided to try to process it."

"Yes."

"Were you able to lift a latent print from that outside of that window?"

"Yes, ma'am. On the outside I developed latents at that location."

The investigator added that he also processed the inside of the window as well. "And I developed latent prints on the left bottom glass pane."

He told the jury that the prints were sent to a different lab that matched fingerprints, because his unit didn't do the actual matching.

The next photograph Reddick showed Lawrence was of the wineglass that was in the sink in the kitchen of the Cannon house. Lawrence said, when he processed that wineglass for fingerprints, he lifted a partial print from it.

"Now, Officer Lawrence, you also spent some time in what would be considered the master bedroom and the master bath. Is that correct?"

"Yes."

"What evidence, if any, did you collect from those rooms?"

Lawrence said the investigators also collected a carpet that had some red stains on it in one of the bathrooms, but not the master bathroom. There were also some stains in the hallway leading from the master bedroom to the child's bedroom.

"Were you ever able to determine what those stains were?" Reddick asked.

"Those stains were blood—in the hallway. And it also had directionality to it."

"Okay. I'm sorry, I missed a point," Reddick said. "Back when you're talking about the master bathroom and master bedroom, you talked about some reddish stains around the bathroom that didn't test initially for blood, but you thought they potentially could be."

"There were several stains, but they were a small amount," Lawrence said.

Lawrence then told the jury exactly what he found at the crime scene and how he processed the evidence.

When Peter Strianse began questioning the witness, he asked about all the people, including family members and members of the police department, who had been allowed in and out of the Cannon house. The defense attorney's implication was that the scene could have been contaminated.

CHAPTER 16

Up next for the prosecution was crime scene investigator Alicia Primm Mahaney, a civilian employee with the Metro Nashville Police Department. Mahaney, whose name was Primm at the time of Jim's murder, was a member of the CSI unit that helped Officer Johnny Lawrence process the crime scene at the Cannon house.

When she had arrived at the scene, she was assigned to take some photographs, as well as collect evidence.

As the prosecutor questioned Mahaney, Sharon Reddick put a picture on the monitor that the CSI had taken of the tree line in the Cannons' backyard.

"Now, looking at the tree line, if you could, tell the jury what that item is."

"It's a white latex glove, and it's an evidence marker that's hung on the tree branch," she said, adding that she had noticed the glove and marked it.

"Did you notice anything unusual about the way

that glove was hanging there in that tree or shrub?"
Reddick asked.

"It just looked like it had been tossed in there."

"I'm going to show you one more photograph
and ask if you recognize that photograph."

"That was a second latex glove in the same
wooded area," Mahaney said. She told the jury
both gloves were close together, although they
were in different shrubs. Mahaney told the members of the jury that after she photographed the
gloves, she collected them as evidence, following
proper procedure. After she bagged the gloves, she
sealed it and wrote out a property sheet so the evidence could be processed and then turned in to
the property room.

Reddick then put up a photograph Mahaney had
taken of the driveway in the back of the house and
asked if there was something of evidentiary value in
the photo. Mahaney said there was an empty beer
can, which she collected as evidence. She also told
the jury she collected an empty beer bottle from
an empty planter in the front yard, which she
processed in the lab and then turned in to the
property room.

"Now, you also spent some time in the house in
what we've been calling the boys' bedroom—the
room where the closet where the decedent was. Is
that correct?"

"Yes."

Reddick then showed Mahaney some photos of
various items in the room, including the closet
door, and asked her to identify them.

"Now, when you visually observed that door facing from inside the closet, was there something that caught your attention?"

"There was a spot that looked like it could have been blood."

"Okay. And I'm going to show you another photograph. Do you see that spot that looked like it could have been blood in that photograph?"

"Yes."

"And where is that, if you point to the screen?"

Mahaney pointed out the spot on the closet door for the jurors.

"Now, did you also process this door facing for fingerprints?"

Mahaney told the jury that she did process the door and she was able to lift a latent print from the door. In response to a request from Reddick, Mahaney pointed out the approximate location of the spot, which was on the side of the door facing the bedroom.

"In addition to photographing what potentially could have been blood, did you do anything else with regard to that spot there on the door frame?"

"I took a swabbing of it."

"Did you do any kind of preliminary tests to determine if it could potentially be blood?"

"I don't remember doing one, since it was so small. I just collected it."

"Let me ask you this. Were you able to lift a latent print from that boys' bedroom door frame?"

"The closet door, yes."

"Yes."

In addition to processing the boys' closet door

frame, Mahaney told the jurors, she also processed the door frame of Sophie's room and lifted a print from it. She then took the prints and the evidence back to the lab to process them.

"And as part of your responsibility for processing evidence, did you complete an evidence-processing log on those items of evidence?"

"Yes."

"I'm going to put one of these on the monitor so that the jury can see, and just ask you to talk about each of the items of evidence that you processed and what you did . . . starting with the Budweiser beer can."

"Of course, it's pretty self-explanatory by the types of headings it has," Mahaney said. "I just put the one Budweiser beer can, the date I brought it into the lab, the date I processed it, the time I started, the specific process type and the time I ended it. I took swabbings from the mouth in the top of the beer can, and then I processed it with magnetic fingerprint powder."

Mahaney told the jurors she was able to develop latent prints on the can and turned those prints in to the print examiners. She also packaged the swabbings from the mouth of the beer can and turned them over to the property room. She also took swabbings for DNA from the mouth of the beer bottle that she collected in the Cannons' front yard at the scene and processed it with fingerprint powder. But she was unable to develop any latent prints from the bottle.

"The second evidence-processing log involves

other items of evidence that were taken from inside the home. Is that correct?"

"Yes."

"If you could tell the jury, which items of evidence you processed and what you did with each of those?"

"One box of American Red Cross latex gloves. I processed the outer part with magnetic powder. There were prints that I lifted from the exterior of the box," she said. "And then I used a chemical called Anhydrone on the inside of the box and on the top around the top edge. And [the log] says I developed latent prints from it."

"And, again, those prints were . . . submitted [for processing]."

"Yes. If it was developed with Anhydrone, we probably scanned those prints. And pictures were made from them."

"And what other piece of evidence did you process?"

"A Clorox bleach bottle with a cap."

"And . . . did you actually observe that Clorox bleach bottle at the scene?"

Mahaney answered affirmatively, saying she saw it next to Jim's head. She told the members of the jury that she processed the bottle with magnetic powder, but she didn't find any latent prints on it. She also collected what looked like a hair or a fiber from the handle of the bottle. She photographed it, secured it in "like some kind of paper fold, to where it can't get out in a loose bag. I taped it up, secured it and put it in another bag. I labeled all that, and turned it in to the property room."

* * *

On cross-examination Peter Strianse showed Alicia Mahaney the photographs she took from the tree line, where the latex gloves were found.

"It was one glove that was hanging in the trees. Is that right?"

"Yes."

"And then there was one glove that was on the ground?"

"It was in the brush."

Strianse then asked Mahaney about the glove that was hanging in the tree.

"Did you measure the distance from the ground to the branch?"

"No, I didn't do any diagrams, so I didn't measure."

"So no measurement was made from the ground to the branch?"

"Not by me."

With that, Strianse ended his cross-examination and the witness was excused.

The next witness called by the prosecution was Rhonda Evans, a civilian crime scene technician with the Metro Nashville Police Department.

Evans told the jury that she had been assigned to assist Officer Johnny Lawrence in processing the crime scene at the Cannon house. She also said Detective Putnam had given her a bag of Kelley's clothing to take back to the property room. She then explained that she had been called back to the lab to process Kelley's rented Pontiac.

"And were you able to lift any latent prints from either the exterior or the interior of the vehicle?" prosecutor Sharon Reddick asked.

"I believe I only developed prints on the exterior of the vehicle."

"So you attempted on places within the interior, but weren't able to actually develop prints?"

"That's correct."

On cross-examination Peter Strianse first asked Rhonda Evans about Kelley's clothes and shoes in the bag that Detective Brad Putnam had collected.

"He went over and interviewed Mrs. Cannon, and she turned over some items to him voluntarily. Is that right?"

"That's correct."

"And then he drove them from the Elmington apartment over to Bowling, where you were. Is that right?"

"Yes, that's correct."

"And put them in your care and custody. Is that right?"

"Yes, sir."

Strianse then asked Evans about a mark someone had made on Kelley's high-heeled shoes, indicating what appeared to be a spot of blood.

"Someone had marked where there appears to be a blood spot under one of the toes in the front of the shoe. Did you mark that?"

"I did not mark those. I took photos of them."

The defense attorney then asked Evans about Kelley's jeans that were in the bag Putnam had handed to her.

"And what brand are those?"

"They say they're Mossimo Supply Company."

"And what size are they?"

"Size one."

"And then you were also given from Detective Putnam a white tank top. Is that right?"

"That's correct."

"And is this the tank top that he turned over to you?"

"Yes, it is."

"And what did you do with those items of evidence after you collected them and logged them in?"

"After I collected them, I took them back to the ID lab and removed them from the packages and took photos of them," Evans told the jury. "Then I repackaged those items and transported them to the property room and submitted them."

Strianse then asked Evans to tell the jury the brand and size of Kelley's tank top. She said it was a Daisy Fuentes top and it was a size small.

This line of questioning was most likely intended to remind the jury that Kelley Cannon was such a small woman she couldn't have possibly overpowered her husband and murdered him.

The next witness for the prosecution was Linda Wilson, an identification analyst with the MNPD. Her job was to identify latent fingerprints by trying to determine their sources. Wilson said she had been with the department for twenty-six years and worked in identification for fifteen years.

"I enter latent prints in AFIS, which stands for Automated Fingerprint Identification System," she told the jury. "I communicate with court officials and detectives, and I maintain our latent print files."

"In your capacity as a latent print examiner, were you asked in July of 2008 to examine a number of prints recovered from a crime scene at Bowling Avenue?" Reddick asked.

"Yes, I was."

"In this case were you also given some known prints of particular individuals specifically related to this case or potentially related to this case?"

Wilson said she was given Jim's fingerprints and the police already had Kelley's prints on file. She added that Sergeant Freddie Stromatt also gave her the fingerprints of Kelley's friend James Dean Baker. In addition to those known prints, Wilson told the jury she was also given some latent print cards of prints lifted from around the crime scene and from items collected from the crime scene.

Wilson told the members of the jury that a number of the prints didn't have enough ridge detail to allow her to compare them to anyone.

"And what are some of the things that can affect whether or not a print lifted might have value to you for examination purposes?" Reddick asked.

"Well, it just depends on the receiving surface or whether or not the person has sufficient moisture or substances on their hands to leave a print, or that person could have worn gloves," Wilson explained.

"Now, a large number of the prints that were provided to you had no value, but there were also several that had value for identification purposes, correct?" Reddick asked.

"Yes."

"And some of those you were able to make iden-tifications, and some you were not?"

"Correct."

"Now you've already told us that you had com-parison prints specifically from three individuals potentially related to this crime scene. And you also had a database that you could compare prints to?"

"Correct."

"Now, is it fair to say that in this case you did not have comparison prints for everyone who had ever been in that house at Bowling?"

Wilson said although it would not be possible to have comparison prints for everyone who had ever been in the Cannon house, she did have compari-son prints of Jim and Kelley.

The prosecutor asked Wilson about the prints that she was able to identify from the water bottle found in the boys' bedroom.

Wilson told the jury the fingerprints on the water bottle belonged to Jim Cannon. She also said the print lifted from the closet door in the boys' room belonged to Kelley Cannon.

"Were there any other prints identified from that door frame to anyone else?"

"No."

"Then you were also able to make an identifica-tion on a print from the baby's room door frame, correct?"

Wilson said the print on the door frame in Sophie's room belonged to Jim.

Then Wilson told the jury members that the other prints that were lifted from the left front outside window, as well as a print on the left inside windowpane on the open front window, were identified as belonging to Kelley.

"Were there any prints from that window, either inside or outside, that were identified to anyone other than Kelley Cannon?" Reddick asked.

"No, there were not."

Now it was Peter Strianse's turn to question Linda Wilson.

"Ms. Wilson, let me ask you a question. You've been doing this for a long time, haven't you?"

"Yes, I have."

"If you were to go out to my house today—and I've lived in that house for probably fifteen years or so with my wife and three children—would you expect to find my fingerprints, my wife's fingerprints, and my children's fingerprints at that place?" Strianse asked the witness, his motivation obvious.

"Probably."

"And how long does a fingerprint stay in a particular location?"

"There's no way to determine how long a print will stay on a surface."

"But if I touch a surface and somebody doesn't clean it or wipe it away, it could be there for a long time?"

"It's possible."

CHAPTER 17

Amy Huston, Jim and Kelley's friend, took the stand next.

Amy, a product manager for AT&T, told the jury she had known Jim since the early 1990s. Then, when he started dating Kelley, Jim brought his new girlfriend into their group of friends. And Kelley became one of their friends.

The witness told the jurors that Kelley and Jim had been having problems for some time, but the first time he talked to Amy about these difficulties was early in January 2008.

"And were you aware at some point that Mrs. Cannon actually moved out of the house?"

"Yes. My understanding is that she was actually removed from the house."

"Now, prior to Mr. Cannon's death in June, when would the last time you had spoken—and I'm talking about prior to June—when would have been the last time you would have spoken with Mrs. Cannon?"

Amy said that Kelley had called her in April,

when she got out of rehab. She then told the jurors how her relationship with Kelley had soured. It was the same story that she had told Detective Putnam shortly after Jim's death.

Amy then told the jury about that night in June 2008 when Kelley called her to meet at BrickTop's.

When she finished telling her story, prosecutor Miller asked Amy if Jim was a big man. She said he was not. In fact, she said, both Jim and Kelley were small people.

During his cross-examination Peter Strianse went over Amy Huston's version of what happened when she met the defendant at BrickTop's.

"I think you told the jury that that weekend of Sunday, June twenty-second, that you had been out of town in Atlanta. Is that right?"

"Yes, I had been."

"So you came home and had sort of gone to bed early to be ready for your workday the next day. Is that right?"

"Correct. I had been shopping and going out to dinner with friends in Atlanta and had a long drive back and was tired."

"And Kelley called you about eight o'clock. Is that right?"

"Yes, it was sometime right around eight o'clock. I would have to look at my cell phone records to see the time."

"And I think you told the police that she was distraught and upset in that phone call?"

"Yes, that is correct."

"She said that she didn't really have anybody to turn to. And she viewed you as a friend."

"Yes."

Strianse then questioned Amy about her relationship with Jim and Kelley.

"Now, you were godmother, you told us, to Sophie, so you spent a lot of time at the Cannon home. Is that right?"

"Yes, I spent time there—probably at least one time a week. And we talked regularly."

Strianse's line of questioning next centered on whether Amy thought Jim was more than a social drinker and if he could hold his liquor.

"I'm just trying to say he's not the kind of guy that would have one or two drinks and be stumbling around?" the defense attorney posited.

"No."

It seemed that through his questions, Strianse wanted to let the jurors know that even if Jim had had a few beers or wine on the night he was murdered, he wouldn't have been intoxicated enough for Kelley to overpower and strangle him.

Strianse then questioned Amy about the night she met Kelley at BrickTop's. He asked her how long they were there and mentioned the fact that Kelley had had three glasses of wine in about ninety minutes.

It seemed as though Strianse wanted the jury members to think Kelley had been a bit too intoxicated to overpower and strangle her husband.

Kelley's attorney next turned his attention to the cut that Kelley had on her hand when she arrived at the restaurant.

"You told us that Kelley was late because she had cut her hand or something?"

"Yes, that is correct."

"And when she showed up at nine-thirty, she had a Band-Aid on her finger. Is that right?"

"Yes."

Why was it important to remind the jurors of the cut on Kelley Cannon's hand? Maybe Strianse wanted them to know that she didn't get the cut trying to murder her husband by strangling him with a ligature. Or maybe he wanted them to wonder why the cut didn't bleed when she was wrapping the ligature tightly around his neck.

Erin Dutton, the custodian of records for the Metropolitan Nashville Emergency Communications Center, took the stand next for the prosecution.

As the custodian of records, Dutton kept the recordings of all the 911 calls that the emergency center received.

"And were you asked to locate and provide a recording of a 911 call made from Bowling Avenue on May 21, 2008?" Sharon Reddick asked.

"Yes."

"I'm going to show you an item and ask if you can recognize this item," Reddick said.

Just at that moment Peter Strianse asked the judge if the attorneys could approach the bench. The judge agreed.

"Your Honor, my recollection is when we had the evidentiary hearing on July 8, 2009, Ms. Reddick said that the 911 call would have to be redacted in some way. That's been a long time," Strianse said. "Well, I've got the transcript, if you want to see it. And I don't know what would need to be taken out before we play it. If the state was concerned enough at the hearing to say it needed to be redacted—"

When Katrin Miller said she didn't recall that, Strianse again offered to get the transcript.

"I might have said it, but I would have been wrong," Sharon Reddick said. "Because we listened to it again."

"Yeah. I mean, we've listened to it in light of your orders," Miller told the judge. "There isn't anything in there that you thought needed to be redacted."

Strianse got the transcript and read a portion of it: "'The State's position is that the recording would be offered as part of the proof related to the incident. We are aware however that there are probably some portions of that recording that need to be redacted.'"

"What portions are those?" the judge asked.

When Reddick said she didn't know, the judge asked Strianse if he had listened to it. He said he had not.

"All I'm saying is, Judge, at that point you hadn't issued an order. We were having the hearing and " Miller said.

"All right, now, this is the call that came in at the police department that Jim Cannon is talking. Does he talk about her assaulting him?"

"Uh-huh," Miller said.

"There you go," the judge said. "Remember, I've said that the assault—what he said about—of course, it's the 911 call. That's different."

"You said in your order with regard to the officers," Reddick said, "the tape is coming, the officers can't testify about the assault."

Strianse then asked if the court could hear the tape without the jury present. The judge agreed.

"Ladies and gentlemen, we need to take up an issue outside your presence," the judge told the members of the jury. "We'll take a few minutes and sort of have a comfort break. And we'll have you back in as soon as we can. Again, I'm aware of the time frame we have to meet. If you'll step out for just a minute."

"We're talking about the 911 tape," the judge said after the jury members left the courtroom. "In terms of the ruling that I made at the time . . . I basically indicate, this is related to a material issue. But it does come in for motive, identity, absence of mistake, common scheme, basically relationship of the parties. I'll again instruct the jury otherwise. But the 911 tape and the statements to Officer Ward prior to his coming back, I said were admissible. I have recently revisited that, but only as to the issues of when Officer Ward went back and talked to Mr. Cannon. So everything up to that I allowed in as being nontestimonial. . . . So we just need to hear it to make sure, right?"

After they listened to the tape, the judge informed the attorneys that before the tape was played in open court, she would instruct the jury members that they were to consider it only as it related to the "relationship of the party, complete story, identity and motive."

* * *

The members of the jury were brought back into the courtroom and Sharon Reddick resumed questioning Erin Dutton.

"I had handed you an item and asked you if you recognized that item. And is that a recording of the 911 call that came from Bowling Avenue on May 21, 2008?" Reddick asked.

"Yes."

"Before we play it, ladies and gentlemen of the jury, again I'm going to advise you how you receive this evidence," the judge said. "This contains some allegations that Mrs. Cannon was involved in other criminal activities or might have been involved in something else. You are, again, only to consider this as it provides a complete story of the crime that you've heard about and it's logically related to or is necessary for a complete account, the relationship of the parties, the identity—the defendant's identity, her motive. So you may only consider it for that reason."

MNPD officer George Ward was called to the stand to testify about responding to the domestic disturbance at the Cannon house on May 21, 2008. Ward testified that on his way to the Cannons', he was receiving information from Jim relayed through dispatch. When Ward arrived, he saw a black SUV driven by Kelley Cannon turning left out of the driveway. She looked right at the officer and continued on her way out of the driveway. His lights were already on, so Ward activated his siren and pursued the defendant. After the defendant reached a speed of seventy miles per hour, Ward stopped chasing her because he was in a residential area. He also didn't want to endanger the child he believed was in the car with Kelley.

When he got back to the Cannon house, he spoke with Jim about what had happened. Jim told him Kelley had assaulted him before taking their youngest child and leaving. Using OnStar, officers eventually located the defendant and retrieved the baby. This wasn't the first time Ward had met Kelley, he told the jury. He said Kelley called the police in February and said that Jim had kidnapped Tim and Henry, because he had picked them up after school.

After Ward was dismissed, the judge adjourned the trial for the day.

The next morning the jury heard the testimony of Metro Police lieutenant Matthew Pylkas.

During his testimony Matthew Pylkas told the jurors that on May 21 OnStar was able to direct police to within one hundred yards of Kelley Cannon's car. They found it parked at the Hampton Inn at Franklin Road and Old Hickory Boulevard. But when they checked with the hotel staff, they learned no one by the name of Kelley Cannon had checked in. After the police described Kelley to the staff, they were able to direct them to her room.

The police used an access key the staff had given them to enter Kelley's room. Kelley, who looked a bit like she was under the influence of something, had Sophie with her. The cops asked why she had run from them. She said she just had to get out of there and away from Jim.

"I asked her why she would run from the cavalry, when the cavalry is coming to help. I told her she would have been safe with the police," Lieutenant Pylkas said. "She muttered a vague reference that she didn't really care for or really appreciate the police."

The police then took Kelley into custody on the outstanding warrants. Pylkas said the next time he saw Kelley was on June 25, when he arrested her on the outstanding warrants for taking her kids in violation of Jim's order of protection.

On cross-examination, referring to the incident on May 21, 2008, Peter Strianse asked Lieutenant Pylkas why he didn't write up his report on it until August 18.

"So how many months later is that? Five months later or so?"

"Roughly. Yes, sir."

"Okay. But you didn't make a contemporaneous report of what you did on May twenty-first. Is that right?"

"Not that exact day. No, I don't believe I did."

"Did somebody ask you to, five months later, put together a report of the May twenty-first incident?"

"I don't recall how it came about that I was doing that, to be quite honest with you."

"I mean, you didn't roll out of bed on August eighteenth and say, 'Gee, I need to do a report from an incident five months ago,' did you?"

Although it hadn't even been three months since

Jim's murder, the defense attorney seemed to be deliberately making the time span appear longer than it really was.

"I wouldn't be able to speculate on how I came about filling out the supplement report."

"But that's typically not the way that somebody does a report of an event, waiting five months to do the report, is it?"

"It depends on your involvement, what it is that you know, how a case is progressing," Pylkas said. "There's a lot of different factors as to why. I was not the one that was filling out the primary incident report, which is the overall official report that evening."

Pylkas explained that in many cases the officers or detectives in charge filled out the primary report. In this case, although Pylkas was not the primary, he still couldn't explain why he filled out the report in August.

Strianse questioned Pylkas about the day when he found Kelley in a room at the Hampton Inn. The first thing he wanted to know was whether Kelley appeared drunk.

"And you went to a room. I assume you knocked on the door?"

"We got to the door, yes."

"And how did you gain access?"

"We had an access key."

"And did Mrs. Cannon appear drunk to you, or anything like that?"

"As far as my experience of being on the police department, it appeared that she was acting possibly under the influence of something. But as far as to be able to give you a medical diagnosis, I couldn't give you a medical [diagnosis]."

The lieutenant then admitted that he hadn't included that piece of information anywhere in his report.

"And she was driving that day. Is that right?"

"Yes."

"And did you give her any field sobriety tests or anything like that to see if she had been driving under the influence from Bowling over to this hotel?"

"Not that I can recall."

"Okay. She told you that the reason that she left was that she just had to get out of there and she had to get away from Jim. Is that right?"

"Yes, sir."

"And you said something in your testimony that she told you that she didn't really care for the police. Is that right?"

"Right."

"Didn't she also tell you that the reason she had some apprehension about the police was that she had been arrested by the police—that Jim had had her arrested?"

"Yes, she did."

"And you put that in your report. Is that right?"

"Yes, sir, I did."

Strianse then questioned Pylkas about the three outstanding warrants against Kelley for violating the orders of protection against her. He asked the officer if the orders of protection actually prohibited Kelley from having contact with the children or just with Jim.

"You would probably have to ask Detective Putnam

on that," the witness said. "As far as I remember, the overall incident of all the goings-on that had been taking place, it's my understanding that it involved the children. But as far as knowing exactly why that particular night, it would be mere speculation on my part."

Strianse then read from one of the orders of protection. "'You shall not telephone, contact, or otherwise communicate with the petitioner,'" he said. "Is that right? [So] based on your experience, assuming that Mr. Cannon was the petitioner on the order of protection, then clearly she's to have no contact with him. Is that right?"

"If he was the petitioner," Pylkas said.

"But in terms of the minor children, the order of protection merely says she's not supposed to threaten or harass her minor children. Is that right?"

"I don't know. I didn't read the violation."

"And you're not familiar with the order of protection and the law that—"

"I don't know what happened in this particular case," Pylkas said, interrupting Strianse's question. "I wasn't part of the ex parte hearing, the service of it. My involvement was that it was communicated to me that there was three violations for an order of protection and that someone needed to be found."

"You've seen an order of protection before, haven't you?"

"Yes."

"Let me show you, Lieutenant Pylkas, the order of protection that formed the basis of the warrants that you told us about," Strianse said. "And you've seen the orders of protection before. Is that right?"

"Yes, sir."

"Look up in the upper left-hand box that says 'petitioner,'" Strianse told the officer, showing him Jim's order of protection against Kelley. "That's James Malcolm Cannon. Is that right?"

"Yes, it says that."

"And he would be the petitioner. And then there are listed minor children protected under this order. Do you see that?"

"Yes, sir."

"And then the respondent, of course, would be Mrs. Cannon. Is that correct?"

"Yes, sir."

"And then take a look at the directives, or the orders, if you will, to the respondent or to Mrs. Cannon," Strianse told Pylkas. "It says, number one, 'You shall not commit or threaten to commit abuse, domestic abuse, stalking, or sexual assault against the petitioner or the petitioner's minor children.' Is that right?"

"Yes, sir."

"And then take a look at number two. 'You shall not telephone, contact, or otherwise communicate with the petitioner.' Is that right?"

"Yes, sir."

"It doesn't say anything about not having any contact with her minor children," Strianse said. "The only thing she's prohibited to do with her minor children is not to assault them in some way?"

At that point Sharon Reddick objected, saying Strianse's line of questioning was asking Lieutenant Pylkas to make a legal conclusion.

The judge agreed and told Strianse to move on.

* * *

When the defense attorney was finished with the witness, Sharon Reddick had a few more questions for the officer.

"Lieutenant Pylkas, Mr. Strianse asked you if you were able to determine whether or not Mrs. Cannon had activated her OnStar. Were you able to determine, or do you know whether or not Mrs. Cannon attempted to contact the police herself at all on that day, the twenty-first?"

"I do not recall."

"And he asked you a series of questions about your report. At that time, as the lieutenant supervisor, it wasn't typical for you to fill out reports at all. Is that a fair statement?"

"Unless I was directly involved into a crime scene–type situation, it would . . . A lot of times my job is directing resources," Pylkas said. "And unless it's more of a large incident command–type situation, or when I'm at a critical crime scene, sometimes it's not always required of me, no."

"So most cases of this nature—domestic dispute—you're not going to fill out a report?"

"On this particular call it was not unusual for me to not fill out a supplement report, no."

CHAPTER 18

During her testimony Metro Police sergeant Twana Chick told the jury about her role during Kelley Cannon's arrest on June 25.

"Now, how is it that you became involved in that stop?" Sharon Reddick asked.

"My lieutenant came across the air and indicated that he was behind a vehicle and it was being driven by her, and that he was making a stop on Harding [Pike]. And I was close to it to back him up."

Chick explained to the jury that one of her responsibilities was to take pictures of Kelley's car.

"Why was the decision made that the vehicle needed to be photographed?"

Chick told the jurors things were pretty chaotic and the police were trying to accommodate a lot of people.

"There were some issues with some family members being there who had a child who was very ill. And ID was not available at the time. It was going to be several hours before they could come," she told the jurors. "And so the decision was made by the lead investigator that the best thing to do would be to go ahead and photograph it and be able to move things along and accommodate folks."

"And this wasn't a situation where the vehicle needed to be impounded or processed or searched. It was simply a matter of getting the vehicle to somebody that [Mrs. Cannon] felt it would be safe with and getting it out of where it was. Is that correct?"

"Yes. It actually went back and forth. She changed her mind several times about whether to have it impounded in a safe location. She mentioned that a lot. But then the issue came up about contacting— I think it was a brother and seeing about getting it secured that way. So it was back and forth quite a few times. And ultimately we were able to make contact with the gentleman at Vanderbilt."

"And ultimately you allowed it to be her call what happened to that vehicle and the contents. Is that correct?"

"Yes, ma'am," Chick said, adding that she took some pictures of the vehicle before turning it over to Kelley's brother.

Reddick then showed Chick some photographs of the backseat of Kelley's car and asked her to describe the items that were there.

"She had a large amount of cash, and she was concerned about that. And, of course, we're always concerned about it as well. So that's documenting that that is there," Chick said, looking at one photo.

"This vast amount of items that fill up the vehicle, do those appear to have been recently purchased?" Reddick asked.

"Yes, most of them had either tags or they were in bags where it appeared they [had] been purchased."

"And she indicated it was new? She had just purchased all of those items?"

"Yes, ma'am."

"Okay. Now, after photographing that vehicle, did you also take some additional photographs that evening?"

"Yes, ma'am."

Reddick then asked Chick about the injuries she observed on Kelley's left wrist, as well as the discoloration she noticed.

"And what did that dark . . . ?"

"It looked like where you had had an adhesive wrap, you know, tape or a Band-Aid or something that you had on there and you pull [it] off and the adhesive stays on your skin," Chick told the jury.

When Peter Strianse cross-examined Sergeant Chick, he first asked about the confusion when police stopped Kelley Cannon.

"You talked about this confusion as to whether the vehicle would go to what you called a secured tow-in lot or be turned over to the care and custody of her brother, Bobby. Is that right?"

"Yes, sir."

"Was part of the confusion that Bobby wasn't there at the time that she was pulled over? And you-all had to wait for him to get there?" Strianse asked.

"That's part of it. Yes, sir."

"And you had taken her cell phone from her. Is that right?"

"I believe we did have it. That's standard practice."

"And she was unable to call her brother?"

"We were trying to call him for her."

"And as calls would come in on the cell phone, she would ask you, 'Is that my brother Bobby calling?'"

"Yes."

"So the decision could be made as to what was to happen with [Mrs. Cannon's vehicle]?" Strianse asked.

"Yes."

The defense attorney then asked Twana Chick about the items inside Kelley's car. He didn't want the jury to think that Kelley had killed her husband and then had gone on a shopping spree with money she might have stolen from him. He wanted them to think Jim had given Kelley permission to buy the items to furnish her apartment.

"You talked about the items that were inside the Yukon. They came from Pier 1. Is that right?"

"They were in Pier 1 bags and had the tags on them from there, the ones I could see."

"They were basically home furnishings. Is that right?"

"Yes, sir."

"Did she tell you that she was living in a temporary-stay apartment?"

"I would have to refer to my report to see exactly what she said about that. It was a comment about furnishing something," Chick said.

"And that she had made arrangements with her husband to purchase some things to make the apartment a little bit more personal if the kids were going to come over?"

"No, I don't recall that."

"Okay. But you do recall her talking about a personal-stay or a temporary-stay apartment she was in?"

"I recall her mentioning furnishing a place. I don't remember more specifics than that."

"But you do remember her [telling you] she had the stuff because she needed to furnish a place? Is that familiar?"

"That's familiar. Yes, sir."

Strianse then asked Sergeant Chick about the discoloration and cut on Kelley's wrist. He wanted the jury to believe that neither the discoloration nor the cut had anything to do with Jim Cannon's murder.

"And before you took the picture, do you remember she had to take a watch off of her wrist?"

"I do not recall that. I'm sorry."

"You don't remember a watch that had a steel band on it?"

"No, sir."

"You said that you thought that might have been adhesive from a bandage. Is that right?"

"That's what it appeared to be."

"But that's just a guess by you?"

"That's right."

"It could just as easily be oil from the steel watchband. Is that right?"

"It could be."

"And as far as the cut, you characterized it as an old cut. I think you said [that] a few minutes ago?"

"Yes, sir."

"So you don't know when or how she sustained that cut?"

"No, I have no idea."

"You did a report in this case, didn't you, Sergeant Chick?"

"Yes, sir, I did a supplement."

"Do you note anything about the bandage that you thought had been on her wrist at some point in time?"

"I don't think I did."

"And you did a single-space that looks like a page-and-a-half report. Does that look familiar?"

"Yes, sir."

"And you did this almost contemporaneously with this arrest. Is that right?"

"Over the next couple of days. Yes, sir."

"And you didn't mention anything about your suspicions that it was a bandage?"

"No, sir."

"I mean, did you actually feel this area or scrape the area?"

"No. I didn't touch her. No, sir."

CHAPTER 19

The next witness to testify was Aaron Bagley, the bartender on duty on May 29, 2008, when Kelley Cannon walked into the Hickory Falls Grille & Bar in Smyrna, Tennessee, and took a seat at the end of the bar.

"A lady came in and sat at the end of the bar and started to tell me about her and her husband going through a divorce," Bagley said. "She found out she was being cheated on. She had caught him flying women to come see him in other states. [She said] if he tried to take the babies from her that she would kill him."

To Bagley, Kelley seemed very distraught, very angry and very bitter. Not to mention, really emotional and unstable.

"And did you actually spend a good bit of time interacting with this customer?" Sharon Reddick asked.

"Yes, ma'am. Well, I mean, she sat down, and I was a bartender working on tips. And she had a nice wedding ring on her finger, so I kind of spent a little more time with her. She was giving a lot of information out, so you had to listen."

"So you were just being a bartender and listening to her tirade, so to speak?"

"Yes, ma'am."

"While Kelley was waiting, what did she eat or drink while she was there?"

"I believe she ordered salmon, and she drank a Kendall-Jackson Chardonnay."

"And did she drink more than one glass of Kendall-Jackson Chardonnay?"

"I believe so."

"Did she eat her salmon?"

"Yes, ma'am, at the bar."

"Now, did she make the statement about killing her husband more than once throughout the course of the time you were listening to her?"

"Yes, ma'am. She said it in a couple of different contexts—that she was so mad that she could kill him. Then if he took the babies—tried to take the babies from her—that she would kill him."

"Was the length of conversation and the content of conversation fairly unusual for you, even for a bartender?"

"Yes, ma'am."

"Fairly memorable?"

"Absolutely."

"Eventually did she leave?"

"I left before she left."

"Had you ever seen her before that evening?"

"No, ma'am."

"Have you ever seen her after that evening?"

"On the news. Yes, ma'am."

Bagley said he had heard stories about Jim Cannon's murder. Then one night when he was at home watching the news, when Kelley's picture flashed on the screen, he recognized her immediately.

"And what did you do or say when you saw a picture of the woman you had seen in the bar that day?"

"I cursed. I said, 'Holy shit.' Can you say that in court?"

"Well, you just did," the judge responded, drawing more than a few chuckles.

"Sorry."

"And then what did you do?"

Bagley said he called his stepdad, a Metro Police officer, and asked what he should do.

"I knew what I should have done. But it was a high-profile thing, I just felt like I needed to find somebody who could take my statement and take what occurred to me and use it."

"So you made contact with the police?"

"Yes, ma'am."

"And provided them the same information that you have just told us here today?"

"Yes, ma'am."

When Sharon Reddick finished questioning Aaron Bagley, Peter Strianse had a few questions of his own.

"I assume in your work as a bartender you sort of are a bit of an amateur psychologist. Is that right?"

"We hear a lot of people pour their hearts out to us. That's correct."

"A lot of people coming in and blowing off steam and that sort of thing?"

"Sure."

"In fact, that was your initial reaction when you heard this tale of woe from Mrs. Cannon. . . . You didn't really take it very seriously is what I think you had put in your statement that you gave to Detective Putnam. Is that right?"

"Well, I mean, at the beginning it seemed like a woman scorned, pretty upset."

"Because I think you told Detective Putnam that you just kind of paid no attention, because people sometimes say extreme things when they're upset. Is that right?"

"Sure."

"Because you certainly didn't do anything about that comment on May 29, 2008."

"No, sir."

Strianse then asked Bagley why he didn't call the police after Kelley Cannon told him she was going to kill her husband, particularly since his stepdad was a cop.

"You had her credit card information and her name and you didn't pick up the phone to call the police on May twenty-ninth and say, 'I think there's a crazed killer that's here in my bar'?"

"No, sir."

"And you certainly weren't motivated to even call your stepdad on May twenty-ninth to report this."

"No, sir."

"Because you thought, as you put in your

statement, sometimes people say things when they're upset. Is that right?"

"Right."

Strianse then pointed out that Bagley only called after Jim Cannon's murder had already garnered some publicity.

Sharon Reddick, however, tried to counter the defense attorney's contention, but she was shot down by the court.

"Mr. Bagley, in retrospect do you wish you had done something that night you heard her threaten to kill her husband?" she asked.

"Objection," Strianse said.

"Sustained."

The judge dismissed Bagley and called the next witness, Paul Breeding, to the stand. But before Breeding could be sworn in, Peter Strianse asked the judge if he could ask Aaron Bagley one more question. The judge agreed and asked the clerk to bring Bagley back in.

"Step back up. You're still under oath, having barely escaped the courtroom," the judge said.

"You thought you were through, Mr. Bagley?" Strianse asked.

"Sure did."

"I apologize for bringing you back. Did Mrs. Cannon tell you when you met with her on May twenty-ninth, there at Hickory Falls, that she had lost twenty pounds or so?"

"Yeah."

"And do you remember putting in your statement that she looked very skinny and you underlined the word 'very' in your statement. Is that right?" Strianse asked, again trying to portray Kelley Cannon as a small woman, incapable of murdering anyone.

"Yes, sir."

"Thank you."

"Anything further?"

"No," Sharon Reddick said.

"Are you sure?" Aaron Bagley asked.

"Run quickly," the judge said, adding another bit of levity to counter the seriousness of the trial. "Now, Mr. Breeding," Judge Blackburn said, "Mr. Breeding, step around. Raise your right hand to be sworn."

Paul Breeding was an engineer with Gresham, Smith and Partners in downtown Nashville. He also owned a small farm in Wilson County, where he raised cattle. Breeding and Kelley Cannon had been friends for around eighteen years—before she married Jim. Paul also knew Jim, but he met him after Kelley did.

Sharon Reddick then asked Breeding about something that happened on June 22, 2008, the day before Jim's body was discovered.

Breeding said he had received a telephone call on his cell phone from Kelley around seven in the evening and he was outside on his farm. Kelley asked Paul to call Jim. She wanted Paul to ask Jim to call her. Kelley couldn't call Jim directly because of the order of protection.

Breeding called Jim on his home phone and then his cell phone, but he couldn't reach him. So he placed another call to Jim's home phone and left a message, telling Jim to call Kelley because she sounded very upset.

The next day Breeding was sitting in his office in Cool Springs when he got another call from Kelley. It was around two or three in the afternoon. Kelley told Paul the police were at her apartment. She said she had the kids and Jim was dead.

"When you talked to her the day before, she sounded very upset. What was her emotional demeanor when you talked to her on the twenty-third?"

"Very, I guess, unemotional and matter-of-fact."

"Did she ask you to do anything?"

"She wanted to know if I could come over and bring the children something to eat."

"Did you do that?"

"No."

When Breeding got off the phone with Kelley, he said he immediately called her mom.

When the prosecution finished, Peter Strianse rose to begin his cross-examination. The first thing he wanted to know was if Paul Breeding was married. Paul said he had been married for fourteen years.

"Now, you were interested romantically in Kelley Cannon, weren't you, over the years?"

"A long time ago."

"Just a long time ago?"

"Yes."

"In fact, when Jim and Kelley got engaged, you weren't really all for that, were you?"

"That's not true."

"You had feelings for her at the time that she decided to marry Jim Cannon. Is that right?"

"No."

"And you were visiting with her in May of 2008 after she had gotten kicked out of the house. Isn't that right?"

"That's right."

"And you had reconnected with her. You had called her over the Memorial Day weekend. Is that right?"

"Yes."

"And did you call her and tell her that you had driven by the house [on] Bowling and that you noticed that Jim and the kids were not there over the Memorial Day weekend, and there was a lot of clothing that had been dropped off by the dry cleaner stuck on the door?"

"That's right."

"And you determined that at that point in time that she was out of the house at Bowling, had just been released from jail and was sort of tacking between hotels and apartments. Is that right?" Strianse asked.

"That's correct."

"And you began a relationship with Kelley Cannon out at the hotel in Smyrna. Is that right?"

"I was helping her through this situation. I wouldn't call it a relationship."

"Did helping her include having sexual relations with her at the hotel?"

"No."

"Okay. So you never spent the night with her there at the hotel in Smyrna?"

"No."

"Okay. And you were not having any sort of relationship with her at that time?"

Strianse asked Breeding if he knew a person named Rick Greene. When Paul said he did not, Strianse asked if he remembered showing up one morning at Kelley's hotel room in Smyrna and finding Rick Greene there.

"There was someone there. I don't know who it [was]."

"Okay. But she had given you a card key to the room, right?"

"That's right."

"And you felt comfortable coming in and letting yourself in, [in] the early-morning hours, when she was out there. Is that right?"

"The purpose was to check on her to make sure that she hadn't [made a] mistake with some of her medication."

"Oh, you were concerned about her medication levels?"

"Uh-huh."

"And you had driven out to Smyrna to check on her?"

"That's right."

"And this is a woman that you had not had much contact with before May of 2008. Is that right?"

"Not very much."

"Okay. And what moved you to call her in May of 2008?"

Breeding said Jim Cannon had asked him to help Kelley because they were going through a difficult time.

"Were you and Mr. Greene surprised to sort of see each other in that hotel room in the early-morning hours of May 2008?"

"I didn't see him or his face or know who he was."

"But you opened the door?"

Breeding said he saw someone in the room and asked for Kelley. Then he saw a man, so he left.

"But that was not the only time you visited out at the hotel in Smyrna. Is that right?" Strianse asked.

"That's right."

Paul said he visited two or three times and helped her move a couple times. He said he was calling Kelley and seeing her pretty regularly from about May 21 until Jim's body was found on June 23. In fact, he called her a number of times on June 22.

Breeding told the court that Detective Putnam called him after finding his number on Kelley's phone bill. When Breeding talked to Putnam, he didn't tell him he had been in a relationship with Kelley. He just told him that he had been helping her move.

"But you took it upon yourself to drive over to Bowling over the Memorial Day weekend without any contact from Mrs. Cannon to take a look at the house. Is that right?"

"I traveled on that street periodically, and it wasn't a particular trip to go by there."

"You live in Lebanon, but you decide to get in the car on Memorial Day weekend and drive by the Cannon residence? That's your testimony?" Strianse asked, sounding somewhat skeptical.

"The day I drove by there was not on a holiday weekend. I don't know which day it was, but it was a workday. And my work takes me through that area."

"And then that causes you to call Mrs. Cannon?"

"Because I saw the dry cleaning hanging on the door."

Still skeptical, Strianse asked Breeding if he drove by the Cannon house regularly on his way home from work or if that was the first time he had ever done it.

Paul said he often drove around Nashville for work.

"And you're driving around Bowling every day?"

"Sometimes I cut through there to go to see a client in Green Hills."

After trying to cast suspicion on Paul Breeding, Strianse had no other questions.

The next witness was Elliott Webb, a loss-prevention specialist for Walgreens. The court played the videotape of Kelley Cannon walking out of the Walgreens without paying for the box of latex gloves on the night before Jim was found dead. Webb testified that Kelley was seen on the store's videotape at 11:17 P.M.

"I want to ask you a couple of questions about the second segment of the tape. You can see Mrs. Cannon put the box in her arm. Is that right?" Peter Strianse asked.

"Yes."

"And she's not making any effort to hide the box. Is that right?"

"Not that I can tell."

"In fact, she goes and spends a few minutes with the pharmacist. Is that the place where she's walking into? Is that the pharmacy?"

"That would be the consultation window."

"And she spends a few minutes consulting with the pharmacist. Is that right?"

"Uh-huh."

"And while she's, I guess, killing time to see the pharmacist is when she picks up this box. Is that right?"

"I would assume, yes."

"Well, did you see somebody else at the pharmacy window right before she went in?"

"There was a black male there."

"So she was waiting for that man to leave, and then she walks to the window?"

"Yeah."

"And then walks out of the store with the gloves in the same position, just in her arm?"

"I can't answer that from the angle that I saw. I couldn't tell if the gloves were in her arm at that particular time."

"In your review of the video, you didn't see her put the gloves in the purse that she had? She had an oversized purse with her."

"No, I didn't see her put the gloves in there."

Having made the point that Kelley wasn't deliberately trying to steal the latex gloves, Strianse went back to his seat and the witness was discharged.

CHAPTER 20

Detective Brad Putnam took the witness stand next and explained to the jurors that he had retired from the Metropolitan Nashville Police Department some sixteen months earlier after a thirty-two-year career on the force.

He then answered the prosecutor's questions about the day Jim Cannon was found dead. When he first arrived, his lieutenant, Nancy Fielder, and his immediate supervisor, Sergeant Freddie Stromatt, were already on the scene and briefed him about what had happened.

He told the jurors that he conducted a walk-through of the scene and determined that robbery was probably not the motive for Jim's murder. Even though Jim's billfold containing his driver's license and credit cards was missing, his expensive Rolex watch was still in the bedroom where his body was found.

"During your walk-through [of] the house and your investigation in this case, were there any signs of a forced entry into the house?" Katrin Miller asked.

"No, ma'am."

"Was there, however, a window that didn't work properly or a particular window that you were made aware of?"

"Correct."

"Were there some family members that were also there present when you arrived, if you recall?"

"I don't know when the family members arrived. I don't know if they were there before I arrived or not, to be honest with you. I did talk to family members later that day at the scene."

"Do you recall speaking with Mrs. Cannon's mother, Diane Sanders, at some point?"

"Yes, ma'am."

"She was there on the scene. Is that right?"

"Yes, ma'am," Putnam said, adding that Kelley Cannon was not at the scene when he arrived. He told the jurors he soon learned that she was at her condo on Elmington Avenue with her three kids.

"And did you request that Detective Stokes go over to that location and talk to Mrs. Cannon?"

Putnam said he asked Lieutenant Fielder and Detective Stokes to go to Kelley's place to check on the kids and find out how they ended up over there, when Jim Cannon had had custody of them. He also asked the pair to notify Kelley that Jim had been found dead.

"And did you request Detective Stokes to record this conversation?"

"No."

"Okay, he just did that on his own. You are aware that he recorded it?"

"Later on. Yes, ma'am."

Putnam told the members of the jury that some-time later that day he went over to Kelley's condo to talk to her. He wanted to know if she knew of anyone who might want to harm Jim.

"Okay. And when you went over there, did you actually record the conversation that you had with Mrs. Cannon?"

"I did."

Miller then played the audio recording of Putnam's interview with Kelley at her apartment the day Jim's body was found. She asked him to compare the audio with a transcript of the recording. The jury members were also given copies of the transcripts to follow along.

After the recording finished, Miller asked Putnam a couple questions pertaining to the interview with Kelley.

"Detective Putnam, on the tape recording of the conversation we just heard, there's a . . . It sounds like a cell phone that goes off twice with a song playing or music playing. Whose cell phone was that, that was going off?"

"It was, I assume, hers. It was the one in the apartment."

"Was it in the bedroom with you?"

"I can't remember if it was in the bedroom or if it was outside, to be honest with you."

"And did you talk to Mrs. Cannon inside the bedroom?"

"Yes, ma'am," he said, adding that he wasn't sure if the bedroom door was ever completely shut.

Putnam told the jury it didn't seem like anyone ever answered the ringing cell phone.

"And you asked Mrs. Cannon about her father calling the Tennessee Highway Patrol," Miller said. "You had some information before you went over to that apartment on Elmington that her father had, in fact, called the Tennessee Highway Patrol that morning," Miller said. "And you asked Mrs. Cannon to sign a consent to search, and you talked to her a little bit about that. Could you explain to the jury what that is and why you did that?"

Putnam explained that although he could get verbal consent from someone, he would rather have the transaction documented.

"So I was asking her if we could have consent, like I said, to search her apartment, search the house. You know, possibly if it became needed to obtain a search warrant," the retired detective said.

"And you asked Mrs. Cannon what she was wearing the night before when she went to dinner with Ms. Huston and then went over to the house on Bowling and picked her children up," Miller said. "And she initially tells you that she was wearing jeans and a shirt and actually points out those clothing items to you. Is that correct?"

"Correct."

"But then pretty soon after she gives you the jeans and the shirt and the shoes, she says, 'No, I wasn't wearing that. I was wearing a dress.' And you asked her for the dress. Is that correct?"

"Correct."

Then she asked him to identify the clothing he

had collected from Kelley—clothing that, Kelley said, she had been wearing the previous evening.

But Putnam said that wasn't all he had confiscated from Kelley's apartment that day. He told the jurors he also collected a box of Walgreens-brand latex gloves he had found in a paper bag on the living-room floor. One corner of the box had been ripped off. The gloves were significant because the detective knew that the killer wore latex gloves, which were discovered near Jim's body.

Putnam also told the jurors that the police had been unable to search Kelley's rental vehicle initially because her attorney had asked them not to do so—although he gave them permission several hours later. But he said before he left Kelley's apartment, he looked in the car and noticed the corner piece of the Walgreens latex glove box on the front seat and what looked like gauze and a Band-Aid on the backseat. Ultimately the crime scene investigators collected those items for processing.

The detective explained that he drafted a search warrant because he wanted to confiscate the black jeans Kelley wore when he interviewed her at her apartment.

"I wanted to get the black denim jeans she was wearing because there was something about the jeans that was significant to me," Putnam said. "We knew that the killer had used bleach to clean up the scene. . . . When I was at the scene, I could smell a very strong odor of bleach. In the closet there was an empty bleach bottle, approximately about two feet from the victim's head. And the victim, down near the lower extremities of his legs underneath, he was lying on some clothing. The clothing was the children's clothing. And you could see discoloration in the clothing, which would be consistent with bleach droplets. I could relate to that because I've done it myself. And when I was interviewing [Kelley] there at the condo, I noticed there appeared to be, like, a discoloration on the left pants leg around the knee. So I wanted to get the black jeans she had on."

"How come you felt like it was better to get a search warrant to get those jeans than simply asking her if you could have them?" Miller asked.

"You mean at that time?"

"Yes."

"I mean, she wasn't aware that I was interested in the jeans, and I didn't want her to know, since [her attorney] had asked us to stop [the search]. So I didn't want her to know I was interested in them because I was afraid before we could come back that, you know, they would be disposed of."

Putnam told the jurors as he was drafting the search warrant, Kelley drove her friend James Dean Baker to the Cannon house to pick up one of Jim's vehicles for her to use. Baker left with Jim's Yukon. Putnam explained that police didn't want Kelley on the property, which is why she had Baker actually drive the Yukon.

At about twenty minutes of eleven on June 23, Detective Putnam and Detective Stokes went back to Kelley's to serve the search warrant and collect the black jeans. Then after Kelley was arrested on June 25 for violating the order of protection, Putnam told the jurors, he decided to check out the store videos from a number of Walgreens in the area to see if any of them had Kelley on videotape the night Jim was murdered. In fact, she was caught on camera in a local Walgreens at about eleven-nineteen, Sunday night, June 22, walking out of the store with a box of latex gloves like the ones found at her house.

"Okay. And do you recall what she was wearing on that surveillance tape?" Miller asked.

"Well, what is significant is that she was wearing black denim jeans, pullover dark-colored shirt. There was a design on it," he said. "I couldn't see the shoes, that I recall. And she had a pocketbook."

"And does she appear to purchase the gloves? Or tell us how you can identify this box of gloves?"

Putnam told the jury exactly what Kelley was doing while she was in Walgreens.

"And where are the gloves? Could you see them?"

"They're in the bend of her right arm," the witness said.

Putnam said DNA testing on a piece of a latex glove found in the room indicated that Jim's blood was on the outside and Kelley's DNA was on the inside. He said after his conversation with Jennifer Shipman, he decided to collect some additional DNA samples from some other people to eliminate them as suspects.

"Was there some unidentified DNA that had [been] discovered?"

"Yes, ma'am."

"Who did you go to, to get additional DNA samples?"

"From the housekeeper, Ms. Armstrong, Jean

Armstrong, and the two nannies, Maria Cross and I can't remember the other young girl's name. I would have to look at the report. Danielle Storm? Does that seem right?"

"Yes, ma'am. I took oral swabs from them as well, and then also Carrie Porter."

"What was the significance of that?"

"Well, [Kelley] had told me she thought that her husband was having an affair with Carrie Porter. And I just wanted to be able to see if she had anything to do with this or not."

"So her DNA was also submitted to the lab?"

"It was."

"Okay. And did you go back to Bowling Avenue back in September and collect even some additional evidence? Bed skirts [and sheets] from the master bedroom?"

"I did. Yes, ma'am."

"And were those also turned in to the TBI? And the Clorox bottle that was recovered in the closet next to Mr. Cannon's body? There was a hair or fiber sample on that bottle."

"Correct."

Putnam told the jury, the hair was tested for DNA, but the results were inconclusive.

Putnam also told the jury that as part of his investigation he obtained some phone records, including Kelley's.

Miller then showed Putnam a piece of paper and asked him if it was a copy of Kelley's cell phone records that she gave him while he was talking to her during the tape-recorded interview. He said it was.

Then she asked him about a call that Kelley made to her mother on June 22, 2008, at around two minutes after six in the evening—the night before Jim's body was found.

"And does the phone records show how long that phone call lasted between Mrs. Cannon and her mother, Diane Sanders?"

"Yes, ma'am. The duration we're talking about here, it looks like almost fifty-four minutes."

"Almost an hour?"

"Correct. Just less than an hour."

Miller then changed her line of questioning and again asked him about James Dean Baker—most likely to beat Peter Strianse to the punch.

"You testified earlier about this James Dean Baker that assisted Mrs. Cannon in collecting the Yukon from the Bowling address," she said. "And I believe you said it was really Detective Stromatt that kind of handled that. And he's your supervisor. Is that correct?"

"Correct."

"Are you aware of whether or not Sergeant Stromatt requested that James Dean Baker's fingerprints be compared to the fingerprints found in the house?"

"We did."

"And why was that?"

"Well, just the fact that, you know, he was an associate of hers, and he does have a criminal record. That's why we did that."

"Okay. And I believe none of his fingerprints were found in the house. Is that correct?"

Katrin Miller told the judge she was finished questioning the witness. At that point the judge decided to break for lunch.

During Peter Strianse's cross-examination he asked Brad Putnam about all the people who were in the Cannon house the day Jim's body was discovered. He mentioned the housekeeper, two nannies, all the police and EMTs/firefighters—a total of about twenty-three people who actually went into the house. His point was that there was a good chance that they destroyed or contaminated the evidence.

Strianse also pointed out for the jury that when Detective Putnam went to Kelley's apartment to talk to her, she fully cooperated with him. In fact, he said, it was her attorney who declined to give police consent to search her vehicle. He also reminded the detective that Kelley was just as cooperative when Putnam returned with a search warrant to collect her DNA.

"Now, the other women that you took DNA from, that was all done after Mrs. Cannon was charged and locked up. Is that right?"

"I don't remember what specific day I did that. I know it was all done that same week."

"You didn't set about to gather up this other DNA sample evidence from these four women until after she was locked up?"

"Correct."

Through his questioning of Putnam, Strianse

continued to remind the members of the jury just how cooperative Kelley Cannon was with the police.

The defense attorney then questioned Putnam about James Dean Baker.

"And you told us that an individual by the name of James Dean Baker accompanied Mrs. Cannon over to Bowling to pick up the car. Is that right?"

"That's what I read in the report that Sergeant Stromatt did. Yes, sir."

"And I think you told the jury that Mrs. Cannon drove Mr. Baker over there?"

"That's what the supplement that Sergeant Stromatt made out says."

"But by that point in time, the rental vehicle had been impounded. Is that right?"

"Yes, sir."

"And the whole reason why she needed the Yukon was because she didn't have a vehicle?"

"Correct."

"So it's unlikely that Mrs. Cannon could have driven Mr. Baker over there?"

"She could have drove his vehicle over there," Putnam responded. "You've got to have two people, one to [drop] the Yukon off, which would be him, and I assume she drove off in his vehicle."

"Yes, sir."

"Now, Fred Stromatt is the one that dealt with James Dean Baker over at Bowling. Is that right?" Strianse asked.

"Yes, sir. Yes, sir."

"And you talked to Detective Stromatt about Mr. Baker. Is that right?"

"Yes, sir."

Putnam told the jury that Detective Stromatt mentioned that he knew Baker through his brother, who was a firefighter, who worked with Baker at the Metropolitan Nashville Fire Department. Putnam said he knew that Baker had been previously arrested. And because Baker was there helping Kelley pick up the car—and he had an arrest history in Davidson County—Putnam decided to submit his fingerprints to compare with the latent prints that were lifted from the crime scene. But that was as far as he went investigating his background.

"Did you check his marriage and divorce records?" Strianse asked.

Putnam said he did not.

Strianse then asked Putnam to look at an official copy of the Bakers' divorce papers.

"If you would, turn to the last page of the complaint where the signature lines for the attorney would be," Strianse told Putnam, who did as he was asked. "And who does it show as the attorney of record for the wife?"

"Well, I see a signature of James M. Cannon."

"[He] is representing the wife in that divorce?"

"Yes, sir."

"But in your investigation all you did was determine that he had a criminal history and you supplied his fingerprints to the fingerprint ID officer. Is that right?"

Putnam said that was all he did, adding he did not look beyond Baker's criminal history.

Trying to get the jury members to focus on Kelley's friend as a suspect in Jim Cannon's murder, Strianse asked Putnam if he was aware that Baker had been fired from his job as a firefighter. Putnam said he did know that. However, he admitted, he didn't know that Baker had been arrested for stalking and attempted burglary and prosecuted for burglary.

"Were you aware that he had harassed members of the Judicial Drug Task Force?"

"I'm not familiar with any of that information."

"You didn't really check into the background of [James] Dean Baker other than to determine he had an OCA number?"

"Correct."

"But he's the individual that picks up the car for Mrs. Cannon at Bowling, at about nine-fifteen, on June twenty-third?"

"According to Sergeant Stromatt's supplement, yes, sir."

Strianse continued questioning Putnam about Baker, trying to paint him as a viable suspect.

Strianse then tried to introduce into evidence as an exhibit through Putnam that Jim Cannon had represented James Dean Baker's wife in their divorce proceedings some eleven years prior to the murder. The judge, however, wasn't buying it.

"You're going to have to show to me how that's relevant," the judge said. "But you're putting it in through a detective who doesn't know anything about that or how to read it. It's related to a 1997 case in circuit court. You've got to do a better job on relevance before I let you put it in."

"You do realize who Mr. Baker is?" Strianse asked

the judge. "He's the one that was with Mrs. Cannon on the day that the vehicle was picked up."

"So? This is 1997. Relevance to this case? A divorce action that took place in 1997," she said.

"And Mr. Cannon represented the wife," Strianse countered.

"Nineteen ninety-seven. That was ten years—eleven years prior to it. Eleven years. Again, relevance?"

"I think it's highly relevant that the man that is driving around—"

"Mr. Strianse, I'm not letting you put this in our record until you can show me this detective can identify any of that. He just said he couldn't," the judge said. "You had him reading from some papers. He can't do it. It's not coming in through this detective. Simple as that. Okay. We can take this up at some other time, but that's not coming."

Strianse then went back to questioning the detective.

"But you're learning for the first time today that he was involved in a divorce in 1998 [*sic*]. Is that right?"

"Absolutely."

"You're learning for the first time that his wife in that divorce was represented by the victim, James Malcolm Cannon?"

"Absolutely."

"Yes, sir."

"You said the day that you were interviewing her on June 23, 2008, that you noticed her clothing and you noticed her fingernails. Is that right?"

"Yes, sir."

"And that she had short fingernails?"

"Yes, sir."

"And you didn't do or ask for any fingernail scrapings from her that day. Is that right?"

Putnam said he didn't because he believed whoever killed Jim was wearing gloves. But he did take her fingernails from the medical examiner and turned them in to the Tennessee Bureau of Investigation.

Jumping from one subject to another, Strianse then asked Putnam about seizing Jim's cell phone.

"You talked about seizing or getting hold of Mr. Cannon's cell phone. Is that right?"

The witness explained that Officer Lawrence collected Jim's cell phone. However, Putnam said, he didn't take any fingerprints off the phone. But he did get subpoenas for Jim and Kelley Cannon's cell phone records, as well as Kelley's landline.

"When you reviewed the phone records for Mr. Cannon's phone, were you surprised to see that there were some calls made on that phone, which would have been after the date of his death and the time of his death?"

"I don't recall that."

Strianse next asked Putnam to look at Jim's cell phone records. Strianse then pointed out a number of calls that Jim had made to Kelley's landline at her apartment, as well as her cell phone. Kelley's attorney also showed Putnam that Paul Breeding had made eleven calls to Kelley three days before Jim was murdered and she called him once.

"And then you were able to determine that Mr. Cannon called Mrs. Cannon at ten thirty-eight on June twenty-second. Is that right?"

"Yes, sir," Putnam said.

"And then you see a call from Mrs. Cannon's cell phone at ten fifty-two. Is that right?"

"Yes, sir."

"And that was a duration of forty-one seconds. Is that correct?"

"Yes, sir."

"Now, you called Mr. Breeding by seeing that number recurring on Mrs. Cannon's phone bill. Is that right?"

"Yes, sir."

"Did he tell you that he was involved in any sort of relationship with Mrs. Cannon between May and June?"

"No, sir."

"Did you ask him that?"

"No, sir, I didn't."

"Did he submit to any kind of an interview?"

Detective Putnam said he talked to Paul Breeding on July 11 over the telephone, but he never set up an interview with him. He just asked if he knew Kelley Cannon.

"You didn't ask for any DNA from him or finger-prints or any other items of physical evidence from him?"

"No, sir."

"Okay. When you arrived on the scene, I think you told us it was about ten fifty-five and you began doing your work [on] Bowling. Is that right?"

"Yes, sir."

"At about two-fifteen, Mr. Hollins, the divorce at-torney, showed up. Is that right?"

"Yes, sir."

Putnam said he wrote in his report that Hollins brought all the court papers that had been filed for the Cannons' divorce, including the order of protection. After that, Putnam said, he went to Kelley's apartment to talk to her. The detective told the jury that he really didn't go over all the information Hollins had given him before he went to see Kelley.

"The main thing that was brought to my attention was the order of protection," Putnam said.

"Do you remember at some point in the summer—it's undated—that you interviewed Mrs. Cannon's oldest child, Tim?"

"Well, I didn't interview him. A forensic interviewer did. But I was present and listened in on the interview," Putnam told the jurors. "And then, if there was any particular questions I would want her to ask him, she would do so."

"Right. And you participated to a lesser degree in the interview, but you were there?"

"Yes."

"And that was a social worker that had conducted the interview. Is that right?"

"Yes, sir."

Putnam said the interview was conducted on Thursday, June 26, at eleven-fifty in the morning—three days after Jim's body was found.

"And do you remember Tim telling the social worker that he had seen a couch or something—"

"Your Honor, I'm going to object to this line of questioning," prosecutor Katrin Miller said.

The judge asked the attorneys to approach the bench.

"What are you going to ask him?" she asked.

"I was just going to ask him if Tim told the social worker that he had seen a couch turned over and up against the closet," Strianse responded. "Tim testified on direct that his mother would not let him go into the bedroom and pick up a pillow. The inference being that Mrs. Cannon wanted to keep the kids out of the bedroom."

"So you're going to ask what?"

"One question. [At] the interview in the summer, did Tim tell the social worker that he walked through the bedroom and he saw a couch that was turned over and pushed up against the closet," Strianse told the judge.

"That's the only question you're going to ask."

"That's not what he told her, though," prosecutor Sharon Reddick said. "He said he saw it down the hallway."

"We may have to just play the thing," Strianse said. "I thought he said that he saw the couch—"

"You're going to have to get to that very specific spot," Judge Blackburn said. "I'm not letting you play anything else. Are you just trying to stall this out so we don't get to your witnesses?"

"Not at all."

"Okay . . . if you want to play that specific thing, you need to ask the question correctly," the judge said.

"So I want to ask one question, if he mentioned that about . . ."

Peter Strianse was trying to prove that Kelley Cannon did not stop Tim from going in the room where Jim's body was found. But the prosecutors were claiming that in his interview with the social worker, he never said he was in that bedroom but rather that he saw the couch from down the hallway.

"Are there notes about what he said?" the judge asked.

"I don't know. I thought he said the couch was at the front door against the wall, or something like that," Miller responded.

"I don't know what he said. He also said a lot of prior inconsistent statements," Reddick said.

"Make sure your question is accurate," the judge said. "Rephrase your question, Mr. Strianse."

"You told us that you participated or were present when Tim Cannon was interviewed by a social worker on June 26, 2008? Did he tell the social worker that when he left the house, there was a couch that was up against the closet?"

"He stated he saw the couch against his closet," Putnam told the jurors.

"That would be his closet in his bedroom, correct?"

"Yes, sir."

"Just one other question. In your dealings with Mrs. Cannon that day, she was not aggressive or belligerent with you in any way, was she?"

"No, sir."

"She was compliant with you?"

"Yes, sir."

"She was compliant with you, answered your questions, did what you asked her to do. Is that right?"

"Yes, sir."

"That's all."

* * *

On redirect Katrin Miller asked Brad Putnam to clarify the number of people who entered the Cannon home after his body was found.

"And [Peter Strianse] named Officer Swor, Officer Cox, Officer Peebles, Officer Tilly and Officer Johnson as being people who actually went inside the house," Miller stated. "Do you recall that of your own memory, or do you need to look at your file to see if they actually did go in the house?"

"I remember the supplements that—"

"[Who] was the first officer that responded?"

"Officer Swor." After looking at the supplemental reports, Putnam said Swor did not actually go into the house, nor did Officer Torian Cox, who actually watched the back door. Putnam said neither Officer Peebles nor Officer Tilly, who also watched the back of the house, ever went inside the Cannon residence.

"And Officer Andre Johnson, could you look at his report and see if he went in the house?"

"He did not. He guarded the back door."

"Could you look at Officer Jeffrey Poole's supplement and see if he went in the house?"

"No, he did not. He's also one of the officers that went up to the Elmington address as well."

"Now, if you could, please turn to Sergeant Freddie Stromatt's report, please. I'm asking you, following up on the questions that Mr. Strianse asked about James Dean Baker. If you could just review that, and then I've got a question for you."

"Mr. Strianse asked you whether or not you

had interviewed James Dean Baker. You said you had not?"

"Correct."

"Did Sergeant Stromatt interview him?"

"No."

"Did he talk to him?"

"Yes, he did."

"Okay. So he did interview him?"

"He spoke to him. Yes, ma'am."

"Okay. That's all the questions I have, Your Honor."

Defense attorney Peter Strianse wasn't quite finished with Brad Putnam.

"Interview is sort of too strong of a word, isn't it?"

"I don't know what all he asked him. What I'm reading here, he stated that—"

"Okay. That's a report of somebody else," the judge admonished the defense attorney.

"I'm sorry. I'm not asking what Mr. Baker said at all. I'm just saying that from looking at the report that Detective Stromatt put together, it looks like he spoke to him briefly. Determined who he was?"

"Correct."

"And then knew him from his brother who worked for the fire department. That's not in the report, but made a connection [that] this is somebody that might have a criminal record?"

"Yes, sir."

"And then was able to determine at some point that he did, in fact, have a criminal record and had one of these OCA numbers that showed he had been arrested in Davidson County?"

"Yes, sir."

"And that led to Mr. Baker's fingerprints being submitted to the ID section of the Metro Police Department?"

"Yes, sir."

"That's all," Strianse said.

Then it was Katrin Miller's turn again.

"Sergeant Stromatt also asked Mr. Baker if he had anything to do with this?"

"Correct."

"And he said no?"

"Correct."

CHAPTER 21

The next witness was Rick Greene. Greene told the court about how he met Kelley and his relationship with her.

"Directing your attention to June the twenty-third, the day that Jim Cannon's body was found, how did you find out about his death?" Katrin Miller asked.

"A mutual acquaintance of mine and Kelley's called me at work. It had been on the news at five o'clock," Greene said. "And she said, 'Did you see the news?' And I said, 'No.' And she said, 'Kelley killed her husband.'"

Peter Strianse immediately asked to approach the bench. He told the judge he didn't think the jury needed to hear that kind of hearsay testimony. Miller said she didn't mean for Greene to say what he said.

Strianse asked for a mistrial, but the judge denied the request. Instead, she told the jury to disregard that portion of Greene's testimony. Then Miller continued questioning him.

"Based on a friend calling you, did you understand that Mr. James Cannon had been found deceased on June the twenty-third?"

"Yes."

Greene then told the jury what happened when he visited Kelley after Jim Cannon had been found dead.

When Peter Strianse began cross-examining Rick Greene, he immediately tried to paint him as a possible suspect in Jim's murder. He asked Rick what his job was at the Marshall-Donnelly-Combs Funeral Home. Rick told the jury he was the funeral director and embalmer.

"As an embalmer you deal with bodies. Is that right?" the defense attorney asked.

"I do."

"And I think you told the police that you carry gloves around in your car, latex gloves, at all times. Is that right?"

"I do."

Under cross-examination Rick Greene admitted that when the police questioned him about his relationship with Kelley some eighteen months earlier, he never told them the story he just told in court. In fact, the first time he told anyone the story was about a week earlier when he had been visited by investigators from the district attorney's office. When the investigators showed up, Greene said, he asked if he needed a lawyer. He was worried because he had not told the detectives about his conversations with Kelley Cannon.

Greene told the jurors that when he learned that Jim was going to be brought to his funeral home, he didn't think he should have anything to do with the decedent's body.

"So at that time we had a body that had to be taken to North Carolina, and I volunteered to go," Rick Greene explained.

"You told your boss there that you needed to get out of town. Is that right?"

"I told him I felt like it was better that I wasn't there while Jim's body was at the funeral home."

"Because his body was there to be cremated. Is that right?"

"That's correct."

"So you get out of town for three or four days. Is that right?"

"Two days."

"And then you come back to Marshall-Donnelly-Combs, and Mr. Cannon's body is still there. Is that right?"

"That's correct."

"But I think you told the officers that you felt guilty and that's why you left town. Wasn't those the words you used?" Strianse asked.

"Well, I felt guilty because of what had been going on before his death."

"And when you say 'going on before his death,' you were having a relationship with Mrs. Cannon?"

"Yes."

"In the course of you having a relationship with Mrs. Cannon between May and June of 2008, did you literally run into another man, by the name of Paul Breeding?"

"Well, I don't know if you could say 'ran into' him. He came in the room one morning early."

"One morning that you were in the bed?"

"Yes."

"And Mrs. Cannon was in the room?"

"Yes."

"And somebody lets themselves into the hotel room there in Smyrna?"

"Yes."

"And for a moment you thought it was Mr. Cannon. Is that right?"

"Yes."

"I think you told the officers you thought you might have to fight your way out of the room, or something like that?"

"Well, I didn't know what was going on, because I was asleep, and here is this other guy that walks in the room. And I had no idea who it was until Kelley told me who it was."

"And this was somebody that you knew as Paul. Is that right?"

"Only because Kelley talked about him. I never met him."

"Didn't you tell the officers that this Paul person, Paul Breeding, was obsessed with Mrs. Cannon?"

"I said that because that's what Kelley told me."

"And didn't you conclude that he assisted her in some way in this killing? Wasn't that what you told the officers?"

"No, I don't remember."

"You never told the officers that?"

Greene repeated that he didn't remember.

"You didn't tell them that you thought the other guy that you had bumped into in the hotel was involved in this?" Strianse wasn't about to give up.

"I might have said that I had said that to Kelley—that if there was anybody else involved, could it have been him?"

"And these discussions that you had with Mrs. Cannon, where you confronted her about her involvement in the death of her husband, you were drinking every time. Is that right?"

"No, not the . . . not every time. Not the second night that I was over there, when she had the money, I wasn't."

"Didn't you tell the officers that you thought Mrs. Cannon was too small and too physically weak to have done this?"

"I don't remember saying that."

"You didn't tell the officers that you don't think she could have done this?"

"No, I didn't."

"Weren't you telling them that because you thought this Paul person was involved?" Strianse asked, trying to implicate someone else for Jim Cannon's death.

"No, I mentioned Paul's name," Rick said. "The reason that Paul's name was brought up was because before Jim's death it seemed like Paul was in the picture constantly with Kelley. And after Jim's death he was gone. I even asked Kelley, why Paul wasn't around [then]. And she said that it was better for him not to be around now for a while."

"You ran into Paul not only that morning in the hotel room in Smyrna, but he returned another time to Smyrna. Is that right?"

"There was another morning that he called, and he was downstairs."

"Was he in the lobby demanding to see Kelley?"

"That's right."

"And it was at that point that you told the investigators that he was obsessed with her. Do you remember that?"

"Well, yeah, I told them that, but I didn't know. The only reason I said that was because that's what Kelley was telling me. I never met this guy. The investigator showed me a picture of him. And I couldn't swear that it was even him. I've never spoken to him or even been close enough to identify him."

"When this Paul person showed up the second time and was waiting in the lobby, did Mrs. Cannon ask you to leave?"

"She did."

"And you refused at that point?"

"Well, no, I did leave."

"You didn't tell the officers that you refused or the DA's investigator that you refused to leave?"

"Well, I asked Kelley why I had to leave. And she said, 'Because he's obsessed with me, and I don't want him to know you're here.' She went downstairs and talked to him, and after that, I left."

"Do you remember telling the investigators that there was one night you were visiting with Mrs. Cannon out at the hotel in Smyrna that she had received a call from her husband, Jim?"

Rick said that was at her apartment in Cool Springs.

"And that's where she received the call from Mr. Cannon?"

"Yes."

"Do you remember telling the investigators the call came in maybe eleven-thirty or so?"

"Yeah, I know it was late, eleven-thirty or twelve."

Rick said it was a long telephone call and Kelley was very upset. He said she was asking Jim why he was doing what he was doing.

"She said, 'You've taken my kids, you know. Why are you calling, telling me you love me and you want me back, but yet you're doing this to me?' And I sat there about fifteen minutes and I motioned to Kelley. And I said I was leaving. And that was the last time I had talked to her, until the Monday night after his death."

Strianse wanted the jury to see that this conversation was very much like the conversation Kelley told police she had had with Jim the night before his body was found.

"Now, you just gave this statement a week ago. Is that right?"

"Uh-huh."

"You don't remember telling [the police] that you thought they were reconciling and that's why you took your leave?"

"Yes, that's why I didn't call her, because I was hoping that they were getting things worked out. I know we were doing what we were doing, but this wasn't any kind of relationship that I knew was going anywhere, and I didn't want it to go anywhere," Greene told the jury. "And because of the kids and the way things were, I was hoping they were getting back together. That's why I didn't call her."

"And you told the investigators that she had never said anything about wanting to harm her husband?"

"No, she did not."

Finally Strianse asked Rick if he remembered

going to the Green Hills Grille with her in 2008 after she had been released on bond. Strianse said it was December 23. Greene said he did recall it, but he thought it was in the summer.

"And do you remember asking her questions about whether she had any involvement in the murder of her husband?"

"I do."

"And do you remember that she denied adamantly that she had any involvement in it?"

"I don't remember so much denial as her saying that there was something else going on with Jim that she didn't know about."

"Didn't you even tell her you were not wearing a wire that day?"

"I don't remember if I said that or not."

"Didn't she tell you that she couldn't admit to something that she didn't do?"

"Counselor, to be honest with you, that night we were both drinking quite a bit, and I don't remember a lot of what was said that night," Rick Greene said. "I can't testify or swear to anything I said that night."

Katrin Miller next called the medical examiner Thomas Deering to the stand. Deering took the jurors through his autopsy of Jim Cannon. During questioning by Miller the jurors learned that the decedent could have been strangled with the cord to a Motorola cell phone charger.

"And the person that was actually doing the strangulation . . . Would you expect the person doing the strangulation to receive any injuries to their hands as a result of this act?" Miller asked.

"I wouldn't expect it," he said. "They might, depending on how they were gripping the ligature, how they twisted it if they were twisting it. If they were wearing gloves on their hands or had some kind of padding, you wouldn't expect it. If they just held it a certain way and just pulled it—had it looped and pulled—they might not. I can't predict. I can't say that for sure they would have them. They might, and they might not."

During Peter Strianse's cross-examination of Thomas Deering, he asked Deering about the purple coloring in Jim's face.

"And I think you've described that as being a backed-up or congestion of blood. Is that right? And that is not positional, meaning gravity didn't cause the blood to be forced up in his head. It was by virtue of the strangulation. Is that right?"

"Well, particularly because I believe I've seen a picture of how the decedent was found, and he was [found] faceup. And it wasn't faceup with his head hanging down a step or anything. He was fairly level. So that would be probably from the blood stopped during the strangulation, yes."

"From the blood literally being forced into his head from the force of the strangulation?" Strianse asked, again trying to imply that Kelley Cannon just wasn't strong enough to do it.

"Well, 'not allowed to leave' would be a better way to put it. I mean, blood normally goes to the head,"

Deering explained to the jury. "It's not allowed to leave if you close off the veins."

Next the defense attorney peppered Deering with questions about the injuries to Jim's head. During that questioning the ME admitted that although there was some blunt-force trauma to Jim's head, there was no bleeding inside his head, nor were there any subdural injuries—injuries that would have been above the brain and below the tough membrane that holds it together.

Deering also told the jury that the injuries to Jim's head would not have rendered him unconscious.

And if Jim wasn't unconscious, the implication was that he could have fought off and overpowered a small person like Kelley.

Strianse then showed Deering the picture of Jim's face that had been entered as an exhibit and asked him to point out the finger and thumb marks. Deering said there were a number of them. He pointed out a thumb mark, which was larger than the finger. The thumb was sort of leaning against the other fingers, which were, for the most part, all grouped together.

"There's also one here," he said, indicating the finger mark which was shown on the photo. "So there are all these punctuate abrasions that are consistent with finger marks."

"I think you told me that it takes a real commitment to strangle somebody to death. Is that right?"

"Yes, it does."

Under cross-examination Dr. Deering told the jury that the marks on Jim's face could have been caused when Jim's murderer thought it might have been taking too long to strangle him and decided to speed the process along by trying to cover up his nose and mouth. And that could have accounted for the bruises between Jim's lip and his teeth.

The ME told the jury members that the damage to Jim's tongue most likely happened during a struggle with his murderer.

"And you've told us about the eyes—that they were really remarkable in terms of the tremendous amount of pressure that was in his head. Is that right?" Strianse asked.

"Yes."

"And that's the pressure from the blood being forced into the head?"

"Well, not able to leave," Deering said. "So it builds up."

"It builds up, and it breaks the capillaries in the eyes. Is that right?"

"Yes."

"Now, in your experience had you ever seen that much of the petechiae that had been hemorrhaged in eyes in a strangulation case?"

"I just don't remember. I may have, but I remember these ones as very remarkable—remarkable in terms of the force that would be required to get the whites of the eyes filled with blood," Deering said.

Strianse continued to hammer away at Dr. Deering, trying to get the jury to believe that it had taken too much strength to strangle Jim Cannon with a ligature—strength that Kelley Cannon did not possess.

"You put in your report that it could also be manual. And was that just to sort of cover the bases, since there were some scrapes on the side of the neck that perhaps could have been caused by fingernails?"

Deering said that rather than committing himself and saying Jim Cannon could only have been strangled with a ligature, he decided to say Jim could have been strangled manually as well, in case the witnesses told different stories.

Strianse then asked Deering to walk the jury through his dissection of Jim's neck, which he did.

"And what you saw when you did the neck dissection, is it fair to say that there was a large amount of force that was used to cause these injuries?"

"Yes."

"And did you find that whoever the assailant was, was someone that was trying to violently break everything that was in Mr. Cannon's neck?"

"I don't know if they were trying to break it, but they were certainly tightening the ligature tight enough to make sure that it worked."

"And did you tell me that you thought it would have been a considerably strong person that would have inflicted this kind of injury to him?" Strianse asked, continuing to make his point that Kelley just wasn't strong enough to do that.

The doctor, however, explained that it wouldn't necessarily have taken a strong person to strangle Jim with the ligature—just someone who exerted a fair amount of force. Deering told the jury a person could put a lot of force on a ligature just by twisting it and holding it tighter, or by wrapping it around more than once and holding it very tightly and forcefully.

"And depending on the individual, if they're struggling against it, then you can generate a lot of injuries based on the struggle of somebody who has been ligature wrapped," Dr. Deering said.

So although the doctor couldn't determine if the person who wrapped the ligature around Jim Cannon's neck was strong, he did know that the ligature was wrapped fairly tightly.

Under questioning from defense attorney Strianse, Dr. Deering told the jury that at autopsy Jim weighed 163 pounds and was five feet six inches.

"Assuming that he was conscious, and assuming that there was some sort of struggle, would someone Mr. Cannon's size have been able to push away a person that might have been five feet, five feet three, ninety to a hundred pounds?" Strianse asked.

At that point prosecutor Katrin Miller objected, saying that there was no way Deering could know what Jim was capable of doing.

The judge agreed and Strianse moved on, asking Deering about the massive hemorrhaging in Jim's neck.

"Had you ever seen anything so pronounced in all the other autopsies that you had done where there had been strangulations?" Strianse asked, once more implying that Kelley Cannon was not strong enough to have inflicted so much damage to her husband.

"Very rarely. . . . There were bruises everywhere. There was injury all over the neck, and this obviously was a strangulation."

"To cut off the blood or cut off the air may take only six or seven seconds, but to strangle somebody to death would take, what, two or three minutes at a minimum?" Kelley's attorney asked.

"Yes, yes."

Point scored for the defense.

Dr. Deering also told the jury that Jim's voice box had been crushed and compressed against his backbone—meaning that the ligature was tight around his neck—and either Jim was struggling against it or it was being held very forcefully.

Strianse's next line of questioning revolved around exactly how intoxicated Jim was the night he was murdered. The toxicology report indicated Jim's blood alcohol level was .15, twice the legal limit for operating a motor vehicle. But Strianse contended that a blood alcohol level of .15 might not be as significant if someone was a regular drinker or a chronic drinker—someone who drank every day.

"Now, if someone was a regular drinker or a chronic drinker and had developed a tolerance to alcohol, might they be able to function at a higher level at .15 than somebody who is not a regular drinker?"

"Yes."

"Where you and I might be very sloppy at .15, but if we were regular chronic drinkers, we might perform pretty well?"

"I would probably be asleep long before that, but yes," the doctor said.

On redirect Katrin Miller tried to counter some of the points that Peter Strianse had made.

"Dr. Deering, when you use the term 'amount of force' and 'held forcibly,' what do you mean?" she asked. "Are you talking about the strength of the murderer or the amount of pressure being applied to the ligature?"

"Well, it could be either. Certainly, a very, very strong individual can inflict a lot of damage on an individual," he told the jury. "But when you use a ligature, you can put a lot of force along a very narrow band. And without being an overly strong person, you can generate a lot of damage along that band. All you have to do is get it wrapped and hold it. And especially if an individual struggles against it, you could get a lot of injury related to that. So it could be either."

"And what if the ligature was twisted? I mean, wouldn't that kind of set it in place so that it's locked into position, more or less?"

"Yes, like a tourniquet. Just from the amount of injury that seems likely in this case."

"And you were talking about the choke hold and the fact that a person could lose consciousness very quickly. Once the ligature is around the neck and the person has lost consciousness, how difficult—as far as amount of pressure or force—is it to complete the act until death?" she asked.

"All you have to do is just hold it. I mean, you just have to hold the ligature for a couple of minutes and that person will die."

Peter Strianse wasn't quite finished with the witness either.

"Given the injuries that you have seen in this case, which you've characterized as 'remarkable' in your experience, isn't it more likely that the person had to be a powerful, strong person to inflict this kind of damage?" he asked.

"Well, it's not any more likely. I mean, that would be one possibility. The other is that they just got the ligature on and got it tight and held it. And it wouldn't necessarily require a very powerful person to do that."

CHAPTER 22

Special Agent Linda Littlejohn, a forensic scientist at the Tennessee Bureau of Investigation crime lab, testified next. Littlejohn told the jury that Detective Brad Putnam brought her evidence connected to Jim Cannon's murder, including two latex gloves from Jim's backyard, a box of latex gloves from Kelley Cannon's apartment, a box of latex gloves from the crime scene, a latex glove found in the closet near Jim's body, the tip of a latex glove from the bedroom and a piece from a latex glove box found in Kelley Cannon's car.

Littlejohn said she was asked to compare the gloves to determine if there were any differences. She told the court that the box of size-large gloves taken from Jim's house were made by American Red Cross. The gloves taken from the defendant's, however, were from Walgreens and they were "one size fits all."

The agent said Putnam asked her to determine whether the gloves found at Jim's house were from the Walgreens box or the American Red Cross box.

After measuring all the gloves in both boxes, as well as the three gloves found at the crime, Littlejohn determined that the three loose gloves found at Jim's looked like the Walgreens gloves taken from Kelley's apartment and they were also the same size. She also ran a chemical test on the gloves from both boxes, but she couldn't tell any difference between the two.

"So is it your expert opinion that the gloves recovered—the loose gloves, the one in the closet and the two in the backyard—are consistent in size with the box of gloves from Walgreens recovered from the Elmington location?" Miller asked.

"Yes, they are."

Littlejohn told the members of the jury that she also compared a piece of the box of Walgreens gloves that police had found in Kelley Cannon's car to the box of Walgreens gloves taken from Kelley's apartment.

"I was able to match that across the tear line and say that those two pieces at one time had been joined," she said.

During his cross-examination Peter Strianse asked Special Agent Littlejohn if she thought the gloves in each box looked a little similar, even though the American Red Cross gloves were marked "size large" and the Walgreens gloves were "one size fits all." She admitted they did. Strianse was trying to plant the idea in the minds of the jurors that the loose gloves found at the crime scene in the closet and the backyard could have come from the box of American Red Cross gloves also found in Jim's house.

"So if you were to take the box of the American Red Cross gloves and take them out, all the gloves in that box sort of resemble each other. Is that right?"

"Yes, they do."

"And then if you did the same thing with the Walgreens box, if you took them all out, they would randomly resemble each other?"

"Yes, they do."

"And then if you sort of put them all in a pile, sort of both boxes would randomly resemble each other?"

"That's correct."

Littlejohn also acknowledged that her chemical analysis of the gloves in each box indicated that they were made of the same materials.

The TBI special agent told the jurors that she measured the glove taken from the backyard of Jim's house and the glove found in the closet near his body. She said she measured each glove from the wrist to the tip of the middle finger, but she didn't measure the width of the fingers of either glove.

In response to Strianse's questions, the forensic scientist said the length of each glove was slightly different. However, she said the measurements across the hand and the wrist were exactly the same.

"Right down to the centimeter?" Strianse asked.

"Well, let me say they weren't any more than one-sixteenth of a difference."

"So there was some difference?"

"Possibly, but not enough for me to document."

"Did you take into consideration that the gloves could have been stretched in any way if they had been worn?"

"Which gloves in particular?" Littlejohn asked.

"Well, the gloves that you were measuring? The gloves from outside, the two from the backyard and the closet."

Littlejohn told the jurors that she didn't think the gloves had ever been worn. She said that the American Red Cross gloves were larger than the loose gloves she found at the crime scene. She also didn't understand Strianse's question; because whether or not the loose gloves had been worn, they were still smaller than the gloves in the American Red Cross box.

The special agent also testified that the loose gloves, as well as the boxed gloves from Walgreens and the American Red Cross, appeared to be the same color. But she again stressed that the loose gloves and the American Red Cross gloves were not the same size.

"And the measurements you did were with a ruler. Is that right?"

"That's correct."

The prosecution's next witness was Jennifer Shipman, a special agent and forensic scientist with the Tennessee Bureau of Investigation. Shipman told the jury that Detective Brad Putnam brought her some evidence relating to Jim Cannon's murder and asked her to test it for the presence of blood, as well as DNA.

"And what test were you asked to perform on this evidence?" Katrin Miller asked.

"I was asked to detect blood. I was asked to detect vaginal secretions from—potential vaginal secretions from an unknown female. And I was also asked to test for epithelial DNA."

Shipman also said she took a blood sample from Jim Cannon, extracted the DNA and ran it through a machine that read its profile so she could use that known DNA profile to compare to some of the evidence that was submitted. Shipman also tested oral swabs from Kelley Cannon in order to develop her DNA profile.

The special agent told the jurors she tested a swabbing from a wineglass, but she wasn't able to get any usable DNA from it. She also tested some bloodstains; and while she was able to get a DNA profile from those stains, she wasn't able to match the DNA profile to Kelley, the maid or the housekeeper.

"That profile came from an unknown female," Shipman told the jurors.

The witness said she also tested what appeared to be dried red bloodstain flakes that police recovered from the floor in the room where Jim's body was discovered. However, she determined the flakes were not dried blood.

Shipman told the jury one of the items she tested was a pair of jeans.

"And did you run some tests on that pair of jeans?" Miller asked.

"Yes, I did."

"And did you locate any blood on the jeans?"

"Yes, I did."

"And where was the blood located on the jeans?"

"There was a small stain on the left thigh."

"On the front or the back?"

"On the front."

"And were you able to obtain DNA profiles from that small stain of blood?"

"Yes, I did. I actually got a mixture that is consistent with James Cannon and Kelley Cannon."

"Are you able to say if it's James Cannon's blood or Kelley Cannon's blood?"

"That I'm not able to say. They were mixed together."

"Would your results be consistent if James Cannon's blood was initially on the jeans and then Kelley Cannon urinated on the jeans?" Miller asked. "Would that give you that mixed profile?"

"That would be a scenario that could result in that, yes."

The forensic agent said she also tested the two latex gloves found in Jim's backyard. Although she detected a small amount of human DNA on one of the gloves, there wasn't enough to determine from whom it came. She also tested what appeared to be dried blood flakes taken from the floor of the master bedroom, which turned out not to be blood, after all. Shipman told the members of the jury that she tested a pair of women's shoes that tested positive for blood.

The agent testified that tests on the inside tip of the latex glove found just outside the closet where Jim's body was located did not indicate the presence of blood. However, she recovered DNA—DNA that came from Kelley Cannon from the inside of the tip of the glove. When she tested the outside of the tip of the glove, it had Jim's DNA on it, as well as the DNA of another person.

"So it was possibly her DNA, but you just didn't have enough locations to make a definite match. Is that correct?" Miller asked.

"Exactly."

Shipman also told the jurors that Jim Cannon's blood and DNA were on the Motorola cell phone charger found in the boys' bedroom.

During his cross-examination of the witness, Peter Strianse first asked Jennifer Shipman about the testing she did on the wineglass. The forensic scientist told the jury that she had tested a swab taken from the wineglass, but she never tested the glass itself. In fact, she admitted, she did not even take the swab herself.

"And was there enough DNA to test on the wineglass in terms of what you found on the swab?" Strianse asked.

"I tried to get a profile. But, no, there was not enough DNA."

"And was it degraded? Is that why you were unable to get any sort of a partial profile?" Strianse's point was that there could have been DNA from another person on that wineglass—the person who murdered Jim.

"The testing that I do doesn't tell me necessarily whether there is insufficient DNA or whether the DNA is degraded. It could be either one."

The jury again heard that there were bloodstains at the crime scene that didn't belong to Kelley or to any of the other women who were in the house.

Still under cross-examination Shipman said the police on the scene designated certain evidence they collected as bloodstains, and it was her job to test the evidence and determine if it was blood.

The witness also told the jury that she did not find any blood or foreign DNA when she examined Jim's fingernail clippings.

The TBI agent then talked about the testing she did on the tip of the glove found outside the closet near Jim's body.

"You told us that the outside had blood on it. Is that right?"

"So you're calling it 'the outside' because that's the state it was in when you got it. Is that right?" Strianse asked.

"Correct."

"And you said that there was blood on the outside, what we're calling the outside, and that was a conclusion that you reached based on a presumptive test. Is that right?"

"That's correct," Shipman said.

"You don't do a further confirming test to determine that it's blood, do you?"

"Not unless it's specifically requested, no."

"Because you don't want to use up the sample. Is that right?"

"Right."

"Now you indicated that the major contributor was James Cannon. Is that correct?"

"On the outside of the glove, yes."

"And I think if I understand your report, you're saying that there's a combination of two sources on what we're calling the outside of the glove. Is that right?"

"That's correct."

"And then the minor [contributor] you said that Kelley cannot be excluded as a contributor. Is that what you have indicated?"

"That's correct."

Strianse then got the agent to admit that out of thirteen genes in a human profile, there were only two that could have come from Kelley.

"Now, isn't it fair to say that the minor contributor based on what you found in your analysis could really be anybody?" Strianse asked.

"It is not conclusive, which is why I worded my profile the way I did. I'm not saying that it is her, [and] I'm not saying it isn't her. I'm just saying that I could not exclude her based on what I had."

"And statistically—and I don't want to just throw out a number, but I'm going to ask you—couldn't it be as many as a million or more people that could not be excluded as being a minor contributor based on what you found?"

"Yes, that would be consistent with a large number of people."

Strianse then asked Shipman about the tip of the glove again.

"If I understand, you found what you believe to be her skin cells on what we're calling the inside of the glove," he said.

"I did recover DNA from the inside of the glove, yes."

"And, again, we don't know. One man's inside could be another man's outside, as far as the glove?"

Strianse continued, "Now, based on the work that you did, you are unable to tell the jury when that genetic material or skin cells may have been deposited in what we're calling the inside of the tip of that glove?"

Shipman said Strianse was correct, adding that DNA testing can't determine the age of a sample.

"And you certainly don't know how it made its way into what we're calling the inside of that tip?"

"Yeah. I wasn't there."

Strianse next asked Shipman if she had been able to figure out to whom the blood and skin cells on Kelley's jeans belonged.

"It was a mixture of DNA, and I did find blood in that particular location. Which DNA came from blood versus skin cells versus urine versus any other type of fluid—no, I couldn't tell you the specifics," the agent told the jury.

"So you've not excluded that it could be semen as one of the fluids?"

"I don't believe I tested for semen on this. No, I did not test for semen on it."

"And this is another stain, if you will, or quantity of DNA that needed to be amplified before you could do your testing?"

"Yes, all DNA is amplified before it's tested."

The defense then asked Shipman to describe DNA transfer for the jury. He wanted the jury to believe that Jim Cannon's DNA found on Kelley's jeans was the result of DNA transfer.

"[That's] basically that whenever two objects, two people, come into contact, there will be a transfer of some sort between one to the other," she said.

"And describe for the jury the differences between a direct transfer of evidence and an indirect transfer of evidence."

"I think what you're asking about would be two

items coming in contact with each other would be a direct transfer. And then perhaps I touch your shirt and then come over here and touch your shirt, and I could transfer from you to you. That would be an indirect," she told the jury.

"So would a direct be if my finger was bleeding right now and blood from my hand hit the carpet? Would that be a direct transfer?"

"Yes, it would."

"And would an indirect transfer be if the blood that just landed on the carpet was stepped on by someone and they walked out of this courtroom and carried the blood into the hallway or another courtroom?"

"Correct."

"That would be an indirect transfer. Is that why it's important that the crime scene be processed in a very careful manner? Because part of the [transfer principle] is that whenever a person comes into a scene, they bring things into the scene. Is that right?"

"That would be a correct assumption based on—" Shipman was not able to finish her sentence before being interrupted by Strianse, who wanted the jury to believe that the crime scene had been contaminated.

"And whenever they leave the scene, they inadvertently or unwittingly take things out of the scene. Is that right?" the defense attorney questioned.

"Correct."

"I neglected to ask you before. In all of the samples that you tested, did you have to retest any of them?"

"I don't believe so, no."

With that, the state rested its case against Kelley Cannon.

Peter Strianse then asked the judge if the attorneys could approach the bench.

"Judge, did you want me to motion for judgment of acquittal?" Strianse asked.

"That's up to you."

The judge then asked the members of the jury to step out of the courtroom for several minutes while Strianse tried to convince her to acquit his client based on lack of evidence.

Ultimately, the judge denied the defense attorney's motion and asked him if he was ready to call his first witness. Strianse said he was ready, but he asked the judge if she wanted to question Kelley about her decision not to testify while the jury was not in the courtroom.

"Okay, let's go ahead and do that."

Judge Cheryl Blackburn instructed Kelley Cannon to raise her right hand to be sworn in.

"Mrs. Cannon, I want to make sure that you understand, first of all, that you have a constitutional right to testify. That is your choice. You can take advice from your attorney, but you ultimately have to make that decision. So have you discussed with Mr. Strianse the advantages and the disadvantages of testifying?" the judge asked.

"I have."

"Okay. And then after your discussion with him,

did you make a decision about whether or not you wanted to testify?"

"Yes, ma'am."

"And that decision was that you do not want to testify. Is that correct?"

"Correct."

"Okay. And is that your decision?"

"Yes, ma'am."

"Well, we're going to make that part of the record. But I will say this, Mrs. Cannon, if you change your mind between the time he closes your proof, let us know. You can still change your mind. But right now, it is not to testify, correct?"

"At this time."

"Okay. Well, if you change it, make sure you tell him or you tell me."

CHAPTER 23

The first witness Peter Strianse called was Detective Freddie Stromatt, a sergeant who had been with the Metropolitan Nashville Police Department for thirty years.

The day Jim Cannon's body was found, Stromatt was working in the investigative unit of the West Precinct. He was called in to assist with the investigation into Jim's murder. He arrived at the Cannon house around nine or ten in the morning and left about ten or eleven that night.

"I want to direct your attention to the evening hours. Were there arrangements made for Mrs. Cannon to pick up a vehicle at [the Bowling address]?"

"Yes, sir, there was."

"And were you part of those discussions or those arrangements to provide her with a vehicle?"

"Yes, sir, I was."

Stromatt told the jury that James Dean Baker showed up at about quarter after nine to pick up the car for Kelley Cannon. When he checked Baker's driver's license, he learned that Baker had a criminal record for drugs and theft. But he wasn't sure that he had given that information to Brad Putnam.

"Was it you or Mr. Putnam that decided to submit the known fingerprints of James Dean Baker for comparison against some latents that were found at Bowling?" Strianse asked, trying to throw suspicion for Jim Cannon's murder onto Baker.

"That would have been Detective Putnam."

"And you are aware that that was done?"

"Yes, sir."

"That's all."

During her cross-examination for the state, Sharon Reddick asked Sergeant Stromatt if James Dean Baker was automatically considered a suspect in Jim Cannon's death because he was helping Kelley. Stromatt said Baker wasn't considered a suspect when he first arrived. He said Baker was there to help Kelley Cannon get the car.

On redirect Stromatt told the members of the jury about when Baker first got to the Cannon house. Stromatt had asked him if he knew anything about what had happened the previous evening. Baker said he had no idea what had happened.

"Obviously, you were not just going to take his word for it that he didn't have any involvement. Is that right?"

"That's correct. Yes, sir."

"Because you noted that he had an arrest record and made sure that his prints were going to be submitted for comparison. Is that right?"

"Correct."

Sergeant Stromatt told the court that neither he nor any other police officer interviewed Baker in a more formal setting.

"You simply asked for his driver's license to make sure he had one before he drove off in the vehicle. Is that a fair statement?"

"Correct."

Kelley Cannon's attorney next called her friend Pamela "Pam" Brady, who told the jury how she had met Kelley. Pam also said that Kelley had called her on May 21, 2008—the night Kelley had been arrested.

"I made some phone calls for her. And then she was, I believe, at the [Loews Vanderbilt Hotel Nashville] when I came up to visit her for the first time after that," she said, adding that she spent a couple days with Kelley at the hotel.

Pam said Kelley was visibly shaken, and she had night sweats. In fact, she seemed to have pneumonia, which she had been known to have periodically. She was just very nervous and had lost a lot of weight since the last time Pam had seen her. Kelley just looked pale and sick.

"And in terms of her weight, do you have a guess as to what her weight might have been?" Peter Strianse asked, insinuating that Kelley was not strong enough to have murdered her husband.

"I've never seen her that small, so I would say somewhere in the range of ninety pounds, something like that."

"And she seemed physically ill to you?"

"She did. It was difficult for her to communicate.

She was, like I said, visibly shaken, nervous, not communicating very well at all."

"And you spent a couple of days with her at the hotel. Is that right?"

"Yes, sir."

"During the course of that two days, were you present in her room when she received a phone call from James Cannon?"

"Yes, sir, I was."

"What was her reaction when she got that phone call?"

Pam told the jury that Kelley didn't really want to answer the phone because she was afraid that she might be breaching some order of protection or whatever the charges were at the time.

"And she was afraid to answer the phone, but she said, 'He's called so many times, I'm going to see what he wants.' I remember listening to the conversation, [and] she said, 'No, do not come and get me. No, do not come and get me.' I assumed he was saying he would come and get her in the morning. And she was saying, 'Don't come and get me.' And then she was crying, and she said, 'Jim, why are you doing this? Why are you putting me through this? Why are you doing this?' And he just kept repeating, 'Well, I'll just come get you in the morning, and everything will work out.'"

"Now, the next month, June of 2008, did Mrs. Cannon come visit you in Huntsville?" Strianse asked.

Pam testified that Kelley spent the Father's Day weekend at her house in Huntsville, arriving on Saturday, June 14, and leaving on Monday, June 16. When Kelley arrived, Pam said, she looked dazed and confused. Kelley even said she hoped she had the right house.

"She was worse than when I had seen her in May, physically. She was nervous. She couldn't sleep. She had night sweats. The bed was just wet and the pillows were wet."

Pam said Kelley had her personal belongings with her when she showed up at her house. Kelley had a number of bags because she had been staying at various places during her separation from Jim.

"And she was just very scattered," Pam told the members of the jury. "It was really very pitiful, because she had all of her things together and had been carrying these things from place to place for quite some time."

Pam said she offered to clean some of Kelley's things, including her favorite two pillows. The pillowcases had mildew on them because they were continually wet because of Kelley's night sweats. Pam said she cleaned them, but she couldn't get the mildew out.

"The pillows were mildewed as well, but she didn't want to give up those pillows," Pam told the jury members. "It was almost like that was her security blanket. So I just cleaned the pillowcases and put those pillowcases back on the soiled pillows."

"What did you observe about her emotional state that weekend?" Strianse asked.

"She was very disjointed, out of sorts, worried. She was just worried out of her mind. She was concerned about getting an attorney, a civil attorney."

"And did she have a persistent cough?"

"She did."

Pam said Kelley was treating her cough with Delsym

cough syrup—a lot of cough syrup. And she was also using an inhaler because of her asthma.

"Over that weekend did she express any animosity to Mr. Cannon?"

"No, she never expressed any animosity toward Jim in the entire time that I knew her."

"And did you have the occasion over the years to see her interact with her children?"

"Only with Tim. She was a loving mother. He loved her very much. He was a sweet baby. I saw him when he was about three years old. That was the last time I saw him," Pam said.

"When did you first get to meet Jim Cannon?"

Pam said the first time she met Jim in person was a few weeks before he and Kelley got married. She had talked to him over the phone when the couple called to say they were engaged. Between that time and the day he died in 2008, Pam had only seen Jim a few times when she was visiting Kelley.

"In the handful of times that you interacted with Mr. Cannon, what did you observe about his drinking or alcohol habits?"

"He always had a drink in his hand. And I'm not a big drinker. It appeared to be bourbon. I couldn't tell you what brand or anything. But he never appeared inebriated at any time."

During cross-examination by prosecutor Katrin Miller, Pam Brady told the jury that she hadn't seen Jim for about six years. The implication was that maybe he had stopped drinking.

"You are aware that your friend Mrs. Cannon had a severe drug addiction?"

Pam said she didn't know that Kelley was addicted to drugs. However, she was aware that Kelley had fallen down some steps while she was living at the house on Bowling and had a problem with painkillers as a result of that accident.

She also said she didn't know any of the details pertaining to the requirement that Kelley Cannon receive outpatient treatment at Cumberland Heights as a condition of her divorce process.

"So if you saw her the weekend of Father's Day in June, and she was nervous and having night sweats, that could be as a result of her drug addiction, correct?" Miller asked.

"I can't answer that question. I'm not medically qualified to answer that question."

Miller asked Pam about the phone call from Jim Cannon that Kelley received when the two were at the Loews Vanderbilt Hotel Nashville.

"Is it possible he was trying to get her to go back into drug rehabilitation?"

"He didn't mention that in the phone conversation," Pam said.

After a couple more questions Pam Brady was dismissed.

The next witness to take the stand for the defense was Dr. Amanda Sparks-Bushnell, the medical director of the Sparks Clinic and a physician. Sparks-Bushnell had treated Kelley Cannon weekly for depression and anxiety from April 2008 until June of that year. The doctor also told the court Kelley had a panic disorder, as well as some sort of post-traumatic stress disorder.

Trying to reinforce in the minds of the jurors that Kelley wasn't strong enough to kill Jim, Peter Strianse asked Sparks-Bushnell about Kelley's appearance during the months she had been treating her.

The doctor told the jury that during that time Kelley weighed about twenty or thirty pounds less than she did at that moment. In fact, Sparks-Bushnell described Kelley as being so thin that she looked emaciated.

"As I may have mentioned before, during some of the times with Mrs. Cannon, she would have a sleeveless ensemble on, perhaps like a sleeveless shirt with a sweater or jacket as the case may be," the doctor said. "And I remember noting she had— There's not a delicate way to say this, but in our home we call them 'grammy muscles,' where there's extra skin on the back of the arm. Something you would expect to see if someone has had a fairly quick weight loss."

Sparks-Bushnell said that's exactly what had happened to Kelley. She had been ill and had lost a lot of weight fairly quickly. "The skin was loose, particularly, I noted, on the back of the triceps. The other thing I noticed is there was no definition between the biceps muscle, the triceps muscle," she added. "She had thin, thin arms, thin upper body, thin everywhere. Her clothes hung a bit loosely. And, again, she had lost a fair bit of weight. Based on that, I would think her upper-body strength would be even less than one would expect for a woman of her size at that time."

The doctor told the jurors that Kelley often had trouble keeping her appointments, in part because she really didn't have a place to call home. She was bouncing around from Jim's house to a number of hotels and extended-stay apartments. She also explained that she had been treating Kelley with a psychostimulant, Adderall XR and then regular Adderall—medications used to treat attention deficit disorder (ADD), which Kelley had. A side effect of those medications was loss of appetite—something Kelley had already been struggling with. Dr. Sparks-Bushnell told Kelley she might have to take her off the amphetamine (in the Adderall XR) if she didn't get her weight up.

Kelley was also taking Zoloft, an antidepressant with antianxiety effect, used to treat PTSD, as well as clonazepam, an antianxiety medication that can also help with sleep, and Provigil for her ADD. Later on, even high doses of Zoloft weren't working for Kelley. Her anxiety went beyond what the Zoloft could handle, so the doctor prescribed Pristiq, which was in a different class of medication, to treat the PTSD.

Despite her myriad psychological problems, Kelley was not psychotic, even though at one point she had been taking Seroquel, an antipsychotic medication for people with schizophrenia. However, the doctor said, the FDA had also approved Seroquel for people who had bipolar disorder. Although it was sometimes prescribed as a sleeping medication, it had never been approved as such.

During her cross-examination of the physician, Sharon Reddick asked Dr. Sparks-Bushnell when Kelley Cannon had looked as emaciated as the medical director had described to the jury. According to the doctor's testimony, Kelley had looked that way since the first time she had seen her, but she could not recall the exact dates. However, she told the jury, that before Jim's death and right up until the time Kelley was initially arrested for Jim Cannon's murder, Kelley was quite gaunt and emaciated. Then after she had been incarcerated, she put on a fair bit of weight and looked healthier. She didn't look so fragile.

The assistant district attorney general tried to get the doctor to admit that before Jim's death Kelley was drinking, as well as mixing her pain meds and her psychotropic meds with alcohol. The doctor said she was not aware of that.

"Now, you testified to prescribing six different types of medications?"

"Let's see. Zoloft, Adderall XR and Adderall, Provigil—and I'm trying to think what was the other one. Pristiq would have been a separate one to the Zoloft. It would have been in place of Zoloft. So I would think six total, five ran concurrent."

"And those medications include—and I know this is just sort of a lay term and you'll probably want to explain it further—sort of uppers and downers, correct?"

"I'm sorry, no, that would be too broad and too general to be accurate," Sparks-Bushnell said. "Lots of different types of medications do different things."

"And if those were being mixed with alcohol and/or pain medications, that could cause a lot of the behaviors that you described earlier?"

"Potentially, if that were the case," the doctor told the jury.

ADAG Reddick then asked the doctor if she had ever testified for another defendant diagnosed with PTSD who had behaved violently. "In fact, very recently, downstairs you were testifying under a circumstance where a person, one of your patients, did something very violent to a partner, correct?"

"There was a combat veteran who had been diagnosed with post-traumatic stress disorder while in the military in service in Iraq and, yes, during a flashback he had become violent," Sparks-Bushnell said.

"It's a regular part of your practice to do that. Is that a fair statement? To testify on behalf of criminal defendants?"

"Not accurate. It's a regular part of my practice to testify in court, when called to do so. [But] I have been on both the prosecution's side, the defense side. So, I'm sorry, that statement isn't accurate."

Reddick then asked if the doctor was a personal friend of Kelley's or her mother's. The doctor told the jury she was not.

"Would it be unusual in your practice to go to the home of one of your patient's family or go to where they're living?" Reddick asked.

"Not necessarily, no. That would not be unusual. No. If one were doing preparation for a case, if one were doing other matters—I have even been known to make house calls," she told the jury. "Don't let the word get around, please. I don't want a big demand for that. But if I have postpartum clients, in particular, who are confined and unable to come, I have been known to go to the hospital to see them or to their home to see them. It's not regular, but it is not unusual."

"So you don't deny that you went to the home

of Diane Sanders and spoke with her and Mrs. Cannon on the telephone from Diane Sanders's home?"

"Oh, no. Of course not."

With that, Dr. Amanda Sparks-Bushnell was dismissed from the witness chair.

CHAPTER 24

Peter Strianse next called Dr. Jonathan Arden, a forensic pathologist. Strianse had contacted Arden, who was being paid for his testimony, to review the materials concerning Jim Cannon's autopsy and to offer advice to the defense as to the cause of Jim's death, the nature of his injuries and how he thought those injuries occurred.

Strianse asked Arden to give the jury some idea of what information he reviewed to reach his conclusions in this case.

Arden told the jury he studied various documents from the medical examiner, including something called the "report of investigation" by a medical examiner, the autopsy report itself, the diagrams that were a part of or attached to the autopsy report and the toxicology report. He also had some digital photos of Jim Cannon's autopsy and pictures of Jim's body in the closet, as well as some police investigation documents that were attached to the indictment.

The forensic pathologist said in his opinion Jim

was strangled to death with some type of ligature—some long, thin, constricting object—that was wrapped around his neck and pulled tightly.

In Jim's autopsy report and photographs, there were linear marks on various parts of his neck, including each side and the back. The marks were made by someone wrapping the ligature around Jim's neck so it was pressing into his skin, Arden explained.

"And there are several different marks on each area of each side," he told the jury. "So that shows that the ligature either had to be wrapped multiple times, or it moved at some point during the course of causing the strangulation."

Arden also told the jury members that Jim had a lot of internal hemorrhaging and bleeding in the structures of and around the throat—more than what was typical or average for a ligature strangulation.

"And the implication of that is that this indicates that the ligature that was constricting his neck and causing the strangulation was applied with a great deal—a substantial amount of force," Arden told the jury members. "And that force was held in place long enough not only to kill him by strangulation but to have compressed the muscles lying on top of the voice box. Actually, there were areas of bleeding toward the back of the voice box itself. So, in summary, that indicates a substantial amount of force being held there for some extended period of time in order to cause this ligature strangulation."

The pathologist also testified that there was bleeding in some areas of the voice box, or the larynx. He told the jury that the larynx was made up of several different components—a small bone shaped like a horseshoe, which was the hyoid bone, as well as two larger plates of cartilage that came together in the front, which is where you can feel a man's Adam's apple. And then there was the cricoid, the horseshoe-shaped cartilage below that. And each of those was connected with various soft tissues, including muscles and some ligaments.

Arden explained for the jury that there was some bleeding on the right top of the hyoid bone, which was a bit loose. He said there was a question about whether the hyoid bond had been broken, but there was no definitive conclusion. Then down lower in the voice box, there was also hemorrhaging in the ligaments connecting the other cartilages.

"And, again, those structures relative to the throat are deep in the throat," he said. "There's even some hemorrhage along the back of the voice box. So the deeper structures of the throat were affected, not just the superficial tissues that are on the top or near the surface."

What that meant was that someone had exerted a substantial amount of force to cause those types of injuries.

"And what do those findings tell you about the amount of force that would have been needed to accomplish that type of injury?"

"I can't [quantify] this for you in exactly how many pounds it would require," the witness stated. "But I can tell you that from having seen examples, in over more than twenty-five years, one can be strangled and not have this much hemorrhage and not have hemorrhage that goes this deep into the structures of the throat. So that this is an indicator of greater amount of force—even within the spectrum of how much force it takes to strangle a person—this is on the upper end rather than the lower end. So it's a large amount of force. It's substantial force. It's a very tight compression that has to be held there. Again, this is not something that would likely happen in the course of a few seconds, for instance."

Arden told the jury it would take about one minute for someone to cause those injuries—if that person managed to constrict the neck very firmly and tightly with a ligature and maintained that pressure the entire time. Although he said it might take a little longer—as long as three or four minutes—depending on how well the person maintained the pressure and whether the victim struggled or moved, which could have loosened the ligature.

"Do you have an opinion as to how much strength it takes to cause the kinds of injuries that you saw?" Strianse asked.

The paid expert witness told the jury it would take a strong person to be able to pull the ligature very tightly and hold it with a large amount of force. So, he surmised, it had to have been someone with substantial strength.

The doctor said that he also saw some scrapes and abrasions—superficial injuries—on Jim's face, which most likely meant he had been in some kind of fight.

"How about the injuries that were caused by the

wrap around the neck? Was there some movement in what you saw as far as those injuries?"

The doctor testified that there were several linear marks on each side of Jim's neck that indicated the ligature had been moved while it was wrapped around Jim's neck. And that meant that Jim was moving against the ligature.

The witness also told the jury that there was bleeding just outside the surface of Jim's skull bone, also called "scalp hemorrhage," indicating that there was some impact to his head. But he did not have any internal head injury or bleeding.

None of the head injuries, however, was enough to make Jim lose consciousness.

During his testimony Dr. Arden told the jury that there were also hemorrhages or areas of bleeding on the surface of the whites of his eyes. Some of those were pinpoint hemorrhages, or petechial hemorrhages. Some of them, especially in Jim's right eye, had blended together and covered the whole area, which meant for about three or four minutes someone had been strangling him very forcefully.

The autopsy and toxicology reports indicated that Jim's blood alcohol level was .15, which was pretty high. In fact, it was about double the limit that would get someone arrested for driving under the influence in most states. If Jim had been an inexperienced drinker, he would most likely have been severely intoxicated. But if he had been a chronic drinker, he probably wouldn't have appeared to be very drunk.

"He's able to stand here and have a conversation

with you and act pretty normal," Arden said. "On the other hand, if you take him and you check the eye movements, he's not going to pass that test. If you test his reflexes or his reaction times, you could scientifically demonstrate that he's not normal."

Arden also explained that strangling someone with a ligature was a very interpersonal act, requiring one person to be physically in contact with the other person. Unlike using a gun to shoot someone from twenty-five feet away, which did not require any physical contact.

"So it's an immediate person-to-person kind of event. And it, of course, provides them the opportunity for the victim to struggle and fight back, and sometimes you see injuries that are related to that part of the process," Arden said, playing into the defense attorney's contention that Kelley Cannon didn't have any visible injuries when police questioned her after Jim's death.

The first order of business for prosecutor Katrin Miller during her cross-examination of Dr. Arden was to remind the jury that Jonathan Arden was a hired gun for the defense who was being paid $400 per hour as a consultant and $4,000 a day if he had to appear at an out-of-state trial. To date, Arden said, he'd been paid $1,300.

Under cross-examination Arden admitted he had never interviewed Kelley Cannon. He admitted he was not saying that it was physically impossible for Kelley to have strangled her husband, because he didn't know.

In response to ADAG Miller's questions, Arden said that while he was aware that Kelley had worked for a medical examiner's office in Nashville, he had no idea she had assisted with autopsies. Miller's point was that if Kelley had helped out on an autopsy of a person who had been strangled, then she'd probably know more about strangulation than the average person.

Miller then asked Arden if the amount of force it took to strangle Jim Cannon and the amount of strength it took were the same thing. The witness said while they were related, they were not identical.

"And when we're talking about force, we're really talking about the length of time that the ligature is actually applied [with] pressure toward the neck. Would that be correct?" Miller asked.

Arden said that wasn't correct. Rather, he said, force referred to how much pressure was being used to strangle someone, not the length of time. "But when I use the word 'force,' I mean how strongly was the ligature compressing the neck as opposed to a lighter degree of pressure," he testified. He admitted, however, that he was unable to determine exactly how many pounds of pressure were used. But he knew it was a lot because of all the damage to Jim Cannon's neck, as well as the muscles and the tissue inside his neck.

The doctor also told the jury that it was quite possible that Jim lost consciousness within ten seconds. And that meant that whoever was holding the ligature just had to keep the pressure on it to kill him. It didn't require any superhuman strength to hold the ligature in place, once someone had passed out. Arden told the jury it wouldn't take Hulk Hogan to maintain the amount of pressure needed to finish off Jim. Once Jim had stopped struggling, his murderer wouldn't have had to apply a huge amount of pressure at all.

With that, the defense rested.

Next the prosecution called James Dean Baker to the stand as a rebuttal witness. He again told the jury that he met Kelley Cannon when they were in rehab at Cumberland Heights, but he didn't know her all that well. He testified that on the day Jim's body was found, Kelley called him and asked if he could go to Jim's house and pick up a car for her, since the police had confiscated hers. After James got the car, he and Kelley went to get a bite to eat at a local restaurant. During his testimony James said that he spoke with Kelley on the telephone later that night and she told him that the police were wrong and she was not the woman on the Walgreens video.

When Peter Strianse questioned James Dean Baker, he tried to imply that James was a lot closer to Kelley than he admitted. He also reminded Baker that Jim Cannon was his wife's attorney when the two were going through their divorce in 1997. James, however, said he didn't know that until that very morning when his brother mentioned it to him.

Baker reiterated that he had no idea Jim Cannon was representing his wife, even though Jim had requested a restraining order and then an order of protection against him on behalf of his wife.

"Mr. Cannon put in the divorce complaint that he filed for your wife that he was afraid that once you were served, you would get violent. Is that right?" Strianse asked.

"I have no idea about that."

"Well, would looking at the divorce complaint help refresh your recollection about that?"

"Whatever it says is what it says."

"So you're not disputing that if Mr. Cannon wrote that in there, it's in there?"

"I didn't read it real good," James said. "He did me a favor getting me out of that marriage."

"You remember the order of protection because the Metro Police came out to your wife's house. Is that right?" Strianse asked.

"Yes, sir."

"You were there to try to take a car away from your wife. Is that right?"

"It was my car, too."

"And you got behind the wheel with a hacksaw and wanted to saw the club that was holding the wheel. And then the police came out and had to arrest you. Is that right?"

"No, sir."

"You don't remember that?"

"They didn't arrest me."

"Do you remember threatening your wife and telling her you would get her?"

"I didn't tell her that."

The defense attorney then brought up James Dean Baker's criminal record again—he had been fired from the fire department for attempted burglary, as well as using drugs—trying to create reasonable doubt in the jurors' minds as to who really murdered Jim Cannon.

"You were stalking. You were trespassing, doing things like that?" Strianse asked.

"I got charged with that, yeah."

Baker admitted he had been charged with harassing a member of the Twentieth Judicial Drug Task Force, which had arrested him for drugs. He had also been charged with calling the cell phones and pagers of the task force members at all hours of the day and night, harassing them—another reason he was canned from the fire department. He also admitted that at the time of Jim Cannon's murder, he was about to lose his job as an over-the-road trucker.

Strianse then turned his attention to what he perceived was a failing on the part of the police to interview Baker after Jim's murder.

"The only time that you were interviewed in connection with this case was that very brief encounter that you had with the police. Is that right? That night on June twenty-third when you picked up the car?" Strianse asked.

"Yes."

James Dean Baker told the jury that the police

never really checked deeper into his background—even though they knew he had picked up the car for Kelley Cannon and he had a criminal record. And they never asked him to take a polygraph, James said. However, after Sharon Reddick objected, the judge ordered the jury to disregard the information about the polygraph and not use it in their deliberations.

CHAPTER 25

After the judge briefly spoke to the jury, Assistant District Attorney General Sharon Reddick began the prosecution's closing argument.

"Ladies and gentlemen, Mr. Strianse started out his opening statement back on Monday afternoon with a little metaphor, which I admit was cute, about you, the jury, being like tourists riding on a bus. And he cautioned you not to let the state take you for a ride. Today, on Thursday morning, after four days of testimony, some seventy exhibits, and hours upon hours of careful listening by all of you, that I'm certain it has become apparent to all of you that the only person in this whole sad, tragic story that's taken anybody for a ride is Kelley Cannon.

Reddick then went over all the pertinent witness testimony for the jurors. Then she told them that the only verdict in this case was a guilty verdict.

"Thank goodness, her plan only worked so far. It worked well enough to take her children away from their father—once and for all—but not well enough to keep from being caught. And I would submit to you not well enough to keep from being convicted of first-degree premeditated murder. That's what you're here to do, ladies and gentlemen. After careful deliberation, applying the facts to the law, convict her of first-degree premeditated murder," Sharon Reddick said.

Next it was Peter Strianse's turn to try and convince the jury that Kelley Cannon didn't murder her husband.

"When I took this case, I felt like I was already three touchdowns behind, and the game hadn't even started yet. Strianse hammered home the fact that Kelley Cannon just wasn't capable physically or emotionally of inflicting the kind of devastating damage that the ME described. He also reminded the jury that police never even considered that anyone else could have killed Jim. Strianse then pointed his finger at the three guys who were pursuing Kelley and vying for her attention and affection in the spring of 2008, trying to create reasonable doubt in the minds of the jurors.

He asked the jurors why police had not considered James Dean Baker, Paul Breeding and Rick Greene serious suspects. The attorney said police should have investigated the men rather than just focused on Kelley.

He told the members of the jury that they all had to be convinced beyond a reasonable doubt that she did that.

"Now, if you get back there and based on the proof you've heard today about the state of her physical condition, that doesn't make any sense to you, there can only be one verdict. And that's a verdict of not guilty," Peter Strianse said. "If you have a question in your mind about whether she was able to do this, it's your duty to acquit her. Thank you for your attention."

Assistant District Attorney General Katrin Miller stood to give the state's final closing.

Miller told the members of the jury that if they based their decision on the evidence, they would conclude that Kelley Cannon was the only person who killed her husband. Even though Peter Strianse called Greene, Breeding and Baker "the three creeps," they were only Kelley's good friends.

Miller also said that it was ridiculous to believe that the police didn't do a good job investigating Jim's death just because they didn't get Baker's 10-year-old divorce records showing that Jim Cannon was his wife's attorney.

As to Kelley's physical appearance and ability and emotions, Miller said despite Peter Strianse's attempts to paint his client as a very delicate, emaciated woman, she was out drinking the night before Jim's murder, as well as on the nights following the discovery of his body.

As far as the state was concerned, Kelley planned Jim's death, Miller told the jury. She said Kelley would not allow Jim Cannon to take her babies. He was not going to take her children.

She knew she would lose in the divorce the child custody. She knew it because of her drug problem. The only way she could win was to take him out of the picture, and that's what she did. Miller told the jury members that the police did their jobs, and they did it well—well enough to bring the jurors the evidence that they needed to decide whether or not to find Kelley Cannon guilty.

"The decision is yours," ADAG Katrin Miller said. "And I would ask you to consider the evidence, nothing else. A Gypsy didn't do it. Paul Breeding didn't do it. Rick Greene didn't do it. James Dean Baker didn't do it. Jean Armstrong didn't do it. Anybody else? Is there anybody else you've heard of that could have possibly done it? Is there anybody else that the evidence points to that possibly could have done it? No. Only one person did it, and you know who that was."

CHAPTER 26

On April 29, 2010, after deliberating for just about an hour, the jury found Kelley Cannon guilty of first-degree premeditated murder. Kelley received a life sentence in prison. She'll be eligible for parole in fifty-one years.

The family of Jim Cannon released this statement after Kelley's conviction: *We are grateful to have this behind us. We feel that justice has been served, and thank the members of the jury for their careful attention to the facts of the case. Our family appreciates the efforts of the local authorities, and the support and well-wishes of everyone as we return our focus onto our family.*

Kelley's mother, on the other hand, still refused to believe her daughter murdered her husband. Diane Sanders told a local newspaper that there were some things that didn't come out at trial that should have.

Assistant District Attorney General Katrin Miller told the media it was a sad day all around. She said that although justice was served, there were no winners because a man was dead and three children lost their father.

The Cannons' three children were placed in the custody of Jim Cannon's sister, Alison Greer. The guardians caring for the Cannons' three children, along with their aunt, have filed a $40 million wrongful-death lawsuit on their behalf against Kelley Cannon over the murder of their father. The lawsuit was filed in the Davidson County Circuit Court.

The damages alleged in the complaint include "the pecuniary value of Mr. Cannon's life." At the time of his death, his company, Medical Reimbursements of America, was expected to take in an annual revenue of some $20 million, according to probate filings. Previously, the company purchased Jim's share of the company from his estate for $5.2 million.

The children were identified only by their initials in the court filings because their guardian stated in an affidavit filed with the lawsuit that keeping their names out of it was in their best interests as they "cope with the horrible aftermath" of the "tremendous tragedy they have endured." Although the guardian agreed that filing the lawsuit was in the children's "overall best interests," she also said that she strongly believed they risked harm because of it.

Judge Hamilton Gayden put the case on hold pending Kelley Cannon's appeal of her criminal conviction.

Several months after her conviction, Kelley wanted to sell the Cannon home so she could use the money to pay for her appeals, as well as to fight the $40 million wrongful-death lawsuit her sister-in-law had filed on behalf of her three children.

The $720,000 brick home had been empty since Jim's death. Her attorneys placed close to $260,000 in liens against the home to pay their legal fees, according to the Davidson County Register of Deeds.

A quitclaim deed from 2005 indicated Jim signed the house over to Kelley Cannon when they were together. Jim put the house in her name because he had gone through bankruptcy and also had bad credit. But in March 2008, a circuit court gave "exclusive possession" of the house to Jim Cannon when Kelley was ordered to leave the home.

Typically, when one spouse kills the other, the assailant forfeits all rights to the property, under Tennessee law, which applies regardless of wills. However, because Jim quitclaimed the property to her in 2005, Kelley had every right to sell the house. And she did just that. Kelley Cannon sold the home for $500,000 through her brother.

On May 28, 2010, Kelley Cannon filed a motion for a new trial, which the trial court denied on July 9, 2010. She then filed an appeal of her conviction in the state's court of criminal appeals; then in October 2011, a three-judge panel heard oral arguments on the case.

Kelley's appeal centered on a number of issues, not the least of which was whether there was enough evidence presented at trial to warrant her first-degree murder conviction. Kelley's attorney also questioned the legality of the search of Jim's house and whether the trial court was right to deny her motion to suppress evidence recovered from the house, as well as statements she made to police after Jim's body was discovered.

Another matter of concern was if the court should have allowed a state's "expert" witness to testify about simple measurements—done with a ruler—of latex gloves found at the scene of the crime. Peter Strianse questioned whether the court properly refused Kelley's motion to suppress statements she made during noncustodial interviews and whether the court erred by admitting Jim Cannon's previous 911 call into evidence.

Strianse also appealed the judge's decision not to grant a mistrial after Rick Greene offered unsolicited testimony during trial—that someone had told him that Kelley Cannon had killed her husband. At that time the judge just instructed the jury to disregard Rick's statement.

In the state's response to Kelley Cannon's appeal, Benjamin Ball, assistant attorney general (AAG), hit her arguments, point by point.

Kelley contended that the evidence presented at trial was insufficient to support her conviction for first-degree premeditated murder because it was largely circumstantial. Kelley also said that the state didn't rule out all of her theories for Jim's murder, but rather focused on just one theory—that Kelley Cannon did it.

But Ball said that the state wasn't required to

rule out Kelley's hypotheses for Jim's death. And he argued there was enough evidence to support Kelley's conviction.

Not only that, but Ball asserted, when an accused person challenges whether or not there was enough evidence to convict, the standard of review was that *after reviewing the evidence in the light most favorable to the prosecution, any rational trier of fact could have found the essential elements of the crime beyond a reasonable doubt,* he wrote. And the jury, made up of twelve reasonable people, reviewed the evidence and determined Kelley Cannon was guilty beyond a reasonable doubt.

According to Ball, the state was *entitled to the strongest legitimate view of the evidence and to all reasonable and legitimate inferences that may be drawn therefrom.* It was then up to the trier of fact—in this case the jury—to resolve questions about the credibility of witnesses, the weight and value of the evidence, as well as all factual issues raised by the evidence. And it's not up to the appellate court to reweigh or reevaluate the evidence, he said.

The fact was a jury believed the evidence, as well as the state's witnesses, and found Kelley guilty, so it was up to her to show why the evidence wasn't sufficient to warrant a guilty verdict.

Because a verdict of guilt removes the presumption of innocence and imposes a presumption of guilt, the burden shifts to the defendant upon conviction to show why the evidence is insufficient to support the verdict, Ball wrote, referencing a Tennessee court decision.

Ball maintained that circumstantial evidence wasn't really any different from witness testimony, and ultimately it was up to the jury to decide how much weight to give to the circumstantial evidence. It was also up to the jury to decide what inferences to draw from such evidence, as well as the extent to which the circumstances were consistent with Kelley Cannon's guilt or innocence.

On appeal, Ball said, the appeals court "may not substitute its inferences for those drawn by the jury in circumstantial evidence cases." And the standard of review remains "the same whether the conviction is based upon direct or circumstantial evidence."

And there was enough evidence for the jury to conclude that Kelley acted with premeditation and convict her of first-degree murder. The evidence included Kelley's statement to the bartender that if Jim tried to get sole custody of their children, she'd kill him. Then on the night she murdered her husband, Kelley told her friend Amy Huston that the children were "hers" and that Jim could not "have them." Kelley was also angry that Jim would "dare" divorce her and was concerned about maintaining her lifestyle without a job.

Ball then said the jury could have inferred premeditation from Kelley's preparations before the killing, as well as the fact that she concealed the crime and tried not to leave evidence behind.

"Evidence of premeditation also included the particular cruelty of the killing and the very nature of the killing," Ball said. Even though Jim was strangled to death, Kelley also forcibly stuck something in his mouth, most likely to keep him from calling out. The state's position was that even though Jim would have been unconscious seconds after Kelley began strangling him, it took her at least two or three minutes to kill him.

In other words, at that point she had to make a conscious decision to continue to strangle him for several minutes until she determined that he was, in fact, dead. It's almost impossible to imagine a scenario in which this behavior wouldn't be premeditated.

As to Kelley Cannon's point that the state didn't rule out every one of her theories about how Jim was murdered, Benjamin Ball said it didn't have to do that. But even if it had, Kelley's hypotheses were hardly reasonable.

First she said that she was physically incapable of murdering her husband. But the medical examiner testified that it didn't take a lot of strength to strangle Jim with a ligature. And even her own medical expert refused to say she wasn't strong enough to murder her husband by strangling him. Although Kelley said she was much smaller than Jim, the evidence didn't back up her claim. When she was arrested three days after Jim's murder, she weighed 110 pounds; and at the time of his death, Jim weighed 163 pounds and was five feet six inches tall.

The evidence presented at trial also didn't support Kelley's assertion that one of her lovers most likely killed Jim because they wanted to be with her. That's because Rick Greene was the only lover she had and he testified that he didn't have any interest in a long-term relationship with Kelley. And if truth be told, he was hoping that she and Jim would get back together.

In her appeal Kelley also tried to claim that Rick Greene testified that she was in a relationship with Paul Breeding or that he was obsessed with her. But Rick actually testified that he had no idea about Paul's feelings for Kelley because he had never met the man. Contrary to Kelley's claims, Rick didn't talk at all about James Dean Baker when he was on the witness stand. And James Dean Baker didn't testify that he was in an intimate relationship with Kelley, either.

Nevertheless, no matter what kind of relationship, if any, Kelley had had with those men, there was no evidence—circumstantial or otherwise—linking any of her "alleged" lovers to her husband's murder.

In her appeal Kelley Cannon alleged that the trial court erred when it denied her motion to suppress the evidence obtained when police searched Jim's house, because they didn't have a warrant. But the state's view was that the trial court acted within its discretion when it denied Kelley's motion because she couldn't demonstrate that she had any standing to challenge the searches or that the searches were unreasonable.

Benjamin Ball said the trial court was correct to decide that Kelley didn't have any right to challenge a search of Jim's home, because she didn't live there and she didn't have an expectation of privacy there. In fact, she left the house on May 5, 2008, and Jim changed the locks. Kelley agreed she had been out of the house for about three weeks, and that Jim was paying the mortgage.

And the evidence showed that Jim had taken out an order of protection preventing her from entering the home. So even though Kelley couldn't say whether she had a key to the new lock, it was highly unlikely that she did.

Because of all those things, Kelley really couldn't demonstrate that she had an expectation of privacy in Jim's house.

Kelley contended that when Jim died, the order of protection was automatically lifted and she also became the owner of the house. But, Ball said, even though Kelley might have owned the house after Jim died, his privacy interests would not have automatically shifted to her. Not only that, but Kelley never presented any evidence that she believed the order of protection had been lifted after Jim died, or if such a belief would have been reasonable. Kelley, therefore, failed to establish that she had the expectation of privacy in Jim's home in order to challenge the validity of the police searches.

That meant if the searches were legal, then the evidence the police collected without a warrant was admissible in court, because police were responding to a homicide and they only seized items that were in plain view.

"Given that the officers were responding to reports of a homicide, did not know the location of the killer, and found a house freely accessible to anyone who might wish to remove evidence, the officers who entered the home did so under exigent circumstances, and they thus did not need a warrant to collect evidence in plain view," Ball said.

Kelley Cannon also contended that the trial court improperly admitted the testimony of Agent Linda Littlejohn, who gave testimony comparing the latex gloves in evidence, because she was not a scientific expert. The state, however, said the trial court acted within its discretion in allowing Littlejohn's testimony because her background in microanalysis qualified her as an expert witness in that field, and as such allowed her to present her opinion on that subject to the jury. She did not, however, testify as a scientific witness.

Additionally, the testimony Kelley complained about was not scientific testimony, and therefore not subject to analysis as such. At the pretrial hearing Littlejohn testified that she was a forensic scientist specializing in microanalysis and the court allowed her to testify as an expert in microanalysis. The agent then testified about the microanalysis performed on varying latex gloves and concluded that all of the gloves tested had the same chemical composition.

During her testimony Littlejohn also testified that she measured the gloves and compared those measurements. And that's the testimony Kelley complained about. However, that testimony wasn't scientific in nature, either, and did not require an expert scientific opinion.

Littlejohn merely testified that the measurements taken of the gloves recovered from the crime scene were the same as the measurements taken of gloves from Kelley's apartment. At the hearing Littlejohn testified that she used a simple ruler to take those measurements. In other words, she testified to the "physical properties of the evidence that left no room for opinion." It was the state's position that the trial court didn't admit Littlejohn as an expert in measuring; it admitted her as an expert in microanalysis.

Even though the assistant district attorney general asked Littlejohn if it was her "expert opinion" that the gloves were consistent in size, the judge never instructed the jury that the witness was an expert in anything but microanalysis.

In her appeal Kelley Cannon said the trial court was wrong when it denied her motion to suppress the statements she made to police—in part, because they didn't inform her of her Miranda rights. She also said she made one of the statements after she asked for an attorney.

Assistant Attorney General Ball said because Kelley was not in custody when she made her statements, the trial court properly decided that admitting her statements into evidence did not violate her Fifth Amendment rights to self-incrimination.

The only way Kelley's statements to police could have violated her rights would have been if the police had taken her into custody and questioned her without advising her of her rights under the Constitution. Kelley would also have had to "knowingly, voluntarily and intelligently" waived those rights.

Police also talked to Kelley in the bedroom of her apartment during the early afternoon and in the presence of her infant daughter, with her children nearby, not in a police station. When the judge decided to admit Kelley's statements into evidence, he took into account the fact that she hadn't been whisked away to the police station so police could interview her.

The judge also ruled that the tone of the interview was a conversation, not an interrogation, and police never confronted or threatened Kelley. Detective Stokes's recording of the conversation backed up the judge's opinion. The recording also supported the judge's finding that the interview took only a little over an hour.

Additionally, the record indicated that Detective Stokes and Lieutenant Fielder were not in uniform when they talked to Kelley Cannon. And neither of them confronted Kelley with any suspicion of guilt or evidence against her. The judge also determined that Kelley was free to leave at any time. No one was forcing her to talk to the police. Then, at the end of the interview, the two officers didn't arrest Kelley. In fact, after their conversation the police left Kelley at her apartment.

The police also interviewed Kelley again, for thirty-six minutes, at three o'clock on the same day as the first interview. During the second conversation Detective Brad Putnam began by telling Kelley he'd like to find a place to speak away from the children. He also explicitly told her that she was not under arrest and was under no obligation to speak with him. Putnam indicated that they were in the "preliminary stages of the investigation" and only wanted to collect "some basic information."

Then when Sophie became fussy, Putnam asked Kelley whether it was the baby's nap time. He said he'd try to speed up the interview so she could take care of her daughter.

Because the police again interviewed Kelley at her apartment, the judge properly concluded that they hadn't taken her into custody. The court also ruled that based on listening to the recording of Putnam's interview with Kelley, the tone of the conversation was "congenial."

The trial judge also determined that the interview conducted by Detective Putnam did not violate Kelley Cannon's Fifth Amendment right to have an attorney present during questioning.

For one thing, Kelley wasn't in custody. Kelley would only have triggered her Fifth Amendment right to counsel if she had asked for an attorney when she was in custody. And for another, during her interview with Putnam, Kelley only said she would "really like" her attorney to be there. When Putnam asked Kelley if that meant she did not want to speak with him, she responded emphatically, "I do. I do. I do." Kelley then turned the table and started asking Putnam questions.

In her appeal Kelley Cannon also claimed that the trial judge was wrong to admit testimony about her character into evidence. The state's opinion was that the judge properly allowed the evidence because it was "highly probative" of her motive and intent.

Under law, for evidence to be admissible, it had to be relevant. And it had "to make the existence of any fact that is of consequence to the determination of the action more probable or less probable than it would be without the evidence."

AAG Ball said the trial court acted within its discretion when, after conducting a hearing outside of the jury's presence, it determined that evidence of the incident in which Kelley forcibly removed one of their children (Sophie) from Jim was admissible.

The state's theory of the case was that Kelley Cannon killed her husband because he wanted to take their children from her during the course of their impending divorce. Ball pointed out that Kelley even publically said that if her husband tried to take her children, she'd kill him.

Therefore, the evidence that she tried to forcibly remove Sophie from Jim's custody, which resulted in an order of protection that prevented her from being around her children, was highly probative of her motive for killing the victim. The state's explanation of motive was that Kelley Cannon didn't want to lose her kids. And that incident that took place on May 21, 2008, represented perhaps the single most compelling reason that she was likely to lose her children. It also provided Jim with the "ammunition" he needed in a divorce proceeding to help "take" the kids away from Kelley.

Therefore, this evidence was highly probative, according to Ball. The trial court also properly determined that the probative value of the evidence outweighed any potential for prejudice. At worst, the evidence was prejudicial in that it showed that the defendant could resort to punching the victim or tearing his shirt.

Besides, the trial judge instructed the jury that it could only consider this evidence to the extent that it provided "a complete account to the relationship of the parties," and helped to establish identity and motive. Because of that, the trial court acted within its discretion in admitting this evidence.

Kelley Cannon also contended that the trial judge erred by admitting evidence in violation of the Confrontation Clause of the Tennessee and United States Constitutions. The Sixth Amendment of the United States Constitution provides the accused with the right to be confronted with witnesses against her.

The Tennessee Constitution also protected this right. The U.S. Supreme Court held that the Confrontation Clause prohibits the admission of testimonial hearsay, unless the witness who made the statement is unavailable to testify in court and the defendant had a prior opportunity to cross-examine the witness.

The U.S. Supreme Court clarified its position by writing that *statements are nontestimonial when made in the course of police interrogation under ongoing emergency.* The court went on to rule that a 911 call made by the victim of a domestic assault reporting an ongoing incident was nontestimonial.

Therefore, the statements Jim made to the 911 operator were in no way testimonial, and the trial court properly admitted the call into evidence, according to the state. In the call Jim was describing an ongoing emergency as his wife, whom he believed to be under the influence of a substance or suffering from a mental disturbance, tried to forcibly take his infant daughter and drive away in a vehicle.

Jim's worries about her potential mental state were essential to describing the danger inherent in her driving off with a child in the vehicle. Jim spent most of the call giving the operator a blow-by-blow account of Kelley's actions in real time. And a great deal of the phone call consisted of Jim yelling at Kelley and begging her not to take the baby. The purpose of the call was to resolve an ongoing emergency that endangered Jim. It was not a formal statement, and any questioning by the 911 operator was unstructured. Likewise, the operator was talking with Jim to resolve an ongoing emergency, not to secure testimony for a criminal trial.

The trial court properly determined, however, that Jim's statement was not testimonial in nature.

Furthermore, in her appeal Kelley Cannon said that the trial court erred by denying her attorney's request for a mistrial after a witness, Rick Greene, offered unsolicited testimony that someone told him that Kelley had killed her husband. The trial court, however, acted within its discretion in denying this motion and instead instructed the jury to disregard Rick Greene's testimony.

The judge then asked the jurors to raise their

hands if they understood, and all the jurors raised their hands. Juries are presumed to follow the judge's instructions; and since Kelley didn't present any evidence to the contrary, she couldn't demonstrate that Rick's statement affected the outcome of the trial or that the trial court abused its discretion.

Moreover, the judge determined that Rick Greene's testimony didn't really respond to the question the assistant district attorney general had asked him. The question posed to Rick was "How did you find out about [the victim's] death?" Greene responded, "A mutual acquaintance of mine and Kelley's called me at work. It had been on the news at five o'clock. And she said, 'Did you see the news?' And I said, 'No.' And she said, 'Kelley killed her husband.'" Even before Kelley requested a mistrial, the assistant district attorney general, out of the jury's hearing, told the judge, "I didn't mean for him to say that." Indeed, the prosecutor asked the witness a simple question about how he learned about Jim's death. She didn't ask how the victim had died. Rick Greene's testimony was unresponsive, and the state didn't solicit it.

Finally Benjamin Ball said that the state had presented a strong case. DNA evidence not only placed the defendant at the scene of the murder, but it also showed that she was in contact with the latex gloves found near Jim's body. Security video from Walgreens showed the defendant preparing for the murder by obtaining those latex gloves. And the box of Walgreens-brand latex gloves, consistent with those recovered from the crime scene, was in the bedroom of her apartment.

The state also demonstrated motive and intent through testimony that Kelley Cannon threatened to kill her husband if he tried to gain custody of their children. When Rick Greene asked the defendant what happened, the defendant refused to tell him, saying she didn't want him to have to lie.

The state didn't elicit the improper testimony; the state presented a strong case; the trial court immediately instructed the jury to disregard Rick Greene's statement. Accordingly, the trial court acted within its discretion in denying Kelley Cannon's motion for a mistrial.

"For these reasons, the judgment of the trial court should be affirmed," Ball said.

ACKNOWLEDGMENTS

First and foremost, I'd like to thank my former agent and friend, Janet Benrey, who is now on to other pursuits. Thanks for everything. I'd also like to thank my editor at Kensington, Michaela Hamilton, for her help. And a shout-out to some folks in Nashville—Joy Kennedy, Nicole Murphy, Rachel Vance, Benjamin Ball, Katy Miller, John Hollins, Don Aaron, Brad Putnam, Robyn Gornicki-Davis and Roger Randles, a true lifesaver.

MORE SHOCKING TRUE CRIME
FROM PINNACLE